Enrollment Form

☐ *Yes!* I WANT TO BE A *PRIVILEGED WOMAN*.
Enclosed is one *PAGES & PRIVILEGES*™ Proof of
Purchase from any Harlequin or Silhouette book currently for
sale in stores (Proofs of Purchase are found on the back pages
of books) and the store cash register receipt. Please enroll me
in *PAGES & PRIVILEGES*™. Send my Welcome Kit and FREE
Gifts -- and activate my FREE benefits -- immediately.

More great gifts and benefits to come.

_____

NAME (please print)

_____

ADDRESS   **APT. NO**

_____

CITY   **STATE**   **ZIP/POSTAL CODE**

PROOF OF PURCHASE

NO CLUB!
NO COMMITMENT!
*Just one purchase brings
you great Free Gifts and
Benefits!*

Please allow 6-8 weeks for delivery. Quantities are limited. We reserve the right to
substitute items. Enroll before October 31, 1995 and receive one full year of benefits.

Name of store where this book was purchased_____

Date of purchase_____

Type of store:
    ☐ Bookstore   ☐ Supermarket   ☐ Drugstore
    ☐ Dept. or discount store (e.g. K-Mart or Walmart)
    ☐ Other (specify)_____

Which Harlequin or Silhouette series do you usually read?

_____

Complete and mail with one Proof of Purchase and store receipt to:
U.S.: *PAGES & PRIVILEGES*™, P.O. Box 1960, Danbury, CT 06813-1960
Canada: *PAGES & PRIVILEGES*™, 49-6A The Donway West, P.O. 813,
       North York, ON M3C 2E8

SSE-PP5B

▼ DETACH HERE AND MAIL TODAY! ▼

For the first time, he really thought about what he'd done.

He, a man who valued privacy, who hoarded his solitary moments the way some men hoarded gold, had invited a strange woman and her newborn infant into his home. A woman with loads of emotional baggage, an uncertain future and a severely damaged self-image.

Not to mention the baby, and the inevitable nights of crying, and the clutter that always seemed to accompany infants. *Had he lost his mind?*

The baby stirred again, and Adam lifted her into his arms. She blinked her little round eyes, trying to focus on his face. She made a soft sound that was somewhere between a coo and a hiccup.

Adam grinned. Damn. She really was cute. He'd have been out of his mind *not* to take her in. Baby or mother.

Dear Reader,

September is an extra-special month for Special Edition!
This month brings you some of your favorite veteran authors,
three dynamite series and a celebration of special events! So
don't miss a minute of the fall festivities under way.

Reader favorite Christine Rimmer returns to North
Magdalene for the latest JONES GANG tale! THAT SPECIAL
WOMAN! Heather Conway meets her match—and the future
father of her baby—in *Sunshine and the Shadowmaster*.
Gina Ferris Wilkins's new series, THE FAMILY WAY,
continues in September with *A Home for Adam*, a touching
and poignant story from this award-winning author.
Diana Whitney's THE BLACKTHORN BROTHERHOOD
continues with a story of the redeeming power of love in
The Avenger.

And this month, Special Edition features special occasions
in three books in our CONGRATULATIONS! promotion.
In each story, a character experiences something that will
change his or her life forever. Don't miss a moment of any of
these wonderful titles: *Kisses and Kids* by Andrea Edwards,
Joyride by Patricia Coughlin, and from a new author to
Silhouette, *A Date With Dr. Frankenstein* by Leanne Banks.

But that's not all—there's lots in store for the rest of 1995
and Silhouette Special Edition! Not to give away our secrets
yet, but safe to say that the rest of the year promises to bring
your favorite authors in very special books! I hope you enjoy
each and every story to come!

Sincerely,

Tara Gavin
Senior Editor

Please address questions and book requests to:
Silhouette Reader Service
U.S.: 3010 Walden Ave., P.O. Box 1325, Buffalo, NY 14269
Canadian: P.O. Box 609, Fort Erie, Ont. L2A 5X3

Gina Ferris Wilkins

A HOME FOR ADAM

Silhouette®

SPECIAL EDITION®

Published by Silhouette Books
America's Publisher of Contemporary Romance

SILHOUETTE BOOKS

ISBN 0-373-09980-0

A HOME FOR ADAM

Printed in U.S.A.

Books by Gina Ferris Wilkins

Silhouette Special Edition

*A Man for Mom #955
*A Match for Celia #967
*A Home for Adam #980

*The Family Way

Previously published by Gina Ferris

Silhouette Special Edition

Healing Sympathy #496
Lady Beware #549
In From the Rain #677
Prodigal Father #711
†*Full of Grace #793*
†*Hardworking Man #806*
†*Fair and Wise #819*
†*Far to Go #862*
†*Loving and Giving #879*
Babies on Board #913

†Family Found

GINA FERRIS WILKINS

This award-winning author published her first Silhouette Special Edition novel in 1988, using the pseudonym Gina Ferris. Since then, she's won many awards, including the Reviewer's Choice Award for Best All Around Series Author from *Romantic Times* magazine. Her books have been translated into twenty languages and are sold in more than one hundred countries.

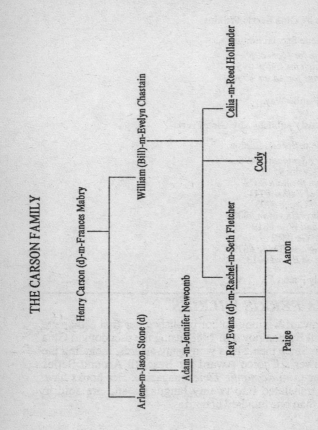

THE CARSON FAMILY

Henry Carson (d) - m - Frances Mabry

Arlene - m - Jason Stone (d)

William (Bill) - m - Evelyn Chastain

Adam - m - Jennifer Newcomb

Ray Evans (d) - m - Rachel - m - Seth Fletcher

Celia - m - Reed Hollander

Cody

Paige   Aaron

Chapter One

Adam Stone nearly jumped out of his skin when the telephone rang late Thursday afternoon.

The instrument had hung silently on the wall of the rather rustic lake cottage for three days; he'd almost forgotten its existence. Its noisy jangle brought him out of the book he'd been enjoying, and out of the self-imposed isolation he'd fought so hard to attain, reminding him abruptly of the real world that existed outside the walls of this cozy haven.

Only Granny Fran had the number where he was staying. She'd promised not to give it out to anyone. Since he knew nothing anyone could say would drag that number out of his stubborn grandmother, he answered the phone with some trepidation, hoping there hadn't been a family emergency in the few days he'd been incommunicado.

"Stone," he said in his habitually curt, my-time-is-precious-don't-waste-it telephone voice.

"It's Granny Fran, dear," a soft, sweet voice informed him. "And there is no emergency, so don't be alarmed."

He exhaled quietly in relief. "Nothing's wrong?" he asked, just to be sure.

"No," she reassured him. "I just wanted to check on you. I have to admit, it bothers me a little that you're out there in that lake cottage all alone in the dead of winter, no one even knowing where you are. What if you hurt yourself or something? What would you do?"

Adam chuckled. "I never knew you were such a worrier," he accused her fondly. "I thought that was Rachel's job," he added, naming his cousin, her eldest granddaughter.

"Ever since Rachel fell in love with Seth Fletcher, she's been too busy and too happy to waste time worrying about the family," Frances replied contentedly. "I suppose that leaves the responsibility to me."

"There's always Mother," he reminded her.

"Oh, heavens, Arlene is much too busy worrying about herself to think about anyone else."

His grandmother's aggrieved tone made Adam wince. "She's been giving you a hard time, hasn't she?"

"No worse than usual."

"Is she nagging you for my number?"

"She's not getting it. There is absolutely no need for you to go rushing back to Little Rock just because her heater isn't functioning properly. Honestly, that daughter of mine is so helpless, it's a wonder she gets herself out of bed."

"Mother's heater is broken?" Adam frowned, thinking of the weather reports for the upcoming late January weekend, predicted to be the coldest of the season, with winter storm warnings issued statewide. "Maybe I'd better—"

"You will do no such thing." Frances cut in, obviously annoyed with herself for mentioning it. "Arlene is perfectly capable of taking care of this. I told her what to do, and she'll do it, now that she has no other choice. I've always said she would be better off—and so would you—if you'd stop catering to her."

"Sometimes it's easier to cater than to deal with the consequences," Adam admitted, picturing all sorts of unpleasant, messy—and time-consuming—scenes.

He didn't try to delude himself that the things he did for his mother were motivated by nobility or unselfish generosity. He simply found it easier to agree with her and pay someone to take care of her requests than to waste time arguing with her.

He'd been called a selfish, arrogant bastard an average of once a day for the past fifteen years or so. There were times when he deliberately did what he could to live up to that title. If nothing else, his attitude made it less likely that anyone else would try to use him the way his mother so often did.

Frances apparently decided there was no need to get into another argument about his mother. "Are you enjoying your vacation?" she asked instead.

"Yeah, it's nice." Adam looked contentedly around the rented cottage with its huge stone fireplace, its worn, comfortable furnishings, its view of acres of uncleared woods and a glimpse of the nearby lake.

This area would be much busier in the summertime, when fishermen and water sports enthusiasts were out en masse, but in late January, the tourist action had all moved to the racetrack in Hot Springs, some thirty miles away, leaving the lake cottage isolated and lonely. Exactly the way Adam had hoped it would be. He dealt with people all day, every day, back in Little Rock—an hour-

and-a-half drive from the lake. Just being alone was a rare and special treat for him.

He smiled at the thought that his friends, family and associates had no idea how close he really was. Most of them were convinced he was taking two weeks in the tropics or some other more traditional winter vacation spot.

"You have plenty of food?" Frances fretted. "If this predicted ice storm hits, you might not be able to drive out of there for a couple of days."

"I have plenty of food. I have my cellular phone in the car in case regular phone service goes out, and there's a stack of firewood higher than my head. I can easily ride out what passes for a winter storm in Arkansas."

"I suppose you know best."

Adam grinned. "Always."

Frances sighed gustily through the line. "I should have known that would be your response."

The most common criticism of Adam was that, in his mind, there were two ways of doing things—the wrong way, or his way. He'd been taking care of others for so long, and had been treated with respectful submission so often, that he had become more than a bit arrogant, a trait he was well aware of, but tended to believe he'd fully earned.

And, besides, he thought with a deepening smile, he *was* almost always right. It just sometimes took him a while to convince others of his infallibility.

His grandmother didn't keep him long on the phone. She told him to have a good rest, made him promise not to call home and risk being pulled out of his much-deserved vacation, then assured him that she, too, had taken precautions against the weather. "But thank you for worrying," she added.

Adam did worry about his grandmother. Though he knew she was in good health and excellent shape for a woman of her years, it bothered him that she still lived alone, an hour's drive from her closest relative. Several times he'd suggested that she move into a nice little house closer to his—hell, he'd even offered to build a guest house on his property for her—but she'd repeatedly, firmly refused. He still fully intended to convince her, given a bit more time and effort.

"Take care of yourself," he said.

"You, too. I love you, Adam."

He grunted a suitable response and disconnected the call. He wasn't comfortable with expressing his emotions in words. He thought his actions adequately demonstrated his concern for his family.

He settled back into the recliner and opened his book again, absently scratching his chin. He hadn't shaved in three days and his straggly beard was beginning to itch a bit. But it was a nice itch, another sign that he had no appearances to keep up during the next week and a half, no expectations to meet.

Outside, the wind began to blow, brushing tree limbs against the walls of the snug little cabin. Heavy clouds obscured the sun, making the afternoon almost as dark as late evening. Illuminated by the soft glow of a reading lamp and the small fire in the fireplace, the cabin was a quiet, cozy refuge from the approaching inclement weather.

Adam sighed in contentment, and lost himself again in the adventure unfolding on the pages of his book.

Jennifer Newcomb's knuckles gleamed whitely against the black steering wheel beneath her tightly gripped hands. Had it not been for the dim green illumination from the dashboard, it would have been pitch-black inside the tiny car.

Heavy, freezing rain and sleet poured down from the dark sky, battering the top of the compact vehicle, competing with the rhythmic *thump-thump* of the valiantly struggling windshield wipers. The steady downpour diffused the headlamps so that their beams glinted off in dozens of different directions, providing more glare than guidance.

The road was a narrow asphalt strip, gleaming like black satin beneath the thin sheet of ice already covering it. Jenny drove at little more than walking speed, fighting the ice and wind and the panic mounting inside her.

She was lost. Somewhere during the past ten miles, she'd obviously taken a wrong turn in her search for a clean, inexpensive place to spend the night. The directions she'd been given over an hour ago had been confusing and hard to remember. What had she done wrong? When had she taken the wrong road? Where *was* she?

She hadn't passed any other cars in what seemed like hours, though it had probably been only twenty minutes or so. There were no lights lining this sorry excuse for a road, and no houses that she could see in any direction. Didn't *anyone* live along here?

When she'd been a teenager, she'd been hooked on old "Twilight Zone" reruns that played on her local television station after school. She felt as though she had entered one of those haunting episodes now. As though civilization as she knew it had disappeared, leaving her alone in this tiny car on an interminable drive to nowhere along this endless stretch of frozen asphalt.

"Stop this, Jenny," she ordered herself aloud, just to hear a human voice. "You'll find help somewhere. And you're not alone," she added, letting go of the steering wheel for a moment to risk a quick touch to her very swollen stomach.

As if to confirm her words, the baby inside her kicked. Hard. The sharp pain in her diaphragm made her catch her breath and clutch the wheel again in a death grip.

"Thanks, kid," she muttered with a humorless laugh. "I needed that. Better than a slap across the face for counteracting hysteria."

The battering of the rooftop intensified, echoing hollowly inside the vehicle. There was a difference in the sound, Jenny realized. The wind had grown stronger, and the temperatures must have dropped. The rain was freezing before it hit the ground, before it pelted her car. She was driving on a deserted road somewhere in south central Arkansas, right in the middle of an ice storm.

She groaned and wasted several precious moments calling herself two or three dozen synonyms for "idiot." If only she hadn't been so damned determined to make this drive alone. If only she'd listened to the well-intentioned advice of friends, co-workers, even concerned strangers. If only she hadn't always been so stubborn, so determinedly independent, so resistant to advice, no matter how well-meant . . .

The car skidded, its back tires fishtailing frantically against the tractionless surface beneath them. Jenny's heart leaped into her throat. She fought the skid, fought the panic, fought the despair.

She didn't stand a chance. Completely out of her control now, the car made several dizzying spins that stopped only when the front fender came up hard against something solid and unyielding.

A tree, Jenny thought, instinctively wrapping her arms around her middle and bracing against the jarring impact. Her seat belt tightened hard against her thighs, where she'd worn it beneath the bulge of her stomach. The shoulder strap jerked her against the back of her seat, taking her breath, but mercifully pulling her away from contact with the steering wheel.

The car's overstrained engine coughed a time or two, then fell silent. The windshield wipers ground to a stop halfway across their path. The headlamps remained on, but the sight they revealed wasn't particularly encouraging. Miles of road. Ice-coated trees. Falling ice mixed now with huge flakes of snow.

For just a moment, Jenny gave in to the urge to cry, the hot, heavy tears cascading down her cold cheeks in a steady stream. But then she made herself stop, drawing a deep, steadying breath.

She'd gotten herself into this mess, she thought angrily. It looked like it was up to her to get herself out. As usual.

She peered through the windshield, hoping for any sign of civilization. The wildly refracted light from the headlamps made her dizzy, but she hesitated to cut them off, suddenly reluctant to face the lonely darkness. Shaking her head at her cowardice, she reached out and pushed in the control. The lights died. The world grew dark around the stalled car, still and quiet except for that steadily falling ice and snow.

"I'm in Arkansas, for crying out loud!" she protested uselessly into the night. "It isn't supposed to do this here. It almost never snows here."

But it was snowing, and the thick, wet flakes were landing heavily on the sheet of ice already coating the ground, making driving more treacherous than ever, even if she could get the car started again, even if she could pull it away from the tree around which her front fender was crumpled.

She pressed her face against the glass beside her and stared intently into the darkness, looking for something, anything, to give her hope. She found it in the distance ahead of her. *Lights*. Just visible through the trees and the storm was a pale gleam of light that could only be coming from a house.

There was no way to tell how far away the house might be. She leaned against the horn, praying its sound would penetrate the storm and the woods and alert someone that she was nearby, that she needed help. Five minutes passed, then ten. No one could hear her. No one knew she was here. She leaned her forehead against the steering wheel, grimly aware of what she had to do.

Common sense told her to stay in the car, bundle up against the cold and pray for someone to find her. Logic reminded her that walking on ice, in a raging storm, in her condition, was an incredibly dumb thing to do, a tragic accident waiting to happen. But she was already cramped and sore from a long car ride, her body jammed tightly into the small space behind the steering wheel. She didn't know how much longer she could sit here like this, hoping for help that might not come along for hours yet.

After all, she thought glumly, no one in his right mind would be out driving in weather like this.

A gust of wind pelted the car with another shower of ice. Jenny shivered as the cold crept inexorably through the glass surrounding her. Another cramp gripped her, twisting her in the uncomfortable seat, dragging an oath from her throat.

She unbuckled the seat belt and reached for the heavy gray wool coat in the passenger seat. Dragging it on, she strained to pull the sides together in front, over the bulky maternity sweater she wore with maternity jeans, knee socks and white leather Keds. When the coat was buttoned, she pulled on knit gloves and a matching knit cap, then wrapped a red-and-white striped muffler around her neck and the lower part of her face.

She took one last look around the interior of the little car, which was crammed almost to the padded roof with boxes and bags and suitcases—everything she owned in the world. And then she put her hand on the door handle.

The first blast of wet, icy wind took her breath away. She dragged in another, forcing her cramped legs out of the car. Her clothing was soaked before she'd even managed to stand upright. One shoe slid on the ice, and she steadied herself frantically against the car, terrified of falling. "I can do this, damn it!" she said, daring the Fates to argue with her.

She looped the straps of her purse over her neck—every penny she possessed was in that worn leather bag—and focused again on that beckoning light.

"I can do this," she said again. And this time the words were a prayer.

Kneeling in front of the fireplace, Adam added another log and poked at the embers, stirring the cheery fire into new life. He considered it a minor miracle that he still had electricity. The inside of the cabin was bright and warm and comfortable, a dramatic contrast to the bitterly cold, dark, icy conditions outside.

He returned to his chair and opened his book. Two novels yet to be read rested on the low table beside him, along with a snifter of fine old brandy. Classical music played softly from the portable CD player he'd brought with him.

For the first time in longer than he could remember, he was utterly content—if only a bit lonely.

The heavy thump on the tiny front porch made him look up from his book with a frown. Falling ice? A broken-off limb from a nearby tree? He'd better check, he thought, setting the book aside reluctantly.

Bracing against the cold, he opened the front door a crack and glanced outside. And then he jerked it open with a fervent curse. "What the—?"

The woman was half sitting, half lying on the edge of the porch, apparently unable to make her way up the three ice-coated steps. Adam had left the porch light on earlier, when he'd brought in a good supply of firewood, and he could see that his unexpected and uninvited visitor was in sorry shape. Wet, icy, gasping for breath, hunched in agony. She looked young, and rather heavy in her thick winter clothes.

Ignoring the stinging sleet and snow that slapped at the skin exposed by his black sweatshirt, Adam knelt beside her. Her lips were blue, her skin dangerously white. There was ice on her eyelashes, on the tips of the wet dark hair that escaped from beneath her knit cap to curl against her pale cheeks. She had one hand pressed to her side, and was supporting herself against the porch with the other.

"Please," she managed to whisper, her voice thin and cracked, her breath catching in ragged sobs. "Wrecked . . . my car. I—I need . . ."

She couldn't finish. But he knew what she needed. Heat, shelter, dry clothing, hot food.

So much for his blessed solitude, his lazy catering to no one but himself. But Adam could no more have turned his back on this woman than he could have changed the weather.

He took her arm. "Come on," he said gruffly. "Let's get you inside."

It wasn't easy to get her to her feet. She was obviously exhausted, and out of shape. They'd made it only half-way to the door when she bent over with a low moan, both arms wrapped around her middle.

"What's wrong? Have you hurt yourself?" Adam demanded, impatient to get her inside where he could check her over.

"Cramp," she whispered, trying to straighten.

He nodded and half dragged, half carried her the rest of the way inside.

He slammed the door behind them, still supporting her sagging weight. He ripped the wet knit cap off her head, exposing a short, tumbled mass of dark curls. He tugged her purse from around her neck and tossed it aside, then unwound the muffler from her throat, hampered more than helped by her groping hands.

"Be still," he ordered her, already reaching for the top button of her coat. "We have to get you out of these wet things so you can get warm in front of the fire."

His words must have sounded appealing to her. She let out a long, shuddering sigh and went still, allowing him to fumble with her sleet-stiffened coat. He slid the heavy garment off her shoulders and released it to fall to the floor. And then he focused suddenly on the body he'd revealed. The very pregnant body.

"Oh, hell," he muttered, even as she pressed her hand to her side and gave another broken groan.

He helped her into the chair closest to the fire. "Are you in labor?" he demanded, fervently hoping she would say no.

As if she'd read his thoughts, she shook her head. "Just cramps," she whispered huskily, her body racked with shivers. "I walked . . . a long way."

Her feet were soaked, the thin leather sneakers no protection against the conditions she'd walked through. He whipped them off, and her thick red knee socks along with them, exposing small, blue-veined feet. He chafed them for a moment between his hands. Her jeans were wet to the knees, but her sweater, which had been protected by her heavy coat, was dry. He reached beneath it.

The woman automatically stiffened and pulled away from his groping hands.

"I'm only helping you out of these wet jeans," Adam told her impatiently. "Your sweater is still dry, you can leave that on, but these jeans have to go. Here," he added, snatching a colorful afghan off the couch. "You can wrap up in this."

It was quite apparent that she hated being in this situation, but she didn't bother to resist him any further. Maybe she'd realized that protests wouldn't have accomplished anything. Adam was determined to take care of her, whether she liked it or not. It was for her own good, after all.

As soon as she was wrapped snugly in the afghan, he hurried into the kitchen and put a kettle of water on to boil, then snatched up a tea towel and carried it back into the living room. He draped it over her head and rubbed energetically at her wet hair. She mumbled a complaint from beneath the towel, but he ignored her.

Her curls were even more wildly disarrayed when he'd finished, but at least they were reasonably dry, he noted in satisfaction. And there was some color coming back into her face, a flush of pink in her cheeks, a heightened brightness in her amber eyes. He didn't care if temper was responsible for those encouraging signs, as long as he could be sure she was all right.

He leaned close to her face and stared intently into her eyes, studying first one, then the other. "Did you hit your head?"

"No, I—"

"Did you fall while you were walking?" he asked, turning his attention to her abdomen. He placed both hands searchingly on her stomach, relieved to feel a strong kick beneath his right palm. It felt as though Junior was healthy—and angry. Adam didn't blame the kid.

He prodded the woman's ankles, which were swollen, but not alarmingly so. "Any sharp pains, or numbness?"

"I'm tired, I'm cold and I feel as though I've been run over by a snowplow, but other than that, I'm fine," the woman replied, sounding a bit peevish. "You can stop pawing me now."

Adam lifted an eyebrow and gave her a look that had made bigger men than he quail.

The woman met his eyes without flinching, her slightly indented chin lifted in a stubborn manner that rather amusingly reminded him of his grandmother.

A shrill whistle sounded from the kitchen. "Water's boiling," Adam said, shoving himself to his feet. "Decaffeinated instant coffee or herbal tea?"

"Tea, please," she said, her head lowering a bit at the subtle reminder that he was doing his best to make her comfortable.

Her hands were still trembling so badly that Adam had to help her get the cup to her blue-tinged lips. He cautioned her to sip slowly; she gave him a faintly resentful look, but complied.

Adam was relieved to see the color slowly returning to her lips, though the occasional shiver still rippled through her. She must have been cold right through to the bone, he thought with a shake of his head.

"What were you doing out on a night like this?" he couldn't resist asking. "The main highway is three miles away. This road runs right into the lake. There are only three other cabins down here, and they're boarded up for the winter. Where'd you think you were going?"

"I got lost," she admitted, staring down into the steaming teacup. "I was looking for the Bide-a-Bye Inn. A guy at a convenience store in Hot Springs gave me directions, but I guess I made a couple of wrong turns. I couldn't find anything in this direction...and then the weather turned so bad and I didn't know whether to turn back or go on. And then I lost control of the car and hit a tree."

"How far from here?" Adam asked, wondering how far she'd walked in that storm.

"I don't know. I could see the lights to your cabin through the trees and I just kept walking toward them. It seemed to take a very long time," she added, her stark tone telling more than her words.

Must have been several hundred yards, at least, Adam thought, amazed that she'd even made it this far. For such a petite woman, she must be a lot tougher than she looked. "What's your name?"

"Jenny Newcomb."

"I'm Adam Stone." He helped her take another sip of the tea, his hands cupped securely around hers on the mug.

Leaning so close to her, he could see that her lashes were thick and dark, her cheekbones high, her nose straight and nicely proportioned. There were shallow indentions at the corners of her soft mouth and that intriguing dimple in her chin. Her complexion was nearly flawless, though still too pale for his comfort.

She seemed embarrassed by his close scrutiny. She squirmed in the chair and pushed the nearly empty cup away. "I don't want any more," she said. "But thank you," she added, the words sounding a bit rusty.

Adam didn't argue with her. He set the cup on a nearby table, then stood looking at her, his hands on his hips. "Okay, Jenny Newcomb," he said, thinking aloud. "What am I going to do with you now?"

Chapter Two

Jenny didn't particularly like Adam Stone's question—nor the other questions it provoked. Who was this man? What was he doing out here alone in a deserted vacation cabin? And what *was* he going to do with her?

She studied him as closely as he'd studied her earlier. He looked rather scruffy, his lean, tanned face unshaven for at least several days. His dark hair was tousled, silvered at the temples, making her estimate his age at somewhere close to forty, give or take a couple of years.

His eyes were dark and intense, bracketed with shallow creases that matched the ones around his unsmiling mouth. There was a small bump on the ridge of his nose; she suspected it had been broken. He was tall and on the thin side, though his shoulders were broad and she had reason to know that he was certainly strong.

She felt a faint flicker of unease at the sudden realization that she was alone in the middle of nowhere with a scraggly stranger. But then she remembered how gentle he had been even when he'd been stripping off her clothes despite her resistance. How he'd steadied her as she'd sipped the tea he'd made her. The slight satisfaction she'd seen in his face when her baby had kicked beneath his cautiously searching hand.

She'd never been a particularly good judge of character—as was evident by her present circumstances—but she decided impulsively that Adam Stone, whoever he was, meant her no harm.

She allowed herself to relax into the comfortable armchair. "I don't know," she said finally, her voice husky from cold and weariness. "What *are* we going to do now?"

"You need some rest," he said. "You're trembling with exhaustion, and no wonder. I have a phone. Is there someone you need to call, someone who'll be frantic with worry about you? Your husband? Family?"

She shook her head. "No husband. And no one is expecting to hear from me," she murmured, then belatedly realized that she'd just made herself even more vulnerable to him, should he be the homicidal type.

Great, Jenny. Why don't you just offer him your money and your life?

Adam sighed, and she couldn't tell if he was equally exasperated with her dangerous candor or annoyed that he was temporarily responsible for her. As her eyelids grew heavier, she found that she really didn't care.

"If I could just lie down for a little while," she said, the words hardly louder than a whisper. Surely a brief nap would clear her mind, grant her a semblance of her usual stubborn self-sufficiency.

"I'll help you into the bedroom," Adam said, reaching for her hands. "You get some rest and then we'll talk about what to do next."

Sounded like an excellent plan to her. Jenny allowed him to hoist her out of the chair, clinging weakly to the afghan in a vain attempt at covering her bare legs, which were exposed from the thigh down by her oversize sweater. She leaned against him as he led her into the bedroom, more from weakness than trust.

The bed hadn't been made since he'd last slept in it. He settled her onto the pillows and pulled a pile of fluffy blankets over her, leaving her cocooned in heavenly warmth. She was aware that he stood for a moment by the bed before he turned and walked toward the door without speaking.

He'd almost left the room when she felt compelled to say something. "Mr. Stone?"

"It's Adam." He corrected her in a soft growl. "Do you need anything?"

"No. I just wanted to say...thank you."

He stood very still for a moment, a tall, solid silhouette in the backlighted doorway. And then he nodded. "You're welcome. Call out if you need me. I'll be in the next room."

She closed her eyes and let sleep claim her, aware even as she lost consciousness that there was something oddly reassuring in the knowledge that this stranger wasn't far away.

So much for peaceful solitude. Adam stood at the window of the cabin, staring out into the night. The winter storm that had seemed to guarantee his peace and quiet earlier now posed more of a trap. There was no way he could drive on the two inches of ice that lay beneath the still-falling snow. It would be dangerous even if he had a four-wheel-drive vehicle; in his Jaguar, it would be downright deadly.

He still found it hard to believe the woman had been out alone on a night like this, lost on rural back roads with no one knowing where she was. She talked like an intelligent woman, but it hadn't been a very bright stunt to attempt. She was damn lucky that she'd ended up here, where he could watch out for her until road conditions improved. She could have ended up stranded alone—or worse, at the mercy of someone less honorable than he.

He had to admit that he was intensely curious about her. Who was she? Was she really as alone as she'd implied when she'd told him that no one knew where she was, or would be concerned by her disappearance? Where had she been going? Where was the father of her baby?

Why had his pulse tripped when he'd knelt in front of her and looked deeply into her amber eyes?

That frivolous and unwelcome question made him scowl and shake his head. Where had such a stupid thought come from?

He turned away from the window, from the frozen landscape outside it, and glanced around the snug cottage. Jenny's coat was still lying on the floor where he'd dropped it, as were her shoes, socks, damp jeans, gloves, hat and muffler. He straightened the room, draping her wet things over chairs near the fireplace to allow them to dry.

He stumbled over something when he bent to pick up her coat. Looking down, he saw her purse, its contents spilled across the hardwood floor.

He hung her coat on the rack beside the door, next to his own heavy parka, then bent to scoop her belongings back into her purse. It would have taken a much more noble soul than he not to give in to his curiosity as he collected her things. Adam had never made any claims to nobility.

A battered billfold revealed a Texas driver's license that gave her name as Jennifer Anne Newcomb, placed her age at twenty-six—older than he'd first thought—and listed a Dallas address.

He didn't rifle through the wallet, though he noted that there were no credit cards or photographs in evidence. He closed it again and shoved it into the purse, along with two lipsticks, a powder compact, a pair of sunglasses, a bottle of prenatal vitamins and a roll of butter-rum Life Savers.

A ragged white legal-size envelope caught his eye; he reached for it, intending to stuff it into the purse with the other things. His attention was grabbed and held by the stack of hundred dollar bills visible through a tear in the envelope. He couldn't resist counting them.

A moment later, his pithy curse blistered the air. What in *hell* was the woman doing driving around by herself with five thousand dollars in cash in her purse? Didn't she know there were plenty of scum who'd kill without hesitation or remorse for this kind of money?

Jennifer Anne Newcomb was obviously in need of a keeper. Unfortunately Adam had always had a weakness for people who seemed to need his always-sensible guidance. He'd have a little talk with her as soon as she woke up, he decided with a sigh, sliding the money carefully into her purse. She was just darned lucky she'd ended up on the right doorstep, he thought again.

He wasn't entirely oblivious to the arrogance in the statement, but he was confident that he could be of great service to her if she'd be reasonable enough to accept his advice.

Adam was in charge again, as he'd been on a regular basis since he was eight years old. By now, he was fully resigned to the responsibility of the role.

Jenny woke with a groan, aware even before she opened her eyes that every inch of her body seemed to be sore. She was accustomed to the various discomforts that accompanied late pregnancy—low back pain, painfully swollen breasts, battered ribs, aching thighs, throbbing ankles—but this was different. She hurt *all over*.

She forced her eyes open, then blinked a few times trying to focus on dark, unfamiliar surroundings. Where was she? Why was it so dark?

Memory returned instantly, and she struggled to sit upright. She'd wrecked her car. She'd made a nightmarish trek over treacherously icy ground, through woods and underbrush, and had landed on the doorstep of an unshaven man holed up alone in a summer cottage. She'd allowed him to strip her and grope her, pour tea down her throat and then tuck her into his bed.

Had she completely lost her mind?

She thought of the money in her purse—every last penny she owned. It would be just her luck to find out that the guy had cleaned her out and left her stranded here.

She had no idea what time it was, how long she'd been asleep, and she couldn't see her watch in the darkness. She tried to turn on the lamp on the nightstand, but nothing happened when she turned the switch.

She frowned, suddenly aware that there was no light coming through the open bedroom door, and that the room was considerably cooler than it had been earlier. She'd been warm enough beneath the pile of blankets, but now that she had thrown them off, she shivered, her bare legs prickling with gooseflesh.

What had happened to the electricity? Had the storm taken it out...or had the scruffy stranger left her stranded here alone, to die of the cold?

Stop it, Jenny. You're letting your imagination get away from you again. Get up and go find out what's going on, for crying out loud.

"Nag, nag, nag," she muttered to that insistent little voice in her head, but she pushed herself to her feet. Her toes curled when they made contact with the cold wood floor. She dragged a blanket from the bed and wrapped it around her shoulders, letting it dangle almost to her ankles. And then she took a step toward the open doorway.

She stopped with a startled cry when a massive dark shape suddenly blocked her path.

"Hey, it's okay," the man said quickly, reaching out to steady her when she stumbled backward. "You're safe with me. Remember?"

The voice was familiar, and so was the face when she finally brought his heavily shadowed features into focus. His name...Adam Stone, she recalled. He'd told her to call him Adam.

"Yes, I remember. What happened to the lights? And the heat?"

"Went out about twenty minutes ago. I've checked the breakers, but I think the problem is with the lines down the road somewhere. It happens often in an ice storm. The weight of the ice causes lines to snap, and it takes a while for the power crews to get them all repaired. I was just coming in to make sure you were warm enough."

"It is getting cold in here," she admitted.

"Come into the living room. I've got a good fire going in there, and it's considerably warmer. Fortunately the kitchen stove is a gas range, so we can have hot water and food."

She moved toward the doorway, but stopped when he spoke again. "Your feet must be freezing on that bare floor. Your own socks are still damp, but I've got some you can wear. Hang on a second while I—ouch," he said when he bumped heavily into a piece of furniture.

She heard the scrape of a drawer opening, then his exclamation of satisfaction. "Here they are," he said, and returned carefully to her side.

"I'll put them on in the living room," she said, impatient to get close to that fire he'd mentioned.

She gasped when he suddenly swung her off her chilled feet and into his arms. She clutched frantically at his shoulders when he began to move. "What are you—put me down!"

"I will. Soon as we get those feet covered," he assured her. "We don't want you getting a chill."

It amazed her how easily he carried her, even as heavy as she was at the moment. He was definitely stronger than he looked.

And he certainly had a tendency to just take over without consulting her first, she added to herself with a frown. If he thought she was the docile, meekly cooperative type just because she must have looked like a wet stray kitten earlier, then he had a lot to learn about her!

He deposited her into the same chair she'd sat in earlier, the one closest to the fire. And then he knelt in front of her and matter-of-factly stuffed her feet into the thick white sweat socks.

"Mr. Stone," Jenny began, trying to reclaim some dignity despite the circumstances. "I appreciate your help, but—"

"Adam." He corrected her as he stood and tucked the blanket carefully around her bare legs. "Are you warm enough now? I have a couple of pairs of sweatpants with drawstring waists that should fit you."

"I'm fine now, though I may take you up on the sweatpants later," she said. "What I wanted to say was—"

He shook his dark head and flashed her an absent smile. "No, don't bother to thank me. It isn't necessary. Are you hungry? I can heat a can of soup."

She *was* hungry, as a matter of fact. The thought of warm soup was enticing enough to almost distract her from what she'd intended to say. And then she remembered. "Yes, that sounds wonderful. But—"

He raised one finger. "Hold that thought. I'll put the soup on. I'm getting kind of hungry myself."

She sighed when he disappeared into what she assumed was the kitchen. The man was harder to talk to than a hyperactive puppy—not that there was anything at all puppyish about his lean face and brusque manner.

She glanced at her watch, surprised to find that it was almost midnight. She'd slept longer than she'd thought. Obviously she was here to stay for the night. She couldn't even begin to imagine what she'd do in the morning. Something told her that Adam Stone would have plenty of suggestions to offer, she thought with a grimace. He seemed to be the type who would.

It was only a few minutes later that Adam came back into the firelit room, carefully balancing a tray that held two steaming mugs and a tube of saltines. "I thought it would be easier for you to drink the soup out of a mug than to try to balance a bowl in your lap," he explained, setting the tray on the coffee table in front of the low couch opposite her chair.

"What lap?" Jenny muttered wryly.

He chuckled. "I hope you like canned chicken noodle soup," he said, handing her a mug and a spoon.

"Sounds good," she replied, trying to remember her last meal. She'd skipped lunch, so she hadn't eaten in fifteen hours. No wonder she was so hungry! She usually tried to take better care of herself.

The soup tasted as good as it had sounded. She sighed in pleasure and downed it as quickly as she could without burning her mouth. Adam ate almost as greedily, making her wonder if he'd missed his dinner because of her. He really was being nice to her—a veritable Good Samaritan. She was grateful, though she was beginning to chafe against his rather autocratic manner.

She suspected he was a man who was accustomed to barking orders and having them followed, which led her to wonder who, exactly, he was and what he did when he wasn't playing the hermit of the lake. A drill sergeant, perhaps?

It was quiet in the cabin, except for the steady *pop-sizzle* of the firewood and the muted sounds of the winter storm that still continued outside, though it seemed to have abated some while she'd slept. There was a strangely intimate feel to dining by firelight with this man, even if they were virtual strangers. She wasn't usually so comfortable with people she didn't know.

"Do you live here full-time?" she asked just to make conversation.

He confirmed her suspicion when he shook his head. "No, I live in Little Rock. I'm just renting this place for a couple of weeks. Taking a vacation, of sorts," he added. "It seemed like a good place to get away from the world and recharge my mental batteries."

"I'm sorry I disturbed your solitude."

He shrugged. "I'm just glad you saw my lights when you wrecked your car. I'd hate to think of you being out in that cold and ice."

She shivered at the thought. "Me, too," she confessed.

He set his empty mug on the coffee table. Jenny placed hers on the end table beside her chair. She sensed before he spoke that he was finally getting around to the questions she knew must be plaguing him.

"What was the name of the hotel you were looking for?" he asked.

She made a face at the silly name when she replied. "The Bide-a-Bye. I was told that it was clean and comfortable and inexpensive, which met all my requirements for tonight. But I think I turned left when I should have turned right somewhere—or vice versa."

"Obviously. There's no place like that around here, that I know of. In fact, I haven't seen anyone since I arrived three days ago."

Not a reassuring comment. "I guess I'll have to call someone to tow my car," she said, thinking regretfully of the expense. "I don't think I'll be driving it away from the tree I wrapped it around."

"I'll look at it as soon as the weather permits," he said. "You weren't too badly shaken by the collision, I hope. You didn't hit the steering wheel or anything, did you?"

"No. I was wearing my seat belt."

He nodded, then frowned again. "Did the seat belt tighten across your stomach? Was there much force?"

"I was wearing it beneath my stomach," she explained. "I'm a bit sore where the shoulder strap tightened across my chest, but I'm sure the baby's fine, if that's what you're worried about."

"Yeah," he admitted. "Since there's little chance of driving out of here for a good twenty-four hours, it's reassuring to know that you aren't in need of immediate medical attention."

"Twenty-four hours?" Jenny repeated in dismay.

"At the least," he repeated. "You haven't looked out lately. It's ugly out there. Two inches of ice with a good three inches of snow on top of that. And since snowplows aren't exactly common equipment in these parts—and particularly on rural roads that are rarely traveled, anyway—we won't be going anywhere until the temperature rises enough for a thaw."

The last she'd heard, the high tomorrow was expected to be only in the low twenties. "It isn't going to thaw tomorrow, is it?" she asked in a low voice.

"Doubtful," he said. "If we're lucky, it'll start melting the day after. It's hard to predict. This is hardly average weather for central Arkansas. Though I remember six or seven years ago, when we got twelve and a half inches of snow in Little Rock," he added conversationally. "The city was basically shut down for days, particularly in the outlying areas."

"They aren't predicting that much snow this time, are they?" Jenny asked apprehensively.

He shook his head. "It's already starting to taper off. The problem, of course, is the ice. I can drive on snow. Ice is an entirely different matter."

"Don't I know it," Jenny muttered, remembering the helpless feeling of being out of control of her sliding car. "I don't suppose you have a four-wheel-drive vehicle equipped with chains?"

"Jaguar," he replied, oddly cheerful about it. "Great car, but useless in this weather."

"Wonderful," she said with a sigh.

"We'll be okay. There's plenty of food for several days, and enough firewood to burn for weeks. Don't worry about it."

"I have to admit that I really feel funny about staying here," she said candidly. "After all, I don't even know you. Maybe it would be better if we tried to call for help. Maybe we could get a tow truck out in the morning, and I could ride to the closest town with the driver."

Adam shook his head. "I'm sure the tow trucks are doing all they can to keep up with the calls they must be getting from stranded motorists. And I really doubt that anyone's going to agree to come all the way out here until these roads clear some. It's just too risky. Besides," he added, not without sympathy, "the phone's dead. I tested it just before you woke up. The phone lines must be down, too."

She couldn't hide her dismay. "But—"

"Jenny," Adam cut in gently. "Face it. You're stuck here for a day or two. I'm sorry, I wish I could take you wherever you want to go. But we'd be foolishly risking both our lives—all three of our lives," he added with a glance at her stomach. "I'm not exactly known for being a gracious host, but I'll try to be on my company behavior while you're here, okay? I swear to you that you have nothing to fear from me."

She bit her lip and eyed his face, finding it difficult to give her trust so easily.

He smiled. It didn't make his hard, dark face look any less intimidating, she decided, but he was obviously trying to put her at ease.

"If the phones were working, we'd call my grandmother," he said. "Granny Fran would assure you that I'm really a decent guy, even though she's convinced that I'm a bit too big for my britches, as she words it."

"Granny Fran?" Jenny repeated, tempted to smile. It was difficult to be wary of someone who talked so easily about his "Granny."

He nodded. "Five feet two inches of pure dynamite. You'd like her, I'm sure. Everyone does."

"Does she live close to here?"

"About a half hour away. She's the only one who has the number where I can be reached—not that it would do her any good with the lines down."

"You must have a high pressure job, to need to get away all by yourself like this," Jenny ventured.

He nodded. "Yeah. You could say that."

"You—um—aren't married?"

"No. Never have been."

"Neither have I." She wondered how he'd react to that, given her condition. Before he should feel compelled to say anything, she heard herself adding hastily, "I came close, a few months ago—" eight, to be exact "—but it didn't work out," she added, looking down at her hands.

"He didn't want the baby?" Adam asked gently.

Her mouth twisted. "He didn't want *me*," she corrected him. "The baby was just something else he didn't want."

Adam studied her face for a moment. "Do you mind if I say that the guy must have been a damn fool?" he asked finally.

She smiled. "No, I don't mind that at all. In fact, I appreciate it. Thanks."

"You're welcome. When's the baby due?"

"Almost another month yet. I plan to be in east Tennessee by then."

"Is that where your family lives?"

"No." She didn't want to talk about her family. "That's where a friend from high school lives. She owns a temporary agency—you know, one of those places people call when they need clerical workers for a limited time?''

He nodded.

''Anyway, she said if I ever wanted a job to look her up. After the baby's born, I plan to find a good day-care center and get back to work as soon as I can.''

''Temporary work doesn't pay very well,'' Adam cautioned. ''No benefits, no retirement.''

He wasn't telling her anything she didn't know all too well. ''I know. But it's a place to start,'' she said. ''I don't have any references to secure a permanent position easily.''

Adam was still looking at her, and his gaze was so perceptive that she was tempted to squirm in the chair. ''You've had a difficult time, haven't you?'' he asked.

She didn't like having him look at her like a charity case. She shrugged. ''Not nearly as rough as some people have it. I've always managed to land on my feet in the past.''

''You're not one of those stubbornly independent types, are you?'' Adam asked suspiciously.

She laughed. ''As a matter of fact, I am.''

He sighed gustily. ''Everyone needs a helping hand at times, Jenny. Keep that in mind, okay?''

She eyed him skeptically. ''I bet you've never asked for help in your whole life,'' she accused him.

He started to speak, then stopped and cleared his throat. ''We weren't talking about me,'' he reminded her.

Which only confirmed her accusation. Adam Stone was the self-sufficient type if she'd ever met one. A kindred spirit, actually, though they probably had little else in common. She just wanted to make it quite clear to him that she was quite capable of taking care of herself—once the roads thawed, of course.

Something told her she had to put her foot down quickly with this man, before he swept her off her feet again.

Chapter Three

Still tired from her ordeal, Jenny soon began to nod in her chair. Adam insisted on helping her move to the couch, where he tucked her in with a pillow and several thick blankets. She murmured a protest at being treated like a sleepy child, but her eyes closed almost before she finished the complaint. She was asleep within minutes.

Adam stood beside her for a long moment, watching her, judging for himself that she was sleeping comfortably, apparently suffering no ill effects from the car accident or the exposure to the cold and damp. Though he was trying to study her with clinical detachment, he couldn't help noticing how beautiful she looked in the glow of the firelight.

Annoyed with himself, he turned away and began to arrange his heavy sleeping bag on the floor in front of the fire. He was still consumed with questions about his uninvited houseguest. He was fully aware that most of them were questions he had no right to ask—but probably would, anyway.

He couldn't see himself just turning this hapless young woman loose to go off on her own with no job, apparently no family to turn to in her time of need. It wasn't in his nature to turn his back on someone in need of his guidance. Whether she realized it or not.

Adding another log to the fire, he slipped out of his shoes and crawled fully clothed into the sleeping bag. He was glad now that he'd impulsively brought it along with him, though he'd had no idea he'd be utilizing it quite like this.

Adam woke several times during the next few hours, each time rising to add a log to the fire and check on his houseguest. Jenny slept soundly, hardly stirring on the narrow, probably uncomfortable couch. She must have been exhausted, he thought in sympathy.

The snow had stopped by Friday morning, but there was still a thick layer of heavy gray clouds that darkened the day and threatened more precipitation. Studying those clouds in concern, Adam tuned in the battery-operated radio he kept in the kitchen and listened as the weatherman predicted more ice and snow by evening.

State police were asking all nonemergency vehicles to stay off the roads, and many roads were closed entirely until crews could clear them. This was the worst winter storm to hit this area in the past decade, the announcer said gravely.

Adam shook his head ruefully. Trust him to pick a time like this for his first vacation in ages. It should have been no surprise to him that he had ended up taking care of someone else on this vacation.

Just for the hell of it, he lifted the telephone receiver to his ear. Still no dial tone. He thought of the cellular phone in his car, but decided there was really no need to try it at the moment. At least it was available in case of an emergency.

He turned on the gas stove and set coffee on to perk. And then he wondered if Jenny liked oatmeal. She would need a good, hearty breakfast when she awoke.

The warmth of the stove felt good in the chilly kitchen. The wooden floor was cool even through his thick cotton socks. He was grateful for the huge stack of firewood behind the cabin, and for the natural-gas stove. They needed all the breaks they could get right now.

A sound from the doorway made him look around. "Good morning," he said, finding his houseguest watching him from across the room. "How are you feeling?"

Still wearing her red sweater and his black sweatpants and white sweat socks, Jenny looked sleepy and tousled, but amazingly attractive, considering the circumstances. She ran a hand through her tumbled dark curls, her expression a bit shy. "Good morning. I'm fine," she assured him.

"Hungry?"

"Starving," she admitted with a slight smile.

"Do you like oatmeal?"

"Actually I do. Is that what you're having?"

"Yeah. Why don't you go on back into the living room where it's warm, and I'll serve breakfast in there when it's ready."

Jenny frowned. "I don't expect you to wait on me, Adam. I'll help you make breakfast."

He shook his head and spoke reasonably. "As small as this kitchen is, we'd only get in each other's way. I can have breakfast ready in just a few minutes."

"But I—"

Sensing that her stubborn independence was forcing her to protest, Adam broke in. "I think the coffee's ready. Why don't you pour us both a cup and carry them into the living room?"

She gave him a narrow look but seemed somewhat appeased at having something to do. She filled two large mugs with the strong, fragrant brew, added creamer to her own, then carried both carefully into the other room while Adam prepared the oatmeal.

They ate in front of the fire, stocking feet curled beneath them, steaming cups of coffee sitting in front of them. The casual atmosphere helped Jenny relax. Adam seemed completely comfortable in her presence, which helped her adjust to the awkward circumstance of breakfasting alone with a stranger.

She watched him circumspectly as they ate. Who, exactly, was this man? From the impressions she'd gathered thus far, she would guess he was a bit of a loner, something she might have suspected even if she hadn't known he'd been vacationing alone in this isolated spot in the dead of winter.

Still, he'd been friendly enough to her, in his brusque, take-charge way. He didn't dislike other people, she hazarded; he simply needed time away from them occasionally.

There was no doubt in her mind that Adam Stone was an inherently arrogant man. He'd shown that tendency from the moment he'd stepped through his front door and rescued her from the storm. Whatever it was he did to earn his living, whatever high-powered, high-stress job had driven him to this quiet refuge, she suspected that he was very successful at it—and that his subordinates jumped at his every command.

There was an air of power about him, an almost visible aura of leadership. What would it be like to be that casually self-confident? she wondered wistfully. That convinced of one's own worth and competence?

She hoped someday to find out for herself.

"Tell me about yourself, Jenny," Adam startled her by saying when they'd finished eating.

She looked at him warily. "What do you want to know?"

He smiled faintly at her tone. "Whatever you want to tell me. It's called making conversation. There seems to be little else for us to do at the moment."

"Oh." That seemed reasonable enough, she supposed. She didn't blame him for being curious. After all, hadn't she just been indulging her own curiosity by speculating about what Adam Stone was really like?

"Are you a native of Texas?" he asked encouragingly, as though to get her started.

She nodded. "Yes. I grew up in a small town fifty miles west of Dallas. What about you? Are you from this area?"

"I grew up in central Arkansas," he acknowledged. "Do you have any brothers or sisters?"

"No. I'm an only child. And you?"

"Only child," he confirmed.

That didn't surprise her. She would have guessed that he'd been either an only child or an oldest sibling.

"Are your parents still living?" he asked.

"Yes," she answered without embellishment. "Are yours?" She figured if he could ask personal questions just to pass the time, so could she.

"My mother is. My father died when I was eight. Do you see your parents often?"

"No," she answered flatly. "Do you see your mother?"

He was obviously amused by her determined, question-for-a-question tactic. "Yes, I see my mother quite often. You aren't close to your parents?"

"No." But that was something she didn't want to talk about. "You seemed quite fond of your grandmother when you mentioned her," she commented instead.

Adam chuckled. "Oh, yeah. Granny Fran's one of a kind. She's in her seventies, yet she can run rings around me almost any day. She keeps a close watch on her family—my mother and me, and her son and his family. She seems to take personal responsibility for the happiness and well-being of her four grandchildren, even though we're all grown now."

"Are you a close family?" Jenny asked, hoping he wouldn't notice the faint hint of wistfulness beneath the question.

He gave the question some thought. "I suppose we are," he said after a moment. "I stay in touch with my cousins, though usually from a distance, since we all lead busy lives. Though I'm the eldest, Rachel, Cody and Celia were my closest approximation to having siblings. We spend most holidays together. We were all together for Christmas, and again for Rachel's wedding on New Year's Eve. Even when we don't see each other for a while, all of them know they can call me anytime they need me and I'll be there for them."

Her hand resting on her swollen stomach, Jenny thought of how nice it must be to know one had a close and supportive family to turn to in times of need.

And then she thought of the interesting way Adam had phrased his observation. "Doesn't it work both ways?"

she asked. "Are they available for you when you need them?"

Adam seemed a bit surprised by the question. "I'm sure they would be," he said. "If I ever needed them, of course."

Ah, yes, she thought ruefully. Adam Stone couldn't imagine himself ever being in a position of needing anyone else. He saw himself as the one others turned to, the one with the answers.

She wondered what it would take to shake this man's supreme self-confidence. And she wondered how he would handle it if he was ever forced to admit that he wasn't invulnerable.

"You said you're going to work for a temporary agency in Tennessee," Adam said, changing the subject. "What work experience do you have?"

This was beginning to sound like an employment interview, Jenny thought with a silent sigh. But, since Adam had taken her in and was feeding and caring for her until she could take care of herself again, she cooperated. "My father owned rental units when I was growing up. I worked in that business from the time I was a teenager—interviewing prospective renters, collecting rent, calling repairmen, even cleaning apartments when necessary."

"Did you like working in property management?"

"Not particularly," she admitted. "But I stayed with it until I was in my mid-twenties. My father and I weren't getting along very well by then, so I moved to Dallas and took a series of clerical jobs. My latest one lasted two years."

Something in her voice must have caught his attention. His dark eyes were focused intently on her face. "What happened?"

She shrugged and patted her stomach. "*This* happened."

"Your baby's father worked for the same company?"

"He was my supervisor," Jenny answered without emotion. "He's divorced, a few years older than I am. We started dating only a few months after I began working for the company. We got along quite well, actually," she added with forced lightness. "I foolishly believed we were headed for the altar—a tidy, happy-ever-after ending. I temporarily forgot that things like that happen only in fiction."

"He hurt you," Adam said. It wasn't a question.

"Yes." *That's enough, Jenny. You don't need to tell him any more.*

But Adam's dark eyes were oddly sympathetic, his deep voice compelling. "Did he break up with you when he found out about the baby?"

"No," she found herself answering. "Even before that, actually. He took me to dinner at one of my favorite restaurants. We had a wonderful evening. I thought I knew how it would end. I was already mentally practicing my acceptance to his marriage proposal."

"But he didn't propose."

She laughed bitterly. "Hardly. He told me that I was a very special person, and that he was very fond of me. And then he told me that he thought we should start seeing other people. We'd been getting too serious, he said. He wasn't interested in remarrying or getting tied down to another monogamous relationship."

"And he'd never mentioned that before?"

She shook her head, her mind replaying that humiliating evening in much too vivid detail.

God, she'd been such an idiot.

"Did you know then that you were pregnant?"

Adam's question penetrated her gloomy thoughts, and she answered automatically. "No. I realized it a few weeks later."

"Did you tell him?"

"Of course."

She winced at that even uglier memory. "He refused to accept it. He accused me of trying to trap him. He even implied that he doubted that he was the father. And then he managed to get me fired from my job—very discreetly, of course."

"So you packed up and headed for Tennessee," Adam said, guessing at the end of the story.

She nodded ruefully, waiting for him to point out, as her friends had, that she'd made a really stupid mistake.

To his credit, Adam didn't say it. "Are you going to demand financial assistance from the jerk?" was all he asked.

Jenny lifted her chin and shook her head. "No," she said proudly. "As far as I'm concerned, this baby has no father. The 'jerk' lost all claim when he pretended it wasn't his."

"You haven't seen him since?"

She made a face. "Once. Two friends took me for a farewell dinner at a nice restaurant in Dallas a couple of weeks ago. He was there, with a tall, slender, stunningly beautiful blonde who had to be at least half his age. He took one look at me in this condition and he almost recoiled in distaste. He managed to greet me politely enough, and then he hustled his blonde away so quickly he nearly left skid marks on the carpet behind them."

Adam rubbed his chin. "I'll send someone to hurt the guy, if you want. Something painful and long lasting."

His tone was so casual, so conversational that Jenny blinked. It almost seemed as though he were serious.

And then she found herself smiling. "That won't be necessary," she said. "I'm quite capable of taking my own revenge, when I want. But thanks for the offer."

"The offer's still open. Keep it in mind."

Still smiling, she looked down at her stomach. "The thing is, I don't want revenge. I did, at first. I hated Carl. But now I don't feel anything for him at all. All I know is, despite everything that's happened, I want this baby. Very much. And somehow, I'm going to take care of it. Alone."

Adam frowned. "With temporary clerical jobs?"

"If I have to," she said coolly.

He shook his head. "You're going to need more help than that. I'll contact my lawyer. You deserve child support, medical and living expenses. There are ways of making—"

"Wait a minute." Jenny broke in abruptly, suddenly angry with herself again for telling Adam entirely too much. How *did* he manage to do that to her?

"You aren't calling a lawyer," she informed him flatly. "I don't want anything from Carl. Or from you, for that matter. I am perfectly capable of taking care of myself."

She couldn't completely blame him for the doubt in the look he gave her. After all, she'd just admitted that she was estranged from her family, that she'd been dumped by a selfish lover, that she'd lost her job, had taken off alone at eight months pregnant on a chance of getting temporary employment, and then had gotten lost and wrecked her car along the way.

She probably *did* sound like a charity case, especially to a man like Adam. But he was wrong. Jenny was a survivor. She and her baby would get along just fine, once she got away from this desolate cabin and back on the path she'd chosen.

She could tell he intended to argue. He even opened his mouth to do so, but she cut him off by gathering her breakfast dishes and rising awkwardly to her feet. "Since you cooked, I'll wash up," she said. "Would you like more coffee before I empty the pot?"

Adam hesitated, then stood. "I'll help you with the dishes."

"You said yourself that the kitchen isn't big enough for two," she said pointedly. "Pour yourself a cup of coffee and sit by the fire. This won't take me long."

She thought for a moment that he was going to argue about that, too. Instead he frowned, muttered something unintelligible and carried his cup into the kitchen for a refill.

Grateful for the brief respite, Jenny took her time with the dishes. She spent most of the time silently berating herself for letting Adam Stone somehow persuade her to tell him her whole life story.

She was determined that he wouldn't manipulate her so easily again during the brief time she would be spending with him until she could move on.

Adam stared moodily into the fire, his coffee growing cold in the mug on the low table beside him. He was thinking of the tale Jenny had told him, wondering what kind of moron could have treated her like that, wondering why she couldn't turn to her parents for help. He pictured something similar happening in his family—to his younger cousin Celia, for example.

Suppose Celia's recent whirlwind romance had gone sour, leaving her unemployed and facing single parenthood rather than happily married. There was no way in hell she'd have found it necessary to strike out alone in search of a job. Everyone in the family would have offered assistance, from cash to job references to baby-sitting.

The front door of every home would have been opened to her—including Adam's, for that matter. Celia would not have been alone. And neither would anyone else in the family during any similar time of need.

Why didn't Jenny have that same support from her own family?

A wave of unexpected fury crashed though him as he thought of the way she'd been treated by her bastard of a former lover. What he wouldn't give for just ten minutes with the son of a . . .

Realizing the direction his thoughts had taken, Adam looked in surprise at his clenched fist.

He deliberately loosened his fingers, telling himself to calm down. It wasn't as though he were personally involved, after all. This wasn't someone from his own family, but a woman who was little more than a complete stranger to him. He would do well to keep that in mind.

Jenny Newcomb fully believed that she would be getting back on the road as soon as the ice melted and her car was repaired. She probably expected Adam to see her off with a cheery wave and then promptly put her out of his mind.

She didn't know him, of course. Those who did could have told her she was wasting her time trying to brush off his assistance. There was no way Adam was going to send this woman off on her own until he was absolutely certain that she would be all right. It just wasn't in his nature to turn his back on anyone who could benefit from his efficacy—even when his assistance wasn't exactly requested.

The morning passed quietly. Jenny had been gratified to discover that Adam had several excellent mystery novels on hand. Adam seemed pleased that she shared his love of a well-crafted suspense story; he highly recommended the one he'd finished the day he'd arrived at the cabin.

Jenny curled up on the sofa with the book and began to read in the grayish, but sufficient, natural light streaming through the cabin's windows. She was grateful for something to do to distract her from her problems. Adam sat in the chair closest to the fireplace and opened the book he'd been reading the evening before.

They sat for several hours in companionable silence. Adam rose occasionally to add more wood to the cheerfully popping fire. Each time he asked Jenny if she needed anything—something to eat or drink, another pillow or blanket. She politely refused, thinking that for a rather gruff man, Adam could be surprisingly thoughtful. He seemed to be accustomed to the role of caretaker, though Jenny was far from comfortable with the position of being cared for.

She was much more accustomed to taking care of herself.

She didn't even realize she was sleepy until Adam touched her shoulder and softly said her name.

Blinking, she brought his face into focus, wondering why he was leaning so close to her. "What is it?"

"You fell asleep," he said with a slight smile. He held up the book she'd been reading. "You dropped your book."

"Oh." Embarrassed, she straightened, realizing she'd slumped against the arm of the couch.

He rested one hand against her shoulder. "Lie down and get comfortable," he urged her. "You probably need a nap."

Rubbing her cramping right calf with her right hand, Jenny pressed her left hand to her side, where the baby seemed to be kicking a message in Morse code against her ribs. "You don't understand," she said wryly. "There *is* no getting comfortable when you're in this condition."

Adam chuckled. "I can imagine."

"No. Trust me, you can't."

"Okay, I can't," he agreed cooperatively. "Lie down, Jenny. Get some rest."

She reluctantly allowed him to ease her down onto the sofa, her head on the pillow he fluffed for her. Again, she wondered how Adam would react should he ever find himself in need of assistance.

She would bet he would like it even less than she did now.

"Are you warm enough?" Adam fretted, tucking the two thick blankets around her.

"I'm fine. Thank you," she forced herself to say with a semblance of patience.

Adam paused with his hand spread across her stomach. He grinned suddenly. "The kid can kick, can't he?"

Flushing a bit at the intimacy of their position, Jenny nodded against the pillow, feeling her baby thumping forcefully against Adam's palm. "Yes. A future soccer player, I think."

Adam didn't seem to be in any hurry to move away. "Boy or girl?"

"I don't know. I haven't had a test to find out."

"Any preference?"

"Not really. Like most expectant mothers, I'll be content either way as long as it's healthy."

Adam laughed softly as the baby kicked again and then slid into a leisurely somersault. "It seems healthy enough to me."

And then he straightened. "Get some rest," he said, his manner suddenly brusque and bossy again. "I'm going to pour myself a cup of coffee and finish my book."

She made a face and closed her eyes, thinking with a fleeting surge of resentment that she would like to be around someday when Adam Stone found himself forced to beg.

It would take at least that to make him understand how it felt not to always be the one in control.

Jenny's first thought when she awoke was that she'd slept much longer than she'd intended. The room was so dark—had she slept the entire day away?

A sound from the doorway into the kitchen made her rise to her elbow and look around. Adam was just coming into the room, bundled up in a heavy parka, his nose reddened from cold, his dark hair wind tossed. The hems of his jeans were wet, and he'd obviously left his boots at the outer door, since he was wearing only thick socks on his feet. His arms were loaded with oddly familiar-looking bags.

"You've been out to my car," she said, shoving herself awkwardly upright.

He nodded. "Yeah. You really did a number on that front fender. Your car looks like it's trying to become one with an oak tree."

She groaned. "I don't think I want to hear about that right now."

He dumped the bags in one corner of the room and shrugged out of his snow-powdered parka. "Okay. I won't tell you that the car's probably totaled."

"I appreciate it," she replied dryly. She ran a hand through her tousled curls and looked again toward the darkened window. "What time is it?"

Adam glanced at his watch. "Just after two." Following her glance toward the window, he added, "It's starting to snow again. I was listening earlier to the battery-powered radio in the kitchen. The weather bureau is predicting another couple of inches tonight."

"Damn." So much for getting out of here anytime today, Jenny thought.

"Jenny, there's a cellular phone in my car. I was thinking about calling my grandmother later to make sure she's okay, and to let her know I'm all right. Are you sure there's no one you want called?" Adam asked. "Won't your parents be worried if they don't hear from you?"

"I told you, I haven't talked to my parents in almost a year," she said coolly. "They aren't expecting to hear from me."

He glanced at her stomach. "Do they know about the baby?"

"No."

"Jenny—"

She pushed herself to her feet. "I have to go to the bathroom," she said bluntly.

Caught off guard, he hesitated. "I'll fix us something to eat," he said after a moment. "I'm sure you're getting hungry. I know I am."

Jenny nodded and headed for the bathroom without looking at him again. He'd learned more about her than she'd intended to tell him already, she thought. She wasn't willing to tell him any more, no matter how curious he might be.

They were, after all, only strangers stranded together temporarily. The snow would end soon, and somehow or another, Jenny would be on her way again. Adam Stone could forget he'd ever met her.

She was sure it wouldn't take him long, though something told her she wouldn't forget him quite so easily.

Chapter Four

Pleased to have her own clothing available now, Jenny washed up and changed into a cheery red-and-blue plaid maternity sweater and blue knit maternity pants with thick red socks. She brushed her dark curls the best she could and even added a light touch of makeup. She wasn't primping, she assured herself; it was simply good manners to try to look somewhat presentable for her host.

Adam smiled when she appeared in response to his call for lunch. "You look very nice," he told her.

She felt like an idiot for blushing. She knew exactly how she looked. Like a red-and-blue plaid hot-air balloon. Still, she managed to say politely, "Thank you."

"I've made grilled cheese sandwiches and canned cream of tomato soup. Is that okay?"

"It's fine. Thank you. But you really don't have to wait on me, Adam. It's not as if I'm an invited guest."

"Don't be ridiculous," he replied. "I have to eat, anyway."

Jenny found that she had very little appetite, but she tried to eat, since Adam had gone to the trouble of preparing the meal. She had to make an effort to keep up her end of the light conversation during lunch; for some reason, she was awfully tired today.

Must be the bizarre circumstances she'd landed herself in this time, she thought ruefully.

Though Jenny offered, Adam insisted on washing up after the meal. "You look a bit pale," he said, studying her face much too perceptively. "Why don't you just sit by the fire and rest awhile? Take a nap, if you like. It's not as if there's anything more exciting to do."

She allowed herself to be persuaded to stay by the fire, though she didn't want to nap. She opened the book she'd been reading earlier and tried to stay awake as she concentrated on the story. And then a commotion from the kitchen brought her head up sharply, her sleepy eyes suddenly wide.

There was a loud thud, and a crash of breaking glass, followed by a low string of curses. Concerned, she tossed the book aside and hurried to investigate.

Adam stood on one foot by the sink, broken glass scattered on the floor around him. He was bent over his left foot, which he held in his hand as he balanced awkwardly against the counter behind him. Jenny noticed at a glance that his once-white sock was already turning red with blood. She gasped.

"Stay back," he said, motioning toward her own stocking feet. "There's broken glass everywhere."

"You're hurt," she said, approaching him cautiously.

"I knocked a glass off with my elbow and then stumbled onto it," he explained, his stubbled jaw hardened by pain and self-disgust. "Jenny, be careful. It won't do any good if you cut yourself, too."

"I'm not going to cut myself," she said, reaching for the broom propped in one corner of the utilitarian kitchen. "Keep still a minute while I sweep this out of the way," she ordered. "Don't put your weight on your foot, there could be glass still embedded in it."

"There is," Adam grunted, picking at the bottom of his bloody sock.

"Leave it alone. I'll look at it."

Adam scowled, and Jenny could tell he didn't like being the one on the receiving end of orders. As she swept the last of the glass into a neat pile, she mused that she rather liked being the one giving the orders for a change.

Jenny bustled Adam into a chair at the kitchen table, then told him to stay there while she fetched the first-aid kit from the cabin's only bathroom. "And leave that foot alone," she added over her shoulder as she left the room. "I'll take care of it."

Adam ignored her, of course. He carefully peeled the sock away from his bleeding foot, wincing as shards of glass peeled away with it. How could he have been so stupid? He never did careless things like this. What had he been thinking of when he'd clumsily knocked the glass to the floor and then brought his foot right down on top of it?

Jenny reappeared at that moment, a white plastic box in one hand and a frown on her face. "I told you to leave it alone," she said with a long-suffering sigh, as though she'd known very well that he would do no such thing.

He shrugged. "I was just looking at it."

She knelt in front of him, made awkward by her condition, and yet oddly graceful at the same time. He was still wondering how she managed that when she took his foot in her hand.

Suddenly uncomfortable with the situation, Adam straightened abruptly. "Look, you don't have to do this. I can handle it."

"Be quiet," she said absently, intently studying the jagged cut that lanced across the pad of his foot. "There's still a piece of glass in here. I'm going to have to take it out. See if there are any tweezers in that kit, will you?"

Adam lifted an eyebrow at her tone.

When had she gotten so cool and bossy? Did medical emergencies always bring out this side of her? Darned if she didn't sound exactly like the head nurse back at the hospital; the one who didn't like him very much and had never made much effort to hide her feelings.

He glanced into the first-aid kit, finding new tweezers still wrapped in sterile paper. "Really, Jenny, this isn't necessary," he said. "I can—"

She took the tweezers from him and ripped open the paper wrapping. "I'll need an antiseptic next," she said, ignoring his words as she bent over the cut. "And a large adhesive bandage. You don't want to get this cut dirty. I've heard that feet are particularly vulnerable to infections."

He thought briefly of informing her that he didn't need supermarket-magazine medical advice from her; that he had several degrees in medicine and was actually considered an authority in some venues. He opened his mouth to speak, but a gasp of pain escaped him instead of the words he'd intended.

"Damn it!" he said when he was capable of coherence again. "That hurt."

Holding a large sliver of bloody glass clasped in the tweezers, Jenny looked up at him, her amber-brown eyes soft with sympathy. "I know," she murmured. "I'm sorry. I couldn't help it."

He was immediately overcome by an almost irresistible urge to apologize in return for snapping at her. Funny. He could hardly remember the last time he'd actually apologized to anyone. He grunted instead. "It's okay."

She looked back down at his foot. "Now it's bleeding even worse," she fretted, reaching for a gauze pad. "It could probably use stitches."

No way was Adam letting her near him with a needle and thread. "It doesn't need stitches," he assured her quickly. "It's just a glass cut. It'll stop bleeding in a minute."

"But—"

"Just pour on some antiseptic and slap a Band-Aid on it," he said gruffly. "It'll be fine."

He wanted to curse again when she carefully and oh so slowly poured the antiseptic over his wound, making sure she saturated the area completely. It burned like fire, hurt worse than when he'd stepped on the glass in the first place. Any other time, he'd have expressed his displeasure in pithy, colorful terms. He bit his tongue to prevent the words from escaping.

He couldn't easily explain his uncharacteristic forbearance. Maybe it was the solicitousness on Jenny's pretty face as she bent so industriously over him, despite the discomfort she must be feeling in that ungainly position. Maybe it was the gentle touch of her cool fingers against his skin.

Or maybe it was the realization that this was the first time anyone had fussed over him in too many years to count. And, to his surprise, he rather liked it.

Stupid, of course. Adam was a caretaker by nature. Always the one in command, the one who looked out for everyone else. It had been his role since he was eight years old, one he'd long grown accustomed to, wouldn't change even if he could. But—just this once—it felt sort of nice to let someone else take care of *him*. If only for a few, fleeting moments.

Jenny finished her task and then started to rise. She gave a muffled groan as she stumbled, thrown off-balance by her added bulk. Adam stifled a grin and gave her a hand, pulling her easily to her feet. She made a face. "Thanks."

"Don't mention it."

Jenny set the first-aid supplies on the table, then turned toward the doorway. "I'll get you a clean pair of socks."

She was gone before he could tell her not to bother. Her added weight certainly didn't slow her down much, even if it did make her a bit clumsy, Adam thought wryly.

He couldn't help wondering what she'd looked like before pregnancy had distorted her figure. He'd bet she was naturally slender and graceful, judging from her fine bone structure. It wasn't hard to guess what her jerk of an ex-lover had seen in her. After all, even under these circumstances, Adam was fighting an entirely inappropriate attraction to her.

What Adam *couldn't* understand was how anyone could purposefully hurt her.

The storm began again early that evening, arriving in a gust of wind and a heavy curtain of wet, icy snow.

Still without electricity, Adam and Jenny were staying close to the fire. The skies had darkened, and there was no longer enough natural light for reading. Adam had unearthed an old-fashioned lantern from a storage room at the back of the cabin, along with several cans of fuel. The lantern and the firelight gave the room a bright, golden glow in the center, which faded to deep shadows in the corners.

The fire crackled and popped and the lantern hissed softly, the sounds lulling Jenny into a near stupor.

Realizing she was falling asleep—how could she possibly be sleepy again?—she roused to ask Adam, "How's your foot?"

He looked up from his book. "Mmm? Oh, it's fine. Hardly sore."

"Good." She shifted in the chair, trying vainly to get comfortable.

"Are you hungry? You haven't eaten much today."

"I'm not at all hungry right now. But, please, don't wait for me. If you're hungry..."

He shook his head. "No. I'm fine." He closed his book and set it aside.

"I didn't mean to disturb your reading."

"I'm getting tired of reading," Adam admitted. "I'm not used to this much inactivity."

"What had you planned to do to entertain yourself while you were here—before the storm hit, I mean?"

He shrugged and made a sheepish face. "Just sit around and read. For some reason, that idea greatly appealed to me last week."

"You must lead a very busy life."

"Yeah. Is your back hurting? You keep squirming around and rubbing it."

She dropped her hand, not having realized she was massaging her lower back until Adam brought it to her attention. "My back hurts all the time these days," she confessed. "I suppose it's just all part of the condition I'm in."

"Would you like me to rub it for you?"

She blinked. The thought of Adam Stone giving her a back rub—the image of his big, strong hands moving slowly against her skin—sent a funny feeling through her. A shivery, not entirely unpleasant feeling that made her frown in self-reproval.

Whatever had gotten into her? Was temporary insanity also a part of this condition?

"No, thank you," she said politely, but firmly. "I'm fine."

"Do you play gin rummy?"

Now that seemed safe enough. "Yes. Do you have a deck of cards?"

"There are several decks, as well as a couple of board games, on the top shelf of the linen closet. I guess the management is prepared for bouts of cabin fever when the weather turns bad."

She smiled and motioned toward the lantern. "It seems the management is prepared for all sorts of contingencies."

"Yeah. I'll have to thank the manager for that when we finally get out of here."

Jenny thought about his words while Adam went off to fetch the cards, limping only a bit on his bandaged foot. He was beginning to sound impatient to leave, she thought. She couldn't blame him, of course—trapped in a cabin in the woods with a pregnant stranger in the middle of a winter storm could hardly be his notion of an ideal vacation.

She should be eager to get out of here herself.

She couldn't imagine why she wasn't.

Adam was gone a bit longer than she'd expected. When he returned, he had a deck of cards tucked into his shirt pocket and steaming mugs gripped in each hand.

"I made us some tea," he said. "It seems to be getting cooler in here, despite the fire."

She nodded and tucked her feet more tightly beneath her. "I'd noticed that," she admitted.

He set the mugs on the coffee table, plucked an afghan from the couch and briskly smoothed it around her. "Better?"

Flustered by his casual attention, she nodded and avoided his eyes. "Yes. Thank you."

He murmured a response while he carefully pulled the coffee table in front of her, tossed a couple of throw pillows on the floor on the other side and settled onto them, facing her from across the low table. "I'll deal," he said.

Jenny nodded and reached for her tea.

She should have expected that Adam would take advantage of the opportunity to find out more about her during the card game. He seemed to be awfully curious about her—and not at all reticent about asking questions that others might have considered overly inquisitive.

"Why don't you get along with your father?" he asked from out of the blue.

Jenny frowned at the cards in her hand. "I just don't," she said shortly. "You forgot to discard."

"Oh. Right." He tossed a three of clubs onto the table and sipped his tea before asking, "What about your mother? Do you get along with her?"

"About the same as I do with my father. And I'd rather not talk about this right now, Adam."

He didn't seem offended. "Fine."

He picked up the ten of hearts she'd just discarded. "Have you thought of any names for your baby?"

There was no following his line of thinking. At least she didn't mind talking about the baby—as long as he didn't start offering unwanted advice again. "I've given it some thought, of course. But I haven't made any decisions yet."

"What are some of your possibilities?"

She couldn't imagine why he'd want to know. He must be just trying to pass the time, she decided. "For a boy, I like Nicholas," she told him. "Or Ashley."

"Ashley?" Adam repeated, wrinkling his nose. He shook his head. "Too sissy. The other boys would eat him for lunch."

Exasperated, Jenny frowned at him. "Did I ask your opinion?"

"No, but you obviously need it. Trust me, this is a guy's judgment. Don't name the kid Ashley unless you're prepared to teach him self-defense before he starts kindergarten."

"That's a sexist, archaic viewpoint."

He shrugged. "Probably. But, still, I'd stick with Nicholas if I were you. Nick's a good name. A boy could live with that one."

"I can't tell you how much I appreciate your insight," Jenny said dryly.

Her sarcasm passed right over his handsome dark head. "Don't mention it. How about if the kid's a girl?"

"Tiffany, maybe."

"Too cute. She'll grow up someday, you know. You want her grandkids to have a grandmother named Tiffany?"

Jenny couldn't help being ruefully amused.

Adam Stone was something else, she mused. Was there any subject he didn't consider himself an expert about? "How about Jane?"

"Too plain."

"Kate?"

"Too common."

"Phoenix."

"Too *un*-common. Whoever heard of anyone named Phoenix?"

Jenny laughed. She couldn't help it. "Well, what name *do* you like?"

Adam gave it a moment's thought, taking the question seriously—as she should have known he would. "Melissa," he said finally. "I like Melissa."

She looked at him suspiciously. "An old girlfriend?"

"No. As far as I know, I've never actually known anyone by that name. I've just always liked it."

"Maybe you'll have a daughter of your own someday and you can name her Melissa."

Adam blew a skeptical breath through his nose. "I doubt it."

Jenny raised an eyebrow at the certainty in his tone. "You don't want children?"

He shrugged. "I like kids okay, but I don't expect to have any. It takes two to make one, you know."

Jenny winced. "I know."

He cleared his throat. "Well, anyway, I don't expect to be married. My job keeps me extremely busy, away from home for long hours—nights and weekends included, when necessary. Not many women are willing to settle for what little time I have left over to give them. The few women I've gotten involved with have all ended up leaving in frustration after I've been forced to stand them up a few too many times."

Jenny started to ask just what he did for a living that kept him so terribly busy, but a loud crash from outside made both of them jump. "What was that?" she asked. "It sounded like it was right outside the window."

Adam had already gone to investigate. "The ice is building up in the trees again," he said somberly. "The weight is breaking limbs. Let's just hope nothing comes down on top of us during the night.''

"What a comforting prospect," Jenny said, drawing the afghan more snugly around her.

"Sorry. I was just thinking out loud. This cabin is sturdy enough. We should be fine.''

A thought suddenly occurred to her. "Did you ever get around to calling your grandmother?"

He shook his head. "I tried. There's no cellular service. I don't know if it's due to the dense woods here or because a tower's down somewhere.''

"So we're completely cut off from all communication," she said quietly.

He nodded. "I'm afraid so.''

The temperature in the room seemed to drop ten degrees. "How long do you think we'll be stranded here?" she asked.

"It's hard to tell," Adam admitted. "Probably another couple of days, at least. These roads aren't great in the best of weather, and they're too isolated to receive attention from the county crews when they're probably scrambling to clear the main highways. But we have plenty of wood and supplies, Jenny. We won't freeze and we won't starve. If you can stand being stranded here with me, we'll be fine." He smiled a little, obviously trying to reassure her.

Jenny tried to return the smile. "I don't mind being here with you," she said candidly. "You're the one who has been inconvenienced by having an unexpected guest show up on your doorstep.''

"I'm enjoying the company," he said, and she thought he sounded a bit surprised by the admission. And then he added, "There are people who would be appalled at being trapped in a cabin alone with me. More than a few

who'd weep in sympathy for your plight if they knew
you'd ended up here with me.''

She chuckled. ''You have a reputation of being an ogre,
or something?''

''Let's just say I've been called a pompous, arrogant,
overbearing son of a—er—gun, on a few occasions,'' he
explained dryly.

She widened her eyes dramatically. ''Surely not.''

He sighed heavily, matching her teasing tone. ''I'm
afraid so. Still think you can survive a couple more days
of my company?''

''I'm tough,'' she assured him. ''I can survive anything.''

''Even more of my cooking?''

''Even that.''

He grinned, and she smiled back at him. The room
seemed to grow warmer again, and Jenny forgot to be
afraid.

A moment later, she forced herself to look away from
him. She cleared her throat. ''Um—are we going to finish this game, or what?''

''Oh, yeah. Right.'' Adam picked up the cards he'd
spread facedown on the table. And then he spread them
faceup. ''Gin.''

Jenny sighed and shook her head. ''I should have
known,'' she muttered. ''Has anyone *ever* bested you,
Adam Stone?''

His dark eyes were focused on her face. ''I'll let you
know,'' he said quietly.

After one quick glance at his face, Jenny inexplicably
decided not to ask him to elaborate.

''Tell me more about your cousins,'' Jenny said sleep-
ily as she lay on the couch watching Adam eat a sand-

wich a couple of hours later.

He swallowed and looked at her in surprise. "Why?"

Tucked warmly beneath a pile of blankets, she shrugged against the couch cushions. "Just making conversation," she murmured. "They sound interesting."

"Are you sure you don't want anything to eat?"

"I'm really not hungry right now. But I would like to hear more about your family."

Adam didn't seem satisfied with her refusal to eat, but he let it drop, for now. She knew he would nag her again about it later. "What do you want to know?" he asked, instead.

"Tell me about Rachel." Something in his voice when he'd mentioned that cousin had made Jenny suspect that Rachel was his favorite.

As if in confirmation of her guess, Adam's eyes softened in the firelight. "Rachel," he murmured, and there was a warmth in his voice that made Jenny's throat tighten in a way she couldn't have explained. "She's the eldest of the Carson siblings. She's—hmm—seven years younger than I am, which would make her thirty-one."

Which told Jenny that Adam was a bit younger than the forty she'd guessed. Must be that officious air of his that made him seem older, she mused, watching him as he talked. And those very attractive streaks of silver in the dark hair at his temples.

"Rachel married young and had two children, Paige and Aaron. Cute kids. Her husband died from injuries he sustained in a car accident several years ago."

"How tragic," Jenny whispered, thinking of how hard it must have been for Adam's cousin to find herself alone with two small children to raise. She knew firsthand that it was a daunting prospect to consider raising a child without help.

"I offered to help her out financially, but she's proud and stubborn—rather like someone else I've recently met," Adam said pointedly.

Jenny only smiled faintly and squirmed against the pillows. Her back was hurting worse than usual this evening, though she had no intention of mentioning it to Adam. He fussed enough over her lack of appetite; heaven only knew what he'd do if he thought she was experiencing any discomfort.

"Anyway," Adam continued, taking her silence as an urge to go on, "Rachel recently met a young attorney named Seth Fletcher, and two weeks ago they were married—on New Year's Eve. It was a small, simple ceremony held at Rachel's church in Percy. The whole family was there. The kids were ecstatic."

"Everyone approves of her new husband, I take it."

"Yeah. It was quite an event. Everyone's delighted for Rachel."

"You, too?"

"Sure. Fletcher's a decent guy, from what I've seen, and he's obviously head over heels for Rachel. Seems fond of the kids, too. I think he'll be good for all of them. If not, he'll have me to answer to," he added conversationally.

Hearing the very serious undertone to the lightly spoken words, Jenny shook her head. "Does the family know that you consider yourself their caretaker?"

He only chuckled and washed down the last of his sandwich with a gulp of lukewarm canned cola.

"Tell me about the other two—Cody and Cecilia," she urged, trying to remember the names.

"Celia." Adam corrected her. "She's the youngest. Twenty-four, pretty, impulsive, a bit pampered by the family. Spunky. Mouthy."

"You're nuts about her," Jenny said with a smile.

"Yeah. Which doesn't mean I haven't thought she needed a paddling occasionally. Like this last stunt she pulled . . ." He shook his head.

Jenny was intrigued. "Tell me."

"She ran off to southern Texas with a jet-setting hotel magnate—Damien Alexander. I didn't know anything about it, of course, or I would have done something to stop her."

"Damien Alexander?" Jenny repeated, startled. "The tabloid heartthrob?"

"That's the one," Adam said grimly. "The guy goes through women like a shark through a school of fish. He met Celia when he was on a business trip to central Arkansas, and he started chasing her. I thought she had more sense than to fall for his practiced lines—especially after Rachel and I warned her about him . . ."

Jenny could just imagine Adam's stuffy, indulgent "warning" to his younger cousin. If Celia had any spirit at all, she'd probably jumped into the playboy's arms out of sheer defiance. "What happened?" she asked.

"As I said, Celia went to Texas for a tryst with the guy—but while she was there, she met someone else. An ATF agent on an undercover assignment. Celia got involved somehow in a gun-smuggling investigation, nearly got herself killed in the process. Instead she ended up married."

"To the ATF agent?" Jenny asked, trying to follow the story.

Adam nodded. "She'd known the guy all of two weeks when they eloped. Everyone in the family thought she'd lost her mind. I checked him out, of course. He seems okay. His superiors think highly of him, anyway."

"You checked him out?" Jenny repeated.

"Of course." He seemed surprised that she would ask. "Celia's family. I couldn't take a chance that she'd gotten impulsively involved with someone who would hurt her."

Jenny's mouth tilted downward. "And what about Cody? Have you investigated *his* wife, too?"

"Cody isn't married. And, no, I don't investigate all his dates, if that's your next question. He's perfectly capable of taking care of himself."

"Because he's a man, of course," she said in disgust.

"I didn't say that."

"Then why aren't you as protective of him as you are of your female cousins?" she challenged.

"Who said I wasn't?" Adam asked with a cool smile. "How do you think he got a loan to start a restaurant-dance club in Percy, Arkansas, when everyone else predicted the place would go belly-up within six months?"

"You gave it to him?"

"No. But I spoke with the bank president for him. Sort of guaranteed the loan, I guess you could say."

Jenny searched his face. "Does Cody know you did that?"

Adam cleared his throat. "Not exactly."

"He wouldn't like it if he knew, would he?"

Adam shrugged and avoided her eyes. "Probably not. Fortunately it's never come up. The club has been successful and Cody and his partner haven't had any trouble making their payments, so it's a moot question. And you, of course, wouldn't tell him, would you?"

"How *could* I tell him?" Jenny asked, startled rather than amused by his wry question. "I don't know him, and the chances are slim that I'll ever meet him."

"Uh, yeah. Right," Adam muttered. "I forgot. I just didn't like your implication that I'm sexist."

"Okay, I was wrong. Your arrogance knows no gender boundaries."

He frowned. "Somehow, I don't think that's a compliment."

Jenny giggled softly. "You think about it," she said around a sudden yawn. "I think I'm going to take a nap."

"Are you sure you don't want something to eat first?" he asked, still worried about her lack of appetite.

Her eyes were already closing. "I'm sure," she said. "But Adam?"

"Yeah?"

"Thanks."

She fell asleep, glad she'd managed to let him know that she appreciated his concern, even if she couldn't help teasing him about his techniques. She didn't hear what, if anything, he said in response.

Chapter Five

Unlike Jenny, Adam couldn't sleep. For one thing, after a day of inactivity, he wasn't tired. His foot was a bit sore, but not really painful, so he had no trouble moving around on it. He hadn't finished his book, but he was tired of reading for one day. He'd straightened the kitchen after finishing his sandwich, so there was nothing left to do except sit and listen to the fire pop and the storm rage outside.

He stood occasionally to pace to the windows and check the weather. By midnight, it appeared that the snow was letting up some, but ice still weighed heavily on the trees surrounding the cabin, and there was an occasional crack as overburdened limbs broke beneath the weight.

There would be no leaving this place for several days yet, Adam thought, turning back to his sleeping guest. Fortunately they were safe enough here, pending any unforeseen circumstances.

Jenny seemed to be sleeping restlessly this evening. Her face was pale in the firelight, and there was a little frown between her dark eyebrows. She'd wriggled around until she'd dislodged the blankets that had covered her. Adam knelt beside the couch and smoothed them back over her, careful not to wake her.

His hand lingered at the mound of her belly. Even through the blankets, he could feel her baby moving, kicking lazily. He smiled faintly, wondering how anyone could sleep with that going on inside her.

The baby gave a strong kick against his palm, as though sensing Adam was there and wanting to make sure he had his attention. Adam's smile deepened. "Brat," he whispered.

He wondered if the baby would be a boy or a girl. And whether Jenny had taken his advice about names seriously—she wouldn't really name the kid Ashley, would she?

And then he wondered how Jenny would get by alone with a baby to support, no job, no home, no family to turn to.

His smile vanished, and his jaw tightened.

Over his dead body, he thought grimly, patting the child to reassure it that Adam Stone had no intention of abandoning either the baby or its mother to that lonely fate.

Jennifer Newcomb might not realize it yet, but she had a friend now. And Adam Stone took care of his friends, just as he did his family.

Sometimes whether they liked it or not.

Something woke Jenny before dawn. She wasn't sure what it was. She lay still, eyes closed, listening. The fire was still burning, and there was an occasional distant cracking sound from outside the cabin, but those by now familiar noises hadn't been enough to rouse her from a sound sleep.

She opened her eyes. Adam had put out the lantern at some point, so that the fire provided the only illumination in the room. Adam lay in his sleeping bag near the wood box, obviously prepared to keep the fire going during the night while Jenny slept.

The firelight flickered on his face, causing intriguing shadows to dance across it. Jenny lay for a time just looking at him, wondering about him . . .

And then it happened again. A sharp pain seemed to creep from somewhere behind her to concentrate in her middle. She felt as though her entire body tightened from the chest down, held a moment, then slowly relaxed. She released a slow breath as the discomfort subsided.

What on earth was *that?*

She'd been lying on her side, her knees drawn up as far as possible on the narrow sleeping surface of the couch. She hadn't changed position in hours.

That had to account for it, she abruptly decided. Her body was protesting the inactivity, was asking that she stretch and move around a bit.

Very slowly, she pushed herself upright, aware that she needed to go to the bathroom.

Adam must have been sleeping very lightly. He roused as soon as she rose to her feet.

"What is it?" he asked gruffly, lifting his head.

"Bathroom," she whispered, rather embarrassed. "Go back to sleep."

"Be careful," he warned. "You don't want to trip and fall in the dark."

"I can find my way by now," she assured him.

"Take the flashlight," he urged, motioning toward the coffee table where he kept the flashlight handy during the night. "Do you need any help?"

"Adam," Jenny said, exasperated more than embarrassed now. "I don't need help going to the bathroom. Go back to sleep, okay?"

He chuckled quietly and stretched back out in the sleeping bag. "Yes, dear," he murmured mockingly.

She couldn't help smiling at his exaggerated—and completely unbelievable—subservient tone.

Jenny was washing her hands when the pain struck again. This one was strong enough to double her over. She gripped the edge of the sink to steady herself, still uncertain exactly what was going on.

A sudden gush of warm liquid soaked her knit slacks and puddled around her red-stocking feet. It happened without warning, so quickly and so forcefully that it took Jenny a moment to understand what had happened.

When the realization hit, her first reaction was to panic. "Adam? *Adam!*"

He appeared almost instantly in the doorway, flashlight in hand, as if he'd been waiting for her call. "What is it?"

Dripping, hurting and frightened, she turned to him. Her voice was little more than a whisper. "I don't know what to do," she said bleakly. "Please. Help me."

It was the first time Jenny Newcomb had asked for help—from anyone—in longer than she could remember.

At first Adam couldn't imagine what had happened, only that something was dreadfully wrong. Jenny's face was stark white in the harsh glow of the flashlight, her amber eyes huge and terrified.

And then he saw the liquid. And the way she suddenly clutched her side and grimaced. And he knew.

For one fleeting instant, his first reaction was much the same as hers. Sheer panic.

And then years of medical training kicked in and took control. "Let's get you back into the other room," he said, his voice amazingly calm. "Lean on me, I'll support you."

"My water broke," she whispered, sounding dazed. "And the pain . . ."

"I know." Shifting the flashlight to his left hand, he wrapped his right arm around Jenny's side and urged her toward the doorway. She moved as though in a trance.

"It's not time," she said, and now her voice was sharpened by an edge of incipient hysteria. "Oh, God, it's not time. This can't happen now."

"Jenny," Adam said, tightening his hold on her as he led her inexorably toward the couch. "Calm down. Whatever happens, we can handle it. I'll take care of you."

"What are we going to do? I don't—" She broke off with a gasp and bent into another contraction.

They were coming fast, Adam thought. Much too fast for his comfort. But they seemed to be of relatively short duration, so maybe they had some time yet. There was always the chance the contractions would ease when she was lying down again, though there was little doubt in his mind that she was in labor. He just hoped the process would go slowly enough for him to remember what to do.

He helped her stretch out on the couch, though she wasn't as helpful as she might have been, since she kept trying to get back up. "We should call someone," she said. "An ambulance. A doctor. The police. Anyone."

He pushed her back down against the cushions again, ignoring the damp stain that spread beneath her. He would replace the couch—that was the least of his worries at the moment.

"Jenny, we can't call anyone," he reminded her patiently. "The phone lines are out, remember? We don't even have cellular service."

She pushed futilely at his hands as he groped for the waistband of her soggy slacks. "What are you doing?"

"I'm getting you out of these wet clothes." Despite her resistance, he swiftly stripped her lower garments away, then draped a blanket over her.

"Lie still," he said, when she started to rise again. "I'm going to light the lantern so I can see what I'm doing."

"What are we going to do? Adam, we have to do something! I can't do this now, like this. I just can't!"

Adam set the lantern close to the couch, half his mind busy listing the items he would need at hand during the next few hours, the other half worrying about Jenny's emotional state. He didn't like the frantic look in her eyes, or the raw edge to her voice. This ordeal was going to be difficult enough without her succumbing to hysteria.

"Jenny, calm down," he said again, trying to speak firmly and soothingly. "Everything is going to be okay."

Tears streamed down her face as she clenched with another contraction. "Oh, God, that hurts."

He knelt beside her and gently brushed a wayward curl from her damp forehead, hoping she wouldn't feel the faint trembling in his fingers. "I know, sweetheart."

She caught his hand in hers, her grip almost painfully tight. "I'm in labor, aren't I?"

"Yes. I think it's safe to assume that you're in labor."

Her eyes seemed to grow, dominating her pale face. "What are we going to do? We're stranded here. There's no one to help us."

"We'll handle it," he repeated, trying to sound utterly confident. "Everything will be fine. I'll take care of you."

A fresh wave of tears escaped her, trickling weakly down the sides of her face. "If only we had a doctor..." she whispered.

He raised her hand to his lips, smiling against her fingers. "Jenny, I *am* a doctor."

She frowned, searching his unshaven face with open skepticism.

He supposed he couldn't blame her for doubting him. "I am a doctor," he repeated. "A surgeon, to be precise."

He figured he didn't need to mention at the moment that his specialty was reconstructive plastic surgery. "I know what I'm doing," he added.

He wasn't lying to her. Not exactly, anyway. He had delivered a baby before. Once. A very long time ago, back when he was still a young intern. Of course, he'd been in a hospital, supported by an efficient and knowledgeable medical staff. All the modern medicines and machinery had been available to him, had they been needed. Help had been only a simple request away.

What he wouldn't give for that to be the case now.

Jenny had gone very still, her eyes locked with his. "A surgeon," she murmured, as though that explained a great deal to her.

"Yeah. Surprise."

Her fingers relaxed their death grip on his, though she didn't let go entirely. "You've been surprising me in one way or another since I landed on your doorstep, Adam Stone," she said.

Gratified by the new note of calm in her voice, Adam chuckled and gently squeezed her hand. "I try to avoid being predictable. Now, can you lie here quietly for a moment while I gather a few things we're going to need?"

"Yes." Her cheeks suddenly darkened. "I've been acting like an idiot, haven't I? I'm sorry."

"Forget it." He pushed himself upright, confident now that Jenny's near loss of control had passed. "I'll be right back."

Not wanting to leave Jenny alone for longer than necessary, he rushed through his preparations, snatching the first-aid kit out of the bathroom along with an armload of towels, putting water on to boil in the kitchen for sterilizing his instruments, searching his mind for anything else he might need.

He couldn't believe this was happening. He'd come to this cabin in search of peace and quiet—time to get away and take care of no one but himself. Now he found himself about to deliver a premature baby by lantern light, miles from the nearest hospital, cut off from all communication with civilization.

God help him. And God help that poor helpless baby.

Jenny was panting through another contraction when he rejoined her. He slipped a folded blanket beneath her, then covered the blanket with a clean towel.

He'd scrubbed up as best he could, but he'd found no sterile surgical gloves in the utilitarian first-aid kit. Why the hell didn't he carry a medical bag in his Jag? he asked himself angrily.

When had he gotten out of the habit of being prepared to practice on-the-spot emergency medicine, rather than becoming spoiled by arriving at a hospital to find everything ready for him to step in and do his thing?

He leaned over Jenny, holding her gaze with his. "I'm going to check now to see how far you've dilated, all right? From this point on, you're going to have to help me. No false modesty, no embarrassment, no questioning my methods. That's the only way we're going to get through this."

Jenny moistened her colorless lips with her tongue. "All right," she said weakly. "I'll help you. But Adam?"

"Yes, Jenny?"

"I'm still scared," she whispered.

"So am I," he said, and then held his breath, wondering if he'd made a monumental mistake with the admission.

Her eyes widened a moment, searching his face. And then she managed a very shaky smile. "We're quite a pair, aren't we?"

"Yeah," he murmured on a long exhale, unable to smile in return. "We certainly are."

She held out her hand to him. "Adam?" she said again.

He took her cold fingers in his. "Yes?"

Her smile was gone now, her expression stark. "Don't let my baby die."

The words hit him like a sledgehammer. More than anything he'd ever wanted in his life, he longed to promise her that nothing would happen to her *or* her baby. That he would take care of them both. Every possible disaster flashed through his mind, from stillbirth to congenital deformities. Heart or lung abnormalities in the baby, both common in premature deliveries. Or something happening to Jenny. Hemorrhaging. Stroke.

For the first time in his memory, Adam was afraid that he wasn't in complete control. That this time, there just might not be anything he could do to prevent the worst from happening. And it terrified him.

It galled him to admit his vulnerability, even to himself. He'd be damned if he'd let Jenny see it. She needed him to be strong now, needed to believe in him. And he was going to do everything within his power to justify her faith.

"Trust me, Jenny" was all he could think of to say.

She let out a small, trembling breath. "I trust you."

Adam squeezed her hand and then turned away. Funny. His eyes were burning, and his vision had momentarily blurred. He dashed an impatient hand across his face and went to work.

Adam Stone was in charge again.

Jenny was in labor for hours.

It wasn't so bad at first, once the early panic subsided. With Adam's calm, practical coaching, she began to breathe deeply through the contractions, which held steady for a while at one every ten minutes or so.

The pains weren't comfortable, by any means, but they were certainly manageable. Now she understood why so many women opted for natural childbirth. Anyone with any fortitude at all could handle a little discomfort.

And then the contractions picked up pace, coming now at approximately every five minutes, and lasting a bit longer than before. A little harder.

Jenny caught her breath with an effort after one particularly sharp contraction. "Wow," she said, when she could speak again. "That was a big one."

Adam gave her a look of sympathy. "Mmm-hmm."

"Um—how are things going down there?"

"You've dilated to about eight centimeters. You still have a way to go, Jenny."

"Oh." She took a deep breath. "Okay. No problem."

Adam only shook his head.

* * *

"Damn!" Jenny's voice was gritty as she cursed—not for the first time in the past hour.

Adam carefully disentangled his fingers from Jenny's and shook his hand to restore the circulation. "That one was a bit rough, wasn't it?" he asked carefully.

Still trying to regain her breath, she gave him a look of disgust. "A bit rough?" she repeated. "A bit rough?"

"Well, uh—"

"How would you like it if someone reached inside you and tried to turn you inside out? How would *you* like it if someone took a sharp knife and jabbed it right into your... oh, hell, here comes another one."

"Stop talking and focus on your breathing," Adam ordered her, taking her hand again.

"Why don't you—" But Jenny's words were cut off in a quick intake of breath before she could finish the suggestion, to Adam's relief.

"Tell me—tell me about your practice," Jenny forced out brokenly a while later.

Adam dabbed at her damp face with a cool cloth. "What do you want to know?"

"Anything. Everything. Just—just talk to me," she whispered, frowning determinedly at his face as she clung to his hand and tried to cope with the pain.

"I graduated high school a couple of years early, accelerated my college education and finished medical school at twenty-three," he said without embellishment. "I've been practicing ever since."

"Im-impressive," she managed to say. "Are you a general practitioner?"

"No. I've specialized."

"In obstetrics?" she asked hopefully.

Adam cleared his throat. "Not exactly. Are you warm enough? Would you like another blanket?"

"Are you kidding? I'm melting." She struggled through another contraction, then asked, "What—what *is* your specialty, Dr. Stone?"

Damn. He wouldn't lie to her, of course. "Reconstructive surgery."

Jenny choked. "Oh, my God. You're a plastic surgeon?"

Adam nodded stiffly.

"I suppose that will come in handy if the baby needs a nose job," Jenny murmured. "But, uh—"

"I know what I'm doing, Jenny. Now, be still. I'm going to see if you're fully dilated yet."

"A plastic surgeon," Jenny muttered as Adam lifted the blanket draped over her raised knees. "I should have known."

He ignored her.

"Come on, Jenny. *Push.*"

"I *am* pushing, you—*aagh!*"

"That's it. Hold it, now. Two, three, four, five. All right, breathe. *Breathe,* Jenny."

"Stop telling me what to do!" she shouted.

Both of them were sweating, frazzled and exhausted. Jenny's face was streaked with tears, utterly without color, her mouth drawn into a thin line of misery and fear. Adam felt almost as though he'd suffered every pain with her, though he knew better to say so.

It was killing him to see her hurting. Every time she cried out in her agony, it was as though a knife plunged into him. He cursed endlessly, silently, raging against the twisted fates that had brought her here like this, so vulnerable, so helpless, so totally dependent on him—and he so pathetically unprepared to help her.

All his training, all his knowledge of medications for easing pain were useless to him here. What good did any of it do him if he had no means available to ease her suffering?

He didn't blame her for yelling at him. Couldn't protest her apparent lack of faith in him. He was a plastic surgeon, for God's sake, not an obstetrician. Not a pediatrician. Not a miracle worker.

He wasn't ready for this!

Even as the uncharacteristic self-doubts assailed him, he kept going, urging her on, patiently repeating instructions, vigilantly on guard for anything that could possibly go wrong. So far, so good. No tearing. No excessive bleeding. The baby seemed to be positioned normally, its tiny dark head already crowning.

"Okay, honey, you're doing fine," he said, talking automatically now, hardly aware of what he was saying, all his attention focused on the infant. "Take a deep breath and push. That's it, hold it. You're doing great, Jenny. Really great. I'm proud of you."

She cursed at him. She screamed at the pain. But she listened to him. And she pushed.

And only moments later, Adam held her tiny daughter in his big, trembling hands.

"It's a girl, Jenny. A beautiful little girl."

Jenny sobbed. "Oh, my God. Is she—?"

"Just a minute. Come on, sweetheart, breathe for me," Adam crooned.

Her vision blurred by tears, sweat and exhaustion, Jenny squinted to see, holding her breath. It was sometime after noon on Saturday, and the room was brightened now by watery light from outside. She could clearly see Adam bent over the tiny body in his hands. She could tell he was busily doing something, though she couldn't see what it was.

Her baby hadn't cried.

Jenny bit her lower lip until it bled, oblivious to this new, nearly insignificant pain.

And then she let out her breath in a gasp of relief when the first tiny mew quavered through the silence of the rustic room, followed by a more lusty cry.

"Adam?" she asked in a whisper, almost afraid to speak aloud.

He looked up at her with a weary smile and glittering dark eyes. "She's fine," he said. "Small but perfect, as far as I can tell."

Jenny closed her flooding eyes. "Thank God."

"You did it, Jenny."

Jenny opened her eyes and searched out Adam's gaze. Her own smile quivered. "*We* did it," she said, correcting him.

He laid her still-crying baby tenderly on her stomach. "We're not quite through yet," he murmured. "You get to know your daughter while I finish down here, okay?"

Blissfully counting tiny toes and fingers, Jenny smiled, content to leave everything up to Adam for now.

He had proven himself more than deserving of her trust in him, she thought with a soul-deep wave of gratitude.

Chapter Six

Utterly exhausted, Jenny slept most of the afternoon, dressed in a warm flannel nightgown Adam had pulled from her suitcase and insisted on helping her into. Adam kept close watch over her as she rested. He was concerned by her pallor, but relieved that her sleep seemed natural enough. She wasn't running a fever; the bleeding was still normal; she wasn't in greater pain than was to be expected after childbirth.

The storm was over. A glittering frozen landscape lay outside the cozy cabin. The sun seemed to be trying to push through the thinning gray layer of clouds. Adam could see his car in the driveway, almost covered in a layer of ice and snow. Maybe, he thought optimistically, he'd be able to drive out within the next twenty-four hours.

Please, God, nothing else would go wrong before he could get them out of here.

He'd dragged a huge wooden rocker in from the bedroom. He sat in it now, close to the fire, a tiny swaddled bundle in his arms. He rocked slowly, gently, keeping silent watch over mother and child.

The baby was sleeping. Adam had cleaned her up as best as he could under the circumstances, and wrapped her in a blanket.

He thought she was beautiful.

Her tiny, wrinkled face was pink and healthy looking, her head covered in downy black curls that made her look very much like her mother. She stirred and made a funny face, and Adam tucked her more snugly into the blanket. She settled contentedly into the crook of his arm, her impossibly soft cheek pressed close to his heart.

The kid was going to be spoiled rotten before she was a day old, Adam thought with a wry smile. But he couldn't bring himself to put her down.

"Adam?"

He lifted his head and smiled at Jenny. "Hi."

She was looking at the baby. "Is she all right?"

"She's fine. She's been napping, like her mom. How are you feeling?"

Jenny made a face. "Sore."

Adam rose carefully from the rocker. "Want to hold your daughter?"

Jenny reached out eagerly. "Of course."

Adam tucked the infant carefully into Jenny's arms, then plumped an extra pillow behind Jenny's back. "Comfortable now?"

"Mmm-hmm." Jenny's full concentration was on her child. "She's so tiny," she marveled.

"I'm guessing around six pounds. Small, but not so much that we have to worry. When was your due date?"

"Three more weeks."

"She needs to be examined as soon as we can get to a pediatrician, of course, but from what I can tell, she's going to be just fine. Her breathing's clear, her pulse is steady, her color's good, she's quite active when she's awake. And she isn't in need of a nose job," he added.

Jenny giggled at the reminder of her sarcastic remark when she'd been in labor. "Is that your professional opinion, Dr. Stone?"

"Yes. My professional opinion is that you have yourself a fine baby here, Ms. Newcomb."

"Thanks to you," Jenny murmured, looking up at him with a shy smile.

He brushed off the praise. "I'm going to warm some broth for you. We need to keep your strength up. I want you to get up and move around a little before long."

Jenny winced. "I don't know if that's possible."

He nodded sympathetically. "It won't be comfortable," he admitted. "But trust me, the longer you lie there, the worse it will be when you do get up. And since we need to get out of here as soon as the roads clear somewhat, you need to be prepared to travel."

She sighed and nodded. "I'm sure you're right."

He flashed her a cocky grin. "Haven't you figured it out yet? I'm *always* right."

She groaned and looked down at her baby. "Did you hear that, Melissa? Have you ever heard such arrogance?"

Adam was startled. "Melissa?" he repeated.

Jenny gave him that shy smile again—the one that made his chest tighten, for some reason. "Yes. Do you approve?"

Adam had to swallow hard before he could speak. Even then, his voice was a bit husky. "Yeah. I approve."

Jenny's cheeks were pink. "Good." And then she looked back down at the baby. "She'll probably want to eat soon, won't she?"

And now Adam had an all new reason to clear his throat as he thought of Jenny baring her breasts to feed her child. Man, what was wrong with him today? Had lack of sleep combined with stress to addle his brain?

"I'll—er—I'll warm the broth," he said abruptly, turning hastily toward the kitchen.

Adam made another trek out to Jenny's car later that afternoon, just before dark. A few of her friends from Dallas had given her a baby shower before she'd struck out for Tennessee. There were boxes of disposable new-born diapers, tiny sleepers, baby blankets and even a pacifier packed into her trunk, she explained.

Jenny let out a long breath when the door closed behind him. He'd been incredibly solicitous to her during the day, but it was nice to have a few minutes alone with her new daughter. Adam had helped her into the rocking chair near the fire, leaving her sitting on a soft pillow, a blanket wrapped snugly around her, the baby tucked into her arms.

The first nursing session had been a bit awkward, but successful. Already, Melissa was ready to eat again. Jenny placed the baby carefully at her breast, tucking the blanket more securely around them.

"You're lucky I had planned to breast-feed all along," she told her daughter with a smile. "I'm glad I read up on the procedure before I left Dallas or we'd both be in trouble. We finally found one subject Adam wasn't an expert on."

In fact, Adam had been rather endearingly embarrassed about the whole subject. Jenny had found that secretly amusing, since he'd handled childbirth so easily.

Just the thought of those long, difficult hours made her smile slip away. She couldn't even bear to think about what she'd have done if it hadn't been for Adam. How could she have known when she'd gotten lost and slammed into that tree that her baby's birth was only hours away?

Had she not seen Adam's lights, or had Adam not been a doctor...well, she shuddered to consider the possibilities.

But, she reminded herself firmly, she *had* seen the lights and Adam *was* a doctor—she didn't doubt that now. And he'd taken care of her as tenderly, as skillfully, as thoughtfully as she could possibly have asked.

She was still convinced that Adam Stone was an arrogant, sometimes overbearing man, much too convinced of his own infallibility for his own good. But she would never forget how kind he'd been to her and her daughter during this ordeal that had been sprung upon him.

Adam was a good man, despite his flaws. She knew she'd never met anyone else quite like him.

Melissa was fed and sleeping again when Adam returned, his arms full of packages. "I got everything I could carry," he said, dumping the load near the couch. "How are you two doing?"

"We're fine. But we could really use one of those diapers," Jenny said with a smile. "I think the tea towel you used is pretty well soaked. And my nightgown with it."

Adam grimaced. "Sorry. Here, I'll take care of her while you change."

Jenny placed the baby carefully into his outstretched arms. Funny how confident she felt in doing so, she mused as she pushed herself painfully out of the chair.

"You okay?" Adam asked, steadying her with his free hand.

Jenny nodded. "Just stiff and sore," she said. "But no more than can be expected."

"You're sure?"

"I'm fine, Adam. Don't fuss over me." She smiled again to soften her chiding.

He looked sheepish. "Sorry. It's not every day that I take care of a new mother."

"This new mother can take care of herself, on the whole. But thank you."

He nodded and dropped his supportive hand. Jenny felt inexplicably bereft at its loss.

"She *is* wet, isn't she?" Adam fretted, carrying the baby to the couch. "Don't you worry, Melissa, Uncle Adam's going to take care of that in no time."

"Uncle Adam?" Jenny repeated, amused.

He shrugged. "That's what Rachel's kids call me, even though I'm really a cousin."

Clutching the blanket around her shoulders with one hand, Jenny rummaged through the things Adam had just brought from her car until she found a tiny disposable diaper and a soft, warm sleeper.

"Are you sure you can handle this without help?" she asked, holding the items out to Adam.

He took them with a rather offended look. "I handled delivering her, didn't I? I can certainly handle dressing her. Go put some dry clothes on."

"I wish I could take a bath."

"There's hot water on the stove. Use it to wash up, if you want."

Settling for what she could get, Jenny nodded. "All right. I'll dress in there."

Adam didn't look up from the baby. "Call me if you need help."

She lifted an eyebrow. "I just had a baby, didn't I? I can certainly handle dressing myself."

He chuckled at her deliberate twisting of his own words. "Just thought I'd offer," he murmured, sliding a diaper under Melissa's tiny bare bottom.

She shouldn't be embarrassed, Jenny thought as she hobbled slowly into the kitchen, a clean nightgown tucked under her arm. After all, Adam was as intimately acquainted with her body now as anyone had ever been. And there was certainly no reason to think he'd been flirting with her, even humorously.

Under the circumstances, it was ridiculous to even consider the possibility.

The stress of the day must be getting to her, she decided. She reached determinedly for a washcloth, putting Adam's odd tone out of her mind.

Saturday evening passed quietly, pleasantly. Jenny and Adam spent most of the time watching the baby, taking turns holding her, admiring her.

"She really is beautiful, isn't she?" Jenny whispered, noting how the light from the fire made her baby's skin look like pink alabaster.

"She really is," Adam agreed patiently for what had to be the hundredth time.

Jenny flushed. "Sorry. I don't mean to rave on so about her."

"Rave as much as you like. I think she's gorgeous, too."

Jenny smiled. "You're a very nice man, Adam Stone."

He widened his eyes comically and looked around as though in search of eavesdroppers. "Shh," he said in an exaggerated whisper. "Someone will hear you. I have a reputation to protect, you know."

"Why *do* you work so hard at that grumpy reputation of yours?" Jenny asked curiously.

Adam dropped the posturing. "What makes you think I do?"

She shrugged. "Just a guess. I think you're very careful to keep people at arm's length—outside your family, anyway. I'm just not so sure why you feel the need to do so."

Adam made a rueful face. "Maybe I do, a little. I suppose I find it easier in the long run."

"Why easier?"

"The closer people get to you, the more they seem to want from you," he said nonchalantly. "I have my hands full enough just taking care of my practice and my family."

"Is that why you haven't married?" Jenny asked in concern. "Because you think a wife would be too demanding of you?"

He looked uncomfortable. "I haven't married because I haven't found anyone I *wanted* to marry," he said, correcting her. "But, yeah, I guess you're right in some ways. I work long hours, and hard ones. When I get home, it feels good to be alone for a while, to do what I want, when I want to do it. I don't need anyone else making demands on my time or having unrealistic expectations for me to live up to."

Jenny considered what he'd said. And then she asked, "What's your mother like?"

He groaned. "Don't tell me. Psych 101, right?"

She shook her head. "I never went to college, remember? I'm just curious."

"Okay, Dr. Freudette—my mother is a difficult woman. Ever since my father died when I was eight, she's been a helpless victim of cruel fate. Dad left us with more money than we needed, a firmly established place in society, a nice house and a secure future, but to listen to Mother, you'd think we were destitute and homeless. She seems to be incapable of making important decisions, a chronic hypochondriac and endlessly demanding of attention—mine, and everyone else who'll cater to her for a few hours."

He stopped, cleared his throat, and threw up his hands. "But she's my mother, you know? On the few occasions when I really needed her, she came through for me. It doesn't bother me to look out for her now. Mostly it's a matter of hiring someone occasionally to take care of whatever she wants."

"You needn't explain yourself to me," Jenny said gently, reacting to the slight defensiveness in his deep voice. "I think it's nice that you take care of your widowed mother."

He exhaled slowly. "Sorry. People are always criticizing me for catering to her. My grandmother, much as I love her, is a stubbornly independent woman who has little time for Mother's dramatics. Even my cousins and friends think I spend too much time taking care of Mother, though they consider me generally selfish and self-serving in every other respect. They don't understand, of course, that it's easier for me to take care of her than to deal with the consequences of not doing so.

"So," he added wryly, "I'm still being selfish. Just in my own way."

Selfish? No. Adam wasn't a selfish man, Jenny mused, looking down at her baby as she rocked and thought about his words. Just the opposite, in fact. He'd spent so many years taking care of his mother, his extended family and his patients, that he seemed to have left no time for himself.

He was arrogant, yes. But now she understood that arrogance a bit better. He'd been taking charge since he was eight years old. After thirty years, it was no wonder he considered himself the best candidate for doing so.

Adam stood abruptly, as though the conversation had suddenly lost appeal for him. "I'm going to make us something for dinner. It'll have to be canned soup again, I'm afraid, but at least it's hot and filling."

"Canned soup is fine with me," she said absently, still thinking about all those complex sides to Adam Stone.

Adam took the baby and laid her on the couch so Jenny could eat from the tray he'd brought her. It was practically the first time little Melissa had been put down since birth; she expressed her displeasure with a disgruntled wail.

Jenny automatically reached for her daughter.

Adam stopped her. "She's okay," he said, patting the squirming infant's tiny back. "Eat your dinner."

"But—"

As though to confirm Adam's words, Melissa quieted. She took the pacifier Adam offered her, and a moment later was suckling it noisily as she settled down to sleep.

Jenny noted resignedly that Adam looked smugly pleased with himself—as always.

Jenny ate sparsely, and then was annoyed to find that her eyelids were drooping again. "It seems like all I've done since I've been here is sleep," she grumbled.

Adam laughed. "Well, that and have a baby."

Her chin propped on her hand, Jenny looked at him thoughtfully. "You have a nice laugh, Adam Stone. You should use it more often," she murmured.

To her astonishment, his cheeks darkened a bit beneath his several-days growth of beard. Had she really embarrassed him with the compliment? How interesting.

"I'll clean this up and then we'll get you and the kid down for the night," Adam said, busying himself with the cleanup. "Maybe tomorrow the roads will start thawing."

"Mmm." Jenny looked away then, not wanting him to see her eyes. She wasn't sure exactly what expression he would find in them—but she thought it might look suspiciously like regret.

Oddly enough, she was growing more reluctant all the time to leave this cozy little cabin in the woods.

Adam made a makeshift crib out of a dresser drawer taken from the bedroom, and snugly lined it with blankets. He fussed over the drawer for quite a while, making sure the blankets were taut enough so that they wouldn't get around the baby's face. Finally judging it a safe temporary bed, he took Melissa from Jenny after she'd nursed, and laid the baby in the drawer.

"She seems comfortable enough," he said, watching attentively as Melissa settled down to sleep.

He'd placed the drawer close to where Jenny lay on the couch, near enough to the fire to provide warmth for the night. Jenny smiled as she looked into the drawer-bed. "She looks perfectly content," she assured Adam.

"You'd better get some sleep," he advised her. "She probably won't sleep much tonight. I understand they wake fairly often to eat at this stage."

"You haven't had much rest, yourself, during the past few days," Jenny reminded him. "You were up most of last night delivering the baby, and you spent the night before that waking every hour or so to add wood to the fire."

"I'd have had to add wood to the fire even if I'd been here alone," he reminded her. "As for delivering Melissa—I figure she's well worth the loss of a few hours sleep."

Jenny smiled. "That's a very nice thing to say."

"Yeah, well, don't tell anyone. I still have that reputation to protect, you know."

"Mmm. Someday the truth is going to get out about you, Adam Stone. Everyone's going to find out what a decent guy you are under all that gruffness. And then what will you do?"

"Run," he said with a rueful shake of his head. "Now go to sleep, Jenny. As soon as it's daylight tomorrow, I'll check the roads. Maybe it will warm up enough for us to get out of here."

Jenny sighed very faintly and closed her eyes. Adam stayed up awhile, his dark, brooding gaze moving from Jenny to the baby and back again.

Sunday morning dawned with the first real sunshine Adam had seen in several days. Standing outside on the porch of the little cabin, he looked up at the startlingly cloudless sky and realized that the temperature was slowly beginning to rise. It was probably still only in the twenties—not enough for a thaw today, at least—but by late Monday, certainly no later than Tuesday, the roads should be clear enough for him to attempt to drive out.

And then what?

The first priority, of course, would be to see to Melissa. Had Adam thought the infant was at any risk, he'd have already carried her in his arms to civilization, if necessary. He was confident that she was a healthy, thriving baby, but he wouldn't be completely comfortable until that opinion had been confirmed by someone who specialized in that sort of thing.

After seeing to the baby, Jenny would probably want to do something about her car. Having seen the vehicle twice now, Adam knew it needed extensive repairs. Expensive ones. The five thousand dollars he'd found in her purse—which, he suspected, was all the money she had—would hardly cover the damage. Even if she had excellent insurance—and he tended to doubt that, given her circumstances—it would be weeks before the car was either totaled and replaced, or repaired and roadworthy.

Where would she and the baby stay in the meantime? Who would take care of them?

Or would Jenny simply find another way to get to Tennessee and the tentative, part-time jobs her friend had offered? Would she foolishly try to go by plane or bus with her baby? Try to make five thousand dollars cover the cost of setting up in a cheap apartment, child care, food, miscellaneous expenses? Within a couple of months, she'd be flat broke.

He realized that his fists had clenched at his side, and that his jaw had hardened with what felt like anger.

And he knew, without a doubt, that he wouldn't be putting Jenny Newcomb on a bus or a plane—or even in her own car—without a fight.

He scowled, then widened his eyes as the solution occurred to him. Of course! Jenny needed a job, and a place for her and her baby to live. Someone to keep an eye on them until they were able to fend for themselves.

He just happened to be that someone.

Why else, he figured confidently, would Fate have sent her to him? Obviously he was meant to help her. And help her he would, whether she cooperated initially or not. Adam didn't doubt his ability to outlast her when it came to stubborn persistence.

He turned on one heel and went back into the cabin.

Jenny looked up from the rocking chair where she'd been admiring her child again and gave him an absent, baby-besotted smile. "Your nose is red," she commented.

"It's cold out there," he replied, pointing this out unnecessarily.

"Mmm." She'd already looked back down at Melissa, who was staring back up at her with a fierce baby frown of concentration.

Adam moved to sit at the end of the couch nearest the rocking chair. He leaned forward, his forearms on his braced knees. "Jenny, we have to talk."

Cooing at the baby, Jenny seemed not to have heard him for a moment. And then she looked up, still smiling. "What is it, Adam?"

Her eyes were the most unusual color, Adam thought, distracted for a moment. Especially in the glow of the fire, they were the softest amber, framed by incredibly thick, dark lashes that owed nothing to cosmetics. Her short dark curls were tousled from sleep around her firelight-flushed, unpainted face. Her mouth was full, luscious, those elusive dimples at the corners evident with her soft smile.

She was beautiful. And he couldn't remember for a moment what he'd wanted to talk to her about.

He could hardly remember his name.

And then Melissa made a little mewling sound and Adam jerked himself back to reality, silently chiding himself for being an idiot just because Jenny Newcomb had smiled at him.

"We need to talk about what we're going to do when we leave here," he said, more brusquely than he'd intended.

Her smile faded. "Have the roads thawed so soon?"

"No, not yet."

Had that been a quick flash of relief in her eyes, or was he only projecting his own complicated feelings onto her? He cleared his throat. "But it won't be long before we'll be able to leave here. I figured the first thing we'll do is have the baby checked out. After that..."

Jenny was frowning now. "I'll have to do something about my car," she murmured when Adam paused. "And I'll need to decide how I'm going to get to Tennessee and where I'm going to stay when I get there. Maybe I'll call my friend and have her find me an apartment, if she can."

Adam shook his head, pushing down another quick surge of temper. He couldn't believe this! She really *was* planning to pack up her baby and her meager possessions and strike out alone. Of all the stubborn, foolish, recklessly independent...

"I have a counterproposal for you," he said, forcing himself to speak lightly, calmly.

Jenny immediately looked suspicious. "A counterproposal?"

He nodded. "But first, one question. Are you sure you don't want to take Melissa and go back to your family in Texas? Surely if they knew about her, if they saw her, they'd want to help you."

A cold mask seemed to settle over Jenny's face. "I'm not going back to Texas," she said flatly. "And I still don't want to talk about my family."

He sighed in exasperation, but decided to table that subject for later. "All right. Then here's the situation. I own a fairly large, five-bedroom house in Little Rock. It's a lot bigger than I need just for myself, but I bought it as an investment."

Jenny was already shaking her head. "I'm not moving in with you," she said. "I'm not a charity case, Adam. I don't need you to—"

"Would you let me finish?" he snapped, tension making him cross. He massaged the back of his neck with one hand, feeling the knotted muscles there.

"As I was saying," he went on when she fell silent. "It's a big house. I'm not there much, and when I am, I'm in no mood to cook or do housework. I've had a full-time housekeeper for the past couple of years, but she retired a few months ago."

That part was true. Mrs. Handy *had* recently retired.

"Anyway," he said, before Jenny could speak, "I've been looking for someone to replace her and I've had no luck at all."

That was *not* true. Adam had decided after Mrs. Handy left to make do with take-out food and a once-a-week professional cleaning. He saw no need to tell Jenny that he'd changed his mind about that only a few minutes earlier. "What I'm trying to say is that I want you to consider coming to work for me, Jenny. As my housekeeper."

She looked startled. "Your housekeeper?"

He nodded. "I realize it isn't a glamorous job, but you have to admit it beats temporary clerical work. I'll pay you well, I'll provide room, board and health insurance for you and the baby. You'll be free to attend classes in the evening, if you like, to prepare yourself for a better career. Most importantly, you'll be with Melissa. You won't have to leave her with strangers while you try to work to support her.''

Jenny winced. ''That's not a fair tactic,'' she murmured.

He shrugged. ''It's the truth. Do you really want her to be just another little numbered body in an impersonal day-care center? Can you really go off every morning leaving her crying for her mother while you struggle to make enough to pay for food and diapers?''

He was being shameless, and he knew it. But he also knew that he wasn't saying anything he didn't truly mean.

Jenny had gone pale. ''Of course I don't want that—for me *or* Melissa. But—''

''Then what's the problem? I need a housekeeper, and you need a job. It sounds to me like an ideal solution.''

Jenny moistened her lips. ''Are you sure you need a housekeeper?'' she asked, still suspicious. ''You aren't just making this up as a way of getting me to accept help from you?''

''I need a housekeeper,'' he repeated flatly. ''You'll believe me when you see the shape my house has gotten into since Mrs. Handy left. And I'm tired of eating take-out or restaurant food. You can cook, can't you?''

''Yes, but—''

''And you've had experience with property management, so I assume the household chores are familiar to you.''

''Well, sure, but—''

''My bedroom is downstairs. The other four are upstairs, and I hardly ever go up there, so you and Melissa will have plenty of privacy. As I've explained, I work long hours. I'm gone much more than I'm home, so you won't have to worry about us getting in each other's way.

"Your primary responsibilities will be meals, shopping, cleaning and laundry. My secretary takes care of paying bills and scheduling appointments for me, but there may be the occasional errand I'll want you to run once Melissa's old enough to be more mobile. I won't expect you to sign a contract or anything like that, but I would like you to commit to at least six months and give me a couple of weeks' notice if you decide to leave."

He was keeping this as impersonal and professional as possible, figuring that would make it easier for her to accept. He thought six months sounded like a reasonable amount of time. Surely, by then, Jenny would be in a better position to know what she wanted. And he'd know by then that she and the baby wouldn't be going off helpless and alone.

A lot could happen in six months.

"You're really serious, aren't you? You really are offering me a job."

He made a sound of exasperation. "Yes, Jenny, I'm serious. Why would I be going to all this trouble to convince you if I wasn't?"

She bit her lip. "Will you let me think about it?"

He wanted an answer now. He wanted to put his mind at rest once and for all that she wouldn't be striking out alone for Tennessee, beyond his guidance. But he forced himself to nod and say, "Yeah, think about it. It'll be a day or two before we can leave here, anyway."

"I'll consider it, then." She avoided his eyes by looking back down at the baby.

"Fine." Adam stood. "I'd better bring in some more wood. We're running low in here."

Looking lost in her thoughts, Jenny nodded silently.

Satisfied that he'd made a good start on convincing her, Adam decided to quit while he was ahead.

Chapter Seven

"Oh, God. I look terrible. I'm saggy and sallow and . . . and I'm still fat." Jenny sounded disconsolate as she stared into the bathroom mirror Sunday afternoon. She plucked at her hair. "Look at this. It's limp, dead. I look *awful.*"

Adam had been passing the open bathroom door on his way back from the bedroom, where he'd changed into clean clothes after bringing in a load of wood. He paused in response to Jenny's dispirited complaints, his eyebrows lifting in surprise.

This didn't sound like the Jenny he'd come to know during the past few days, he mused. Not once during their ordeal had she complained or fretted about her appearance. And she hadn't sounded this unhappy even when she'd told him about her recent personal problems.

"You look fine, Jenny," he assured her tentatively, eyeing her pale, but still pretty face. "Not at your best, probably, but you *have* just had a baby. You have to expect that it'll take a little time for you to recover completely.''

She sighed and turned away from the mirror. ''I suppose you're right.''

''Melissa's sleeping?''

Jenny nodded. ''She's in her bed,'' she said, referring to the makeshift crib. ''She's been sleeping a long time.''

''She needs a lots of sleep at this stage. It wouldn't hurt you to get some rest, either.''

''I'm tired of sleeping. And I'm tired of reading, and sitting on the couch in front of the fire. I need something to do. I should be making plans, or making phone calls, or...or something. But I can't do anything stuck here with no phone and no electricity and no way to get anywhere.''

She looked close to tears. Adam nervously cleared his throat and shifted his weight on his feet. Crying women had always made him nervous.

His mother was a master at it.

Maybe Jenny was bored, he thought, clutching at excuses. He understood boredom. After too many years of staying much too busy, he was getting a bit tired of all this enforced leisure time himself.

''Maybe you'd like to make us some dinner,'' he suggested, grabbing at the first chore that occurred to him. ''There isn't much to choose from, but there are plenty of canned goods in the pantry and—''

''You want me to *cook?*'' Jenny broke in incredulously. ''I've just had a baby! I need rest, for heaven's sake.''

He promptly felt like a heel for even making the suggestion. ''Uh—sorry—I—er—''

Mercifully he was interrupted by a thin wail from the other room. Melissa was awake and requesting her mother's presence.

Jenny responded immediately after giving Adam one last reproachful look over her shoulder.

When she was gone, Adam slumped against the wall behind him. *Women,* he thought with a bewildered shake of his head. Who could understand them?

He busied himself for a while to allow Jenny time to recover her equilibrium. When he finally judged it safe, he tiptoed into the living room.

Jenny was sitting in the rocking chair, humming softly, smiling beatifically down at the baby. Adam exhaled in relief. "How's she doing?"

"Fine," Jenny replied absently. "She's just eaten, and now she's getting sleepy again. She makes the sweetest little faces, doesn't she?"

Adam privately thought some of those baby faces were a bit weird. He'd been quite startled earlier when Melissa had crossed her eyes and stuck out her tongue at him.

"Yeah," he had the sense to say, instead. "She's one cute kid."

A little weird, maybe, but definitely cute.

Jenny sighed contentedly, pushed the rocker with one foot and started humming again. Adam didn't recognize the tune, but it was pleasant and soothing. Probably a lullaby.

Reassured that everything was back to normal, he picked up his book, settled onto the couch, and turned to the page he'd last read. A moment later, he was lost in the story, only marginally aware of Jenny's soft singing, the quiet creaking of the rocker, the occasional mews from the baby and the cheery popping of the fire.

Perhaps half an hour had passed when he suddenly realized that something was wrong again.

He glanced up from his book. Jenny was still in the rocker, still holding the sleeping baby, but she no longer seemed content. She looked miserable. A steady stream of tears dripped silently down her cheeks. Her lower lip quivered pitifully.

Adam closed his book. "What is it?" he demanded. "What's wrong? Are you in pain?"

Jenny shook her head. "No, I'm not in pain. Nothing major, anyway," she added, squirming against the rocker's thin seat cushion.

"Then why are you crying?"

She mopped her face with one hand. "I'm not c-crying." She sniffled.

He sighed, clinging to his patience with his fingernails. Adam Stone was not a patient man.

"Jenny," he said firmly. "Tell me what's bothering you."

"I was just feeling sorry for my poor baby," she admitted in a barely audible murmur. "She's so tiny and helpless. And she has such a . . . such a lousy excuse for a mother," she added in a near wail.

"How can you say that?"

"How could I not?" she snapped back. "I got pregnant by a self-centered jerk who has no interest at all in his child. I lost my job, sold everything I had and struck out in the dead of winter—alone—with no secure future ahead of me. And then I wrecked my car and ended up having her here, with no hospital available if she needed one. I've messed everything up from the very beginning. How can I possibly think I can raise this precious little girl alone?"

Somewhere in the middle of her woebegotten monologue, Adam finally realized exactly what was going on
here. Hormone hell. Postpartum blues, combined with a
healthy dose of fear and exhaustion. He should have realized it before—should even have anticipated this devel-
opment.

"Jenny." He leaned forward, forearms on his knees,
speaking in a deep, confident tone. "Calm down. You're
just upset because your hormones are a little crazy right
now. It's quite common after childbirth. It's called postpartum de—"

"I know about postpartum depression," Jenny said
defensively. "And this isn't it. I'm not crazy, Adam. I'm
just being realistic. I *have* made a lot of mistakes. Don't
you dare lie to me and say you don't agree with me!"

He shook his head, fighting a smile that would only
make her angrier. "You aren't crazy. And, yes, you've
made some mistakes. But haven't we all?"

"But I—"

He held up a hand to silence her. "You fell for a man
who didn't deserve you. That isn't a crime, Jenny, it's just
bad luck. As for losing your job, that was through no
fault of your own. From what you told me, the jerk sab-
otaged you. I'm not sure what happened between you and
your parents, but I'm sure it's something that can be
worked out, given time and a little effort on both sides."

He noted the immediate, stubborn expression that
crossed her face. Jenny didn't like talking about her parents.

He really was going to have to find out soon exactly
what had happened there. He couldn't fix it if he didn't
know what was wrong.

He dropped the subject of her family and moved on to
her next complaint. "As for leaving Texas and striking out

alone, maybe it wasn't the safest course to choose, but you obviously had your reasons. You knew there was work for you in Tennessee and a friend to give you moral support. You were doing what you thought best for you and your baby.

"I'm sure you were driving very carefully. The best of drivers have lost control on icy roads. You had the good sense to be wearing your seat belt and to keep your head during the crisis. You made your way to this cabin, where there was food and warmth and shelter waiting for you."

He smiled then, lightening his tone. "It was a stroke of good luck that I happened to be staying here," he couldn't resist pointing out. "Not only am I a doctor—which you have to admit came in handy yesterday—but I'm a generally decent guy who would never hurt you or take advantage of you. I have a full-time job available for you, with room and board and benefits and a safe environment for your baby. All in all, I'd say your bad luck ended when you arrived at my doorstep."

Jenny bit her lip and avoided his eyes. And then, finally, she glanced at him with a rueful smile. "You really are an arrogant man, aren't you, Adam Stone?"

"Yeah," he admitted candidly. "But I'm not such a bad sort."

She let out a long breath. "No," she said. "You're not a bad sort at all."

She was quiet for another few moments. Adam gave her time. He was deeply relieved when she finally smiled at him, looking more like the Jenny he'd come to know.

"I'm sorry," she said. "I *have* been acting crazy. I guess you're right about that hormone thing."

Adam flashed her a deliberately cocky grin. "Jenny," he chided gently. "How many times do I have to remind you that I'm *always* right?"

She shook her head, but her smile deepened. "Definitely arrogant," she muttered. But she was smiling.

Adam felt his throat tighten. This woman had gotten to him somehow, he thought with a trace of apprehension.

He wasn't at all sure what he was going to do about it.

Adam persuaded Jenny to take a much-needed nap after their talk. He took the baby and laid her in the drawer-crib while Jenny stretched out on the couch.

Jenny was asleep within minutes.

Thirsty, Adam made a pot of coffee. He gazed out the window over the battered aluminum sink while he waited for the old-fashioned coffeepot to perk. The temperature must be rising, he noted in satisfaction. There was a steady cascade of water from the roof as icicles slowly melted. It wouldn't be long before the roads were navigable.

He poured himself a cup of the strong, fragrant brew and carried it into the living room. Jenny was out soundly. Melissa was asleep, but restless. He patted her little tummy and she settled down, but he had a feeling it was only a temporary respite.

He took a seat in the rocker and kept an eye on both ladies as he sipped his coffee. He wished Jenny had given him a definite answer about the housekeeping job. He would feel much better knowing everything was settled to his satisfaction.

For the first time, he really thought about what he'd done by offering her the position. He, a man who valued privacy, who hoarded his solitary moments the way some men hoarded gold, had invited a strange woman and her newborn infant into his home. A woman who came with loads of emotional baggage, an uncertain future and a severely damaged self-image.

Not to mention the baby, and the inevitable nights of crying, and the clutter that always seemed to accompany infants. Baby bottles in his European enameled sink, rattles and blocks on his plush, champagne-colored carpeting, tiny handprints on his off-white walls, the smell of soiled diapers or regurgitated milk overpowering the delicate scents of expensive air fresheners.

Had he lost his mind?

Melissa stirred again, her tiny fists flailing as she made soft, disgruntled sounds that weren't quite crying, but threatened to be. Glancing quickly at Jenny, who was still sleeping, Adam set down his coffee mug and lifted the baby into his arms.

Cradling her close, he murmured soothing inanities and settled back into the rocker, which he set into a slow, lulling motion.

Melissa blinked her little round eyes, trying blearily to focus on his face. Her pink mouth puckered, her miniature fingers flexed. She made a soft sound that was somewhere between a coo and a hiccup.

Adam grinned. Damn. She really was cute.

He'd have been out of his mind *not* to take her in. Baby or mother.

Melissa had almost settled back down to sleep when Adam was startled by a knock on the cabin door. He must have been dozing himself; he hadn't heard anyone approaching—either by foot or vehicle.

Jerked awake when Adam stood, Melissa started to whimper. Adam patted her absently as he walked to the door.

"Who is it?" he asked by habit, thinking maybe it was a power lineman—possibly a state trooper investigating Jenny's wrecked car.

The cheery voice that answered was unexpectedly familiar. "Hey, cuz, it's me. Cody. Open up. It's freezing out here."

"Cody?" Adam jerked the door open to find his lanky blond cousin on the doorstep, nose and cheeks reddened by cold, his torso bundled into a heavy, lined suede jacket. "What the hell are you doing here?"

"It's Granny Fran's fault," Cody explained hastily. "I drove down to check on her and she made me—hey! Is that a *baby?*" His bright blue eyes had fixed in fascination on the bundle in the crook of Adam's left arm.

"Of course it's a baby," Adam said crossly, suddenly aware that he was holding Melissa in the open doorway. "Get in here and shut the door, Cody. You're letting all the heat out."

"Of *course* it's a baby," Cody repeated in bewilderment, though he automatically followed his cousin's orders. "How silly of me to act surprised."

Adam led Cody quickly into the kitchen, since he didn't want to disturb Jenny yet. He realized that Cody was still so busy staring at the baby that he hadn't even noticed the woman sleeping on the couch.

"There's coffee," Adam said, nodding toward the coffeepot as he tucked Melissa's blanket more snugly around her in the chilly room. "Pour yourself a cup if you like."

"Thanks. A hot drink sounds good." Still watching his cousin out of the corner of his eye, Cody poured coffee, took a sip, then immediately asked, "Uh—does Granny Fran know about the kid?"

Surprised by the question, Adam shook his head. "No, of course not. Why?"

"Well, she was so insistent on having me drive out here to check on you. She seemed quite worried that she couldn't reach you by phone, so worried that she broke her promise not to tell anyone where you were staying. I thought maybe—"

"No. Granny's just overreacting to the storm, I guess. Trust me, Melissa was a surprise even to me."

"Melissa? That's the kid?"

Adam smiled. "Yeah." He pulled the blanket back enough for Cody to see the baby's face. "Cute, huh?"

Cody stepped closer and leaned over to study the tiny face. Melissa gazed back up at him as though fascinated by this new adult in her short life. "She's a sweetheart," Cody agreed. "I think she has your eyes."

Adam had been looking down at the baby. His head snapped up. "*My* eyes?"

"Yeah. And maybe your nose. Except for the bump you got when you broke yours, of course."

"Cody, I'm not this baby's father."

Now it was Cody who looked confused. "You aren't? Then where did you—?"

"Adam? I thought I heard another voice in here." Jenny stood in the doorway to the kitchen, her dark curls tousled around her face, her amber eyes still heavy lidded from sleep. Her blue sweat suit bagged around her, hiding her figure, but emphasizing her slender bone structure.

Adam found it necessary to swallow. Hard. It was one of those moments when Jenny's natural beauty caught him unprepared, made him suddenly, vividly aware of her as a damn attractive woman, despite everything.

Cody's attention was immediately diverted from the baby. "Well," he said, looking Jenny over thoroughly. "Isn't this interesting." And he began to grin.

Adam gave a mental groan. Cody was notorious for his love of a good joke—especially his own. And Cody had been trying for years to catch his older cousin in an awkward situation; anything, Cody had said repeatedly, to make Adam seem just a little less perfect and a lot more human.

This just might be the opportunity Cody had been waiting for.

"Jenny," Adam said, motioning with his free hand toward Cody. "My cousin, Cody Carson. Cody, meet Jenny Newcomb, and her daughter, Melissa."

"It's a real pleasure to meet you," Cody said, flashing one of his patented, charming smiles. He ran a hand through his thick mop of sandy gold hair, his brilliant blue eyes gleaming with intrigue.

Though Adam knew Cody evaded commitments the way a hypochondriac avoided germs, he was also aware that his cousin had never had any difficulty attracting feminine admiration. He found himself wondering how Jenny was reacting to that megawatt smile.

And then he was angry for himself for even wondering.

"It's nice to meet you, too," Jenny said to Cody, self-consciously smoothing her hair. "Um—how did you get here?"

"I drove. I have a four-wheel-drive Jeep. The roads are still lousy, but thawing. I wouldn't try taking your Jag out for a few days yet, Adam."

"I wasn't planning to," Adam replied. "How about giving us a lift back to civilization? We need to get the baby to a doctor."

Cody's eyes rounded in concern as he turned back to the infant. "Is something wrong? She's so tiny—I hope she isn't ill."

"She isn't," Adam answered. "She's just brand-new. She's only a day old, give or take a couple of hours."

Cody gasped. "A day old? Are you saying you delivered this baby?"

Adam nodded and cradled Melissa a bit closer. "I delivered her."

Cody whirled toward Jenny. "What are you doing standing here in this chilly kitchen? You should be sitting in front of the fire. Come on, let me help you to the couch. Are you okay? Can you walk?"

He had his arm around her shoulders as he fussed over her, already guiding her into the other room.

Adam opened his mouth to tell Cody he was overreacting, but he fell silent when he heard Jenny laugh.

"I'm fine," she said to Cody. "Really. But it's sweet of you to be concerned."

Sweet? Adam followed the other couple into the living room, frowning. When *he* had tried to fuss over Jenny, she'd almost taken his head off. She'd never called *him* sweet.

Of course, *no one* had ever called Adam Stone sweet. But that was beside the point.

Cody made sure Jenny was comfortably seated on the couch, a blanket tucked around her shoulders. "Can I get you anything?" he asked solicitously, for all the world, Adam thought, as though Cody were the host and Jenny his honored guest.

Jenny was still smiling. "Only my baby."

"You bet." Cody spun toward Adam.

Adam dodged Cody's eager hands. "I'll give her the baby," he said gruffly.

"Sure." Cody backed away. "So tell me what happened. How did you end up here with Adam, Jenny?"

Jenny murmured an absent thank-you to Adam as he laid Melissa in her arms. And then she turned to answer

Cody. "Did you see a little blue car hugging a tree a few hundred yards down the road?"

Cody frowned. "No," he admitted. "I was trying to drive and read Granny Fran's directions to the cabin. Her handwriting is terrible. Are you saying you wrecked your car?"

She nodded. "I lost control in the ice storm Thursday evening. Fortunately I saw Adam's lights—the electricity was still on then—and made my way here. He took me in, and he's been taking wonderful care of me ever since."

She smiled at Adam and he immediately forgave her for smiling at Cody. Of course, he still didn't much *like* it.

"And Adam delivered the kid." Cody shook his head in apparent wonder. "That's a far cry from fixing noses, isn't it, cuz?"

He didn't give Adam a chance to answer. Cody knelt in front of Jenny and stroked a finger gently down Melissa's downy cheek. "She's beautiful. Really beautiful. I don't think I've ever seen a prettier baby. Well, except for my sister's kids," he added hastily. "Let's just say Melissa's equally pretty to Paige and Aaron."

"Very diplomatic." Jenny seemed genuinely amused. "I'm sure your sister would appreciate your tact."

"Then it would be the first time she'd ever called me tactful," Cody confessed. And then he stood and turned to Adam. "If we're driving out of here today, we'd better be on our way. The temperature will probably drop again after dark."

Adam agreed. "Are you up to this, Jenny?" he asked. "It won't be a particularly comfortable trip for you, I'm afraid."

"I can take it," she assured him. "Where are we going?"

"To my grandmother's house. We'll stay there while we make arrangements for Melissa to see a doctor and for something to be done about your car."

For once, Jenny deferred to his judgment without question.

Both Cody and Adam insisted that Jenny should stay on the couch with the baby while they loaded the Jeep and secured the cabin. They even made a trek to Jenny's car to retrieve the rest of her things. Adam had explained that he was afraid her possessions would be stolen if they left them unattended in the car after the roads thawed.

In less than an hour, they were underway. Cody drove, Adam sat in the front passenger seat and Jenny in the back seat with the baby, who was securely fastened into the newborn car seat Jenny had received as a shower gift from a group of her former co-workers.

"You must have had a nice shower," Adam commented, thinking of the diapers, sleepers and pacifiers they'd already used out of her gifts.

Jenny, he noted, looked more than a little uncomfortable. Cody was driving slowly and with almost obsessive care, but the storm-damaged road was rough and bumpy. Adam didn't like the tightness around Jenny's mouth or the weary droop of her eyelids. Maybe conversation would take her mind off her discomfort.

"Yes," she answered him. "I had a very nice shower. My friends from work were very supportive during the past few months."

"Are you from around here, Jenny?" Cody asked, glancing briefly in the rearview mirror.

"Texas," she said. "I was on my way to Tennessee when I got lost on this road."

"Tennessee, huh? Got family there?"

"No."

Cody didn't press her for more information. Adam assumed Cody could tell Jenny wasn't eager to elaborate.

Adam almost asked her then if she'd made a decision about his job offer. He changed his mind only because he didn't want to risk quarreling with her in front of Cody.

And they *would* quarrel unless Jenny gave him the answer he wanted to hear.

Melissa squirmed in her car seat and began to fuss. Jenny bent over her, making crooning mother sounds, offering the pacifier, catching the baby's tiny flailing fists in her own loving hands.

Adam became distracted just watching her.

There was a special glow in her amber eyes when she looked at her baby, he noted. A special softness in her musical voice. A special beauty in her face.

He found himself thinking poetically of madonnas and guardian angels. And then, becoming aware of what he was doing, he blinked, scowled and turned around in his seat to face the front again.

Only to look right back over his shoulder at Jenny and the baby.

He never noticed how very closely Cody was watching *him*.

Chapter Eight

It was just past dusk when Cody turned the Jeep into the driveway of a neat frame house. A light gleamed invitingly from the doorway beneath a wide, welcoming front porch. Lace curtains fluttered in the front windows.

Jenny thought it was one of the prettiest little houses she'd ever seen. But she might have been tempted to think that about any place where she could get off this hard leather seat and onto a soft chair or sofa, she thought ruefully.

"Grandma's house," Cody said with a grin over his shoulder. "And Red Riding Hood and the Big, Bad Wolf have come to visit her."

"Assuming Jenny's Red Riding Hood and *you're* the wolf," Adam drawled, "what does that make Melissa and me?"

Cody chuckled, and shot back an answer without hesitation. "Beauty and the Beast."

Regally ignoring his cousin—as Jenny thought he must do fairly often—Adam opened his door. "Don't move, Jenny. I'll help you out."

She'd already reached for her own door handle, intending to let him know she could get out without his help. A moment later, she realized she'd been overly optimistic. She was so stiff and sore, she could hardly move. She needed all the help Adam offered just to climb out of the high sports vehicle.

He put an arm around her to steady her. "Careful," he warned. "There are still patches of ice everywhere."

Shivering, she nodded. She hadn't worn her coat for the heated ride in the Jeep, and her sweat suit was woefully inadequate for the frigid outside temperature.

Adam pulled her closer. "Cody, can you bring the baby?"

Jenny bit her lip as she looked quickly around at Adam's cousin. Could he safely carry a tiny baby over icy pavement? She wanted to say she'd take Melissa, herself, but she was terrified of losing her footing and falling. She rather wished Adam were carrying the baby.

As annoying as he could be, Adam certainly inspired faith in his competence.

She watched anxiously while Cody leaned into the Jeep to unstrap the baby. He wrapped her snugly in a warm layer of blankets before lifting her out into the cold.

Jenny began to relax almost immediately. Cody certainly seemed comfortable enough with the baby in his arms.

"Cody's good with kids," Adam murmured, as though sensing Jenny's misgivings. "He's had a lot of practice with his niece and nephew. They're crazy about him."

Jenny nodded, then shivered again. Instinctively she crowded closer to Adam. He responded by drawing her into the warmth of his denim-and-flannel-covered body. "Let's get you inside," he said, leading her after Cody.

The door opened just as they all stepped onto the porch. A tiny, gray-haired woman in a black-and-silver wind suit rushed over the threshold. "Adam! I'm so glad to see you're all right. I was worried about you out there in the woods during such a storm. I hope you forgive me for sending Cody to—why, goodness! Who's this?"

Adam guided Jenny into the house with his grandmother and Cody. "Jenny Newcomb, this is my grandmother, Frances Carson."

"It's very nice to meet you, Mrs. Carson," Jenny managed to say through cold-stiffened lips.

"You poor dear, you're freezing. I'll put on some water for hot tea. Or would you prefer cocoa?"

"Tea sounds wonderful," Jenny said gratefully.

"Here's someone else for you to meet, Granny Fran." Cody dug into the blankets to expose Melissa's furrowed pink face. "This is Jenny's one-day-old daughter, Melissa. Adam delivered her."

"Oh, my goodness!" The wide-eyed little woman looked from Adam to Jenny to the baby.

Her face promptly softened. "What an angel," she crooned. "Isn't she the sweetest thing? Cody, you be careful with her, you hear? Bring her into the parlor where her mama can hold her in the big upholstered rocker. Oh, my, she's such a dear."

Adam made a rueful face at Jenny. "Just follow Granny Fran and Cody," he suggested. "I'll go make the tea. Granny Fran's going to be too busy admiring the baby to remember it for a while."

Jenny nodded a bit nervously and watched Adam disappear, leaving her alone with these people she really didn't know at all, no matter how nice they seemed.

As Adam had predicted, his grandmother spent some time *oohing* and *aahing* over the baby once Jenny was settled into the rocker with Melissa in her arms. She treated Jenny as a welcome guest, insisting that Jenny call her Granny Fran, as nearly everyone else did, she explained.

Jenny repeated her abbreviated story about being lost on the way to Tennessee, about going into premature labor and Adam's delivery of the baby. She could see the pride glowing in Frances Carson's eyes at her grandson's skill. She obviously adored her eldest grandchild.

Jenny was grateful that neither Granny Fran nor Cody asked about the baby's father. She assumed they guessed that she was unmarried, but there was no condemnation or disapproval in their friendly expressions.

Very nice people.

She looked down at Melissa, who was beginning to make the funny little faces that indicated she would be wanting to eat soon. As much as Jenny regretted her lapse of bad judgment in getting involved with Carl, she could never be sorry about Melissa, she thought wistfully. Already she loved this baby more than she'd ever imagined she could love anyone. Whatever trials lay ahead for them, they'd survive somehow. Together.

Adam came back into the room balancing a tray, which held a ceramic teapot, three cups, a sugar bowl, a plate of what appeared to be homemade cookies and three dessert plates.

"Teatime," he said, by way of announcing his return. "Sorry, Melissa, there's nothing here for you. We'll wait until you're old enough to appreciate Granny Fran's cookies. Nobody makes them better."

Cringing, Jenny saw that Cody seemed intrigued by Adam's implication that Melissa would be around when she was old enough to eat cookies. Despite his rather lazy manner, Cody didn't seem to miss much, she'd already realized.

Granny Fran never seemed to notice. She thanked Adam for bringing the tea, exclaiming sheepishly at her own neglect to do so.

"I was so excited about having a baby in the house again that I forgot all about it," she explained.

"I know you did," Adam said with a smile. "Sit down. Since I made the tea, I'll serve. Cody, how about running out to the Jeep and bringing in the infant seat so Jenny can set the baby down for a little while?"

"Sure thing." Cody was already on his feet and moving cooperatively toward the door.

"She's going to want to eat soon," Jenny warned Adam.

He shrugged. "Maybe she'll wait until you've had time to have a cup of tea."

His grandmother laughed. "Babies aren't known for being patient when it comes to feeding time. Jenny, dear, would you mind if I hold her for a moment until Cody gets back in? I have to confess, my hands have been itching to get ahold of her ever since I saw her."

Jenny couldn't help smiling at the older woman's avid enthusiasm. "Of course I don't mind."

She handed her daughter over confidently. Jenny thought she had never met anyone who looked like a more natural grandmother than Frances Carson.

Adam poured Jenny a cup of tea. "Cream or sugar?" he asked.

She accepted the steaming cup gratefully. "No, thank you. This smells heavenly."

"You have to try some of these cookies," he insisted, piling several on a dessert plate. "They're great."

She thought of the pounds she still had to lose, then looked again at those homemade cookies. Oh, well, she thought, tossing caution to the wind. She could always start dieting tomorrow. "Thank you," she said again as Adam set the plate close at hand on a small cherry-wood occasional table that was almost covered with knick-knacks.

Cody came back in with the infant seat. "Brr," he said dramatically. "It's as cold as a witch's—er—refrigerator out there. Where do you want this?"

Adam reached for the vinyl-and-molded-plastic seat. "Here, I'll take it. Help yourself to tea and cookies."

"I'll do that." Cody promptly grabbed a generous handful of cookies, making Jenny glance enviously at his slender waistline. He couldn't eat like this often, she mused, or he'd never stay so slim.

Adam took the baby from his reluctant grandmother and laid her in the seat. They all held their breaths when Melissa promptly squirmed, screwed up her face and looked all set to cry. They exhaled in unison when she yawned, closed her eyes and fell into a light sleep.

"What can I say," Adam bragged. "I have the magic touch."

Cody sighed gustily and rolled his eyes. "I've heard *that* before," he muttered.

His cousin, as usual, ignored him.

Adam made a production of serving tea and cookies to his grandmother. "Is there anything else you need?" he asked her.

"Yes," she said promptly, her eyes twinkling up at him. "A kiss from my oldest grandson."

He grinned, leaned over and planted a surprisingly tender kiss on her soft, lined cheek. The look that passed

THE EDITOR'S "THANK YOU" FREE GIFTS INCLUDE:

▶ Four BRAND-NEW romance novels
▶ A Porcelain Trinket Box

PLACE FREE GIFT SEAL HERE

YES! I have placed my Editor's "thank you"
seal in the space provided above. Please send me 4 free
books and a Porcelain Trinket Box. I understand
I am under no obligation to purchase any books, as
explained on the back and on the opposite page.

235 CIS AWJN (U-SIL-SE-09/95)

NAME

_____

ADDRESS   APT.

_____

CITY   STATE   ZIP

Thank you!

DETACH AND MAIL CARD TODAY!

THE SILHOUETTE READER SERVICE™: HERE'S HOW IT WORKS

Accepting free books places you under no obligation to buy anything. You may keep the books and gift and return the shipping statement marked "cancel". If you do not cancel, about a month later we will send you 6 additional novels, and bill you just $3.12 each plus 25¢ delivery and applicable sales tax, if any.* That's the complete price, and—compared to cover prices of $3.75 each—quite a bargain! You may cancel at any time, but if you choose to continue, every month we'll send you 6 more books, which you may either purchase at the discount price...or return at our expense and cancel your subscription.

*Terms and prices subject to change without notice. Sales tax applicable in N.Y.

between them was so warm, so loving that Jenny had to look away, a hard lump forming in her throat.

It had been years—if ever—since she'd had that strong sense of family closeness. She could hardly remember her own grandparents.

She realized then that she'd just fallen in love.

She assured herself hastily that her affection was directed toward sweet Frances Carson—and not her complex, unpredictable grandson.

Adam finished his own tea quickly, then announced that he had to make some telephone calls. "I have a friend who's a pediatrician in Hot Springs," he explained to Jenny. "I'm sure he'd be glad to look Melissa over first thing in the morning. I'll also make arrangements about having your car towed and evaluated for damage."

"I can do that," she argued hurriedly. "There's no need for you to—"

He cut her off with a wave of his hand. "I'll take care of it. Is there anyone else you want me to call?"

"No, I—"

"Fine." He'd already turned away. "Guess I'll call the office while I'm at it, make sure nothing's come up there."

"You'd better call your mother," his grandmother said with a touch of sympathy in her expression. "She's been having fits to talk to you for the past few days. She's handled the bad weather just fine, but it gripes her no end that you haven't been around to cater to her."

"I'll call her," Adam said without noticeable enthusiasm.

Jenny was getting a pretty clear mental image of Adam's mother, and it wasn't a particularly comfortable one. How would his mother feel if Jenny accepted Adam's generous job offer? Would she disapprove of her son hiring an unmarried young mother? Would she suspect things that simply weren't true?

Cody was watching Jenny as Adam left the room. "You'll get used to that if you're around him much longer," he said.

She didn't quite understand. "Get used to what?"

"That steamroller technique of his. Adam tends to decide what's best, and then he takes care of it without bothering to consult anyone else involved."

"Adam means well," Granny Fran defended instantly. "He's just—er—"

"Dictatorial." Cody supplied a word.

"Overly zealous." Granny Fran corrected him.

"Arrogant," Cody added.

"Self-confident," his grandmother returned.

"Granny's pet," Cody muttered with an exaggerated scowl.

Granny Fran laughed softly. "Nonsense. I love each of my grandchildren the same, and you know it, you rascal."

Cody chuckled and leaned over to kiss her with a noisy smack. "Love you, too, Gran. Got anything else to eat around here?"

Jenny was glad that the baby woke then, demanding to be fed. It was a nice reminder to her that she was no longer alone.

She had her own family now, even if that family consisted only of herself and one tiny, hungry baby girl.

Adam completed his calls and assured everyone that all arrangements had been made. He didn't give Jenny a chance to ask what, exactly, he'd arranged on her behalf.

"I'd better be going," Cody said with a yawn and a stretch. "It's getting dark out."

"You aren't planning to make that long drive home tonight, are you?" Granny Fran demanded. "It's almost completely dark now, and those highways are still very slick. You should stay right here tonight."

"She's right," Adam said. "It would take you at least three hours to get back to Percy tonight—if you make it at all. You'd be safer staying here.

"Besides," he added with a wry grin. "I need your wheels tomorrow. Granny Fran doesn't have a car, remember? And mine is still snowed in at the cabin."

Cody sighed and shook his head. "Your true motivation reveals itself. If you'd only taken my advice and bought a sensible, practical vehicle like mine instead of that sexy foreign number you just had to have...."

"What can I say? I'm so well suited to sexy cars," Adam quipped smugly.

Cody groaned.

Jenny thought in bemusement that there seemed to be a lot of affection between the cousins, even if it was tinged with exasperation. On both sides.

"That's settled then," Granny Fran said with relief. "Cody, you'll spend the night here. You and Adam can use the twin beds in the back bedroom, the same ones you've always used. Jenny, the front guest room will do for you and Melissa. That's where Rachel and Celia always stayed when my grandchildren slept over."

"I hope I'm not causing you any inconvenience," Jenny said politely.

Granny Fran shook her gray head. "Not a bit. I love having company. I'd better get dinner started. Cody will be hungry again soon—and he's almost as impatient as your daughter when he wants to be fed," she added with a mischievous smile.

"I resent that," Cody said lazily.

"I'm sure Cody's *more* impatient than Melissa," Adam contributed, tongue in cheek.

Chuckling, Granny Fran headed for the kitchen.

"You've made her week," Cody told Jenny. "Granny Fran's never happier than when she has someone to cook for and fuss over."

"Does she live here alone?"

Cody nodded. "My sister Rachel and I live in Percy— that's a couple of hours north of here. Our kid sister Celia recently moved to New Mexico with her new husband. My parents—Dad's Granny Fran's son—live in St. Louis. Adam and his mother, Aunt Arlene, both live in Little Rock, which is about an hour's drive away from here."

"I've tried to get Gran to move closer to me where I can keep an eye on her," Adam said with a slight frown. "I've even offered to build her a guest house next to mine. She won't even discuss it."

Jenny could tell he was quite disgruntled by his grandmother's refusal to fall in compliantly with his suggestions.

"She's lived in Malvern almost all her life," Cody said pointedly. "Raised her kids here. Her church is here, and her friends. She's happy here."

"Still, it would be better if she were closer to me," Adam complained.

"Better for whom?" Jenny couldn't resist asking. "Your grandmother—or yourself?"

Adam turned his frown toward her. Cody gave her a look of approval.

Jenny quickly busied herself folding a baby blanket.

Cody rescued her from whatever Adam might have said. "C'mon, cuz, let's bring in Jenny's things. I'm sure she'd like to get settled into the guest room for the evening."

Jenny was grateful to him for rescuing her from one of Adam's lectures. She sent him a quick smile, which Cody returned warmly.

Adam, she noticed, began to frown even more heavily, though he allowed Cody to drag him away.

"She's lovely," Granny Fran told Adam much later that evening. Dinner had been eaten, the dishes cleared away. Jenny and the baby had retired to the front guest room for the night; Cody was settled in front of the TV in the den, engrossed in a late-night "Star Trek" rerun.

Adam sat in the kitchen drinking hot cocoa with his grandmother, enjoying the rare, quiet time with her. He visited her as often as he could, but, with his demanding schedule, it was too infrequently for his satisfaction. Usually he saw his grandmother when the entire family had gathered for an occasion, such as the past Christmas. The family gatherings were always pleasant, but a bit chaotic. There was rarely time to just sit and chat.

Savoring the peace, and the cocoa, Adam lifted an eyebrow in lazy enquiry in response to his grandmother's comment. "Who's lovely? The baby?"

"Oh, yes, of course. But I was talking about Jenny. What a nice young woman," Granny Fran said. "So polite. Even after all she's been through for the past few days, she still wanted to help with the dishes after dinner. She seemed quite distressed when I refused to allow her to do anything to help."

"She's very independent," Adam explained. "Determined to pull her own weight. I swear, Gran, she's worse than Rachel when it comes to being stubborn and self-reliant.''

"In other words, she refused to let you step in and immediately take charge of her life for her," his grandmother translated indulgently.

Adam frowned. "I wasn't trying to do that. It's just that I could see she needs help and there are several things I can do to help her. She's had a run of bad luck lately, made a few mistakes, and now she just needs some sensible advice. A little guidance, maybe."

"Guidance that you, of course, are eminently suited to offer her."

Adam's frown deepened. "Now you sound like Cody. Am I really so officious?"

His grandmother gave him a lovingly exasperated smile. "Yes, dear, you are. At times. But those of us who love you know that you always have the best intentions. You only want to help those who are less fortunate than yourself. Just as you are unable to turn your back on your mother, no matter how trying she may be at times."

"And *should* I turn my back?" he demanded. "On Mother—or Jenny and her baby?"

"Of course not. You simply have to give Jenny the opportunity to decline your assistance, if she chooses. You can't force your advice on others, Adam, no matter how wise you think it might be."

"I don't claim to be all that wise," he muttered. "It's just that I've had more experience than Jenny. She's young, and vulnerable, right now. I can help her."

"How?"

"I've offered her a job. As my housekeeper."

Frances tilted her head. "Your housekeeper?"

"Yes. You know Mrs. Handy retired."

"Of course. But I thought you'd decided not to re-place her. You said you were home so rarely, you really didn't need a full-time cook and housekeeper."

"So I was wrong," Adam said with a shrug. "Now that I think about it, I *do* need some help around the place."

"And you've come to that realization since you met Jenny."

He avoided her too-knowing eyes by taking a cautious sip of his hot beverage. "It seemed like a convenient so-lution for both of us," he murmured into the mug.

"Hmm. As I said, Jenny *is* a lovely woman."

Adam set down his mug with a thump, barely avoiding splashing cocoa all over her spotless kitchen table. "I didn't offer her a job because I was personally interested in her," he insisted. "Not in the way you've implied, anyway. I just want to help her. I have an opening, she needs someplace to go. What could be simpler? Or more straightforward?"

"So you're *not* personally interested in her? You don't find her attractive?"

"I didn't say that," he hedged, pushing away an all-too-clear image of the way Jenny had looked standing in the kitchen doorway at the cabin, heavy eyed and flushed from sleep. "Jenny is attractive, of course. But I have no intention of anything more than a professional relation-ship with her. We can be friends, perhaps. But that's all."

His grandmother seemed privately amused. "And why is that?"

Adam was growing defensive. He wouldn't have taken questions like this from anyone but Granny Fran. Any-one else—except his favorite cousin Rachel, perhaps—would have already received one of his notoriously curt put-downs. But he had never been able to risk hurting his grandmother.

He answered reluctantly. "For one thing, she's too young for me. By twelve years."

"I was eleven years younger than your grandfather."

Adam eyed her warily. "You aren't matchmaking again, are you? Trust me, you're off course this time. I have no intention of getting involved with anyone right now. I don't have time for a relationship. You know how busy I am with work."

"Sweetheart, there's always time for love," his grandmother admonished.

Love? Who said anything about love?

Gulping silently, Adam held up a hand. "This whole conversation is getting ridiculous," he said as sternly as he dared. "I've offered Jenny a housekeeping position, nothing more. She hasn't even accepted that.

"Jenny's just gotten out of a bad relationship, and she isn't looking for another right now," he explained evenly. "She needs a job, a place to stay, a place to raise her baby until she gets back on her feet and decides what to do with her future. I'm going to do everything I can to make sure she has those things—but it's nothing personal," he insisted. "Anyone would do the same for someone in her situation."

"All right, dear, I won't embarrass you any further. I think it's wonderful what you've done for Jenny, and I'm sure she's very grateful to you."

Somehow, that bothered Adam more than anything she'd said yet. He didn't like thinking that Jenny's feelings for him—casual as they might be—were in any way influenced by gratitude.

"I don't want her feeling grateful to me," he grumbled. "It's a job, that's all. Not charity."

Granny Fran sighed. "You're being very prickly this evening, Adam. It's difficult to carry on a conversation with you."

"Sorry," he said. "Maybe we should change the subject."

"Perhaps we should. Did I tell you I talked to Rachel this morning? She and Seth seem to be settling in nicely. She's so happy."

Adam glanced at her a bit suspiciously, wondering if there was any deeper meaning to her new choice of topics. Deciding he was being paranoid, he relaxed and went along with her. "How are the kids doing?" he asked.

His grandmother eagerly began to fill him in on all the latest family news. Adam listened with forced attention, still distantly uncomfortable after her artless conversation about Jenny.

Adam drove Jenny and Melissa to the pediatrician's office in Cody's Jeep early the next morning, leaving Cody contentedly alone with his grandmother—and her cooking.

Jenny was a bit nervous about this appointment. She wouldn't be able to put her mind completely at ease until Melissa had been thoroughly examined and pronounced healthy.

Adam escorted them into the clinic and gave his name to the receptionist. "I called yesterday," he added. "Max said he would work us in."

The efficient receptionist nodded her head. "Dr. Lawrence told me to expect you. We'll call you shortly, Dr. Stone, Mrs. Stone."

"Oh, I'm not—" Jenny began, but Adam ushered her into the waiting room before she could correct the receptionist's misconception.

"Did you tell her we were married?" she snapped when she and Adam had been seated in adjacent chairs, Jenny holding the baby while Adam leafed through a magazine he'd picked up from a low table.

"Of course not," he answered absently, seemingly interested in an article about Oprah's personal life. "But there was no need to argue with her. It's really none of her business, is it?"

"No, I suppose not," Jenny conceded. Still, it bothered her that the woman had assumed she and Adam were married. She couldn't quite explain why.

Half an hour passed before Melissa's name was called. Jenny was surprised when Adam stood at the same time she did. "Are you coming with us?" she asked.

He nodded, studying her expression. "Do you mind? I thought Max might have some questions about the delivery."

"Oh." That made some sense to her. "Well, you can come with us, then. But Adam?"

"Mmm?"

"Let me talk, okay? I *am* her mother."

He seemed surprised by the request. "Of course you are. You don't really expect me to go in there and take over the examination, do you?"

She didn't answer. Truth was, she did expect just that.

With a sigh of resignation, she followed after him, reminding herself that Adam had, after all, arranged this examination for her.

She supposed she should be grateful.

Chapter Nine

By the end of the day, Jenny had to admit that Adam's brisk efficiency amazed even her. She'd never seen anything like it. He seemed to accomplish tasks almost by simply wishing them done.

It was no wonder he'd gotten just a little arrogant about his own competence.

His pediatrician friend—whom Jenny liked immediately—pronounced Melissa healthy, if a bit small, and utterly beautiful. He took his time with the examination, answered all Jenny's questions to her satisfaction, conferred politely with Adam without leaving Jenny out of the conversation, and saw her off with some helpful advice and reassurances that Melissa would be just fine.

Jenny felt as though an enormous load had just been lifted from her shoulders.

Adam bought her lunch at a small, excellent restaurant in Hot Springs. Melissa slept in her infant seat on a spare chair, receiving plenty of admiring attention from the wait staff and the other diners.

Adam proved that he could be a charming lunch companion. Still glowing from the pediatrician's encouraging words, Jenny thoroughly enjoyed the meal. They'd been fortunate to have had a gas stove and a pantry full of supplies at the cabin, she told Adam, but it was nice to eat food that hadn't come out of cans.

He agreed heartily. "Would you like dessert?"

She shook her head. "I couldn't eat another bite. Besides," she added ruefully, "I still have several extra pounds to lose."

"You don't look it," he said, glancing down at the oversize sweater she wore over knit slacks. "But there's probably not time for dessert, anyway. You have a one-thirty appointment with Dr. Cooper."

"Dr. Cooper?" This was the first time Jenny had heard the name. "Who is that?"

"Dolores Cooper. One of the best gynecologists in the mid-South. You'll like her, I'm sure."

"You made me an appointment with a gynecologist?" Jenny asked in disbelief.

"Yes. I'm reasonably certain that you're in good health, but I'll feel better after you've had a checkup. I'll sit with the baby while you're in the exam room."

"Adam, shouldn't you at least have consulted me about this?" Jenny asked in exasperation.

He looked surprised that she'd even mention it. "Surely you expected this. You have to take care of yourself as well as your child, Jenny. How can you care for her if you neglect your own health?"

She bit her lip. She knew he was right—as always—but she still wished he'd given her the courtesy of discussing his plans with her. "I just think you should have talked to me about it first," she said.

He looked thoughtful for a moment, then nodded. "You're right. I should have. I'm sorry, I was trying to help."

Jenny swallowed a slight gasp of surprise. Adam was admitting he made a mistake—no matter how minor? And he was apologizing.

Something told her he didn't do either very often.

Dr. Cooper—who, as Adam had promised, seemed to be an excellent gynecologist—gave Jenny a thorough examination, suggested a diet and exercise program to follow for the next few months and told her what to expect by way of her recovery. All in all, she assured Jenny—and Adam, who seemed determined to find out for himself—that Jenny appeared to be in good health for a woman who'd just given birth under very primitive conditions.

"Now what?" Jenny asked when she, Melissa and Adam were back in Cody's Jeep. "Have you made me an appointment at a beauty parlor?"

"Very funny," Adam said, but she could tell she didn't have his full attention.

He must be preoccupied planning the rest of my day, Jenny thought with a sigh, lapsing into silence.

By late afternoon, the roads had cleared considerably. The skies were blue, the temperatures almost balmy, compared to the past week. The locals were emerging from their homes, relieved that the atypical winter weather seemed to have passed.

Jenny was startled to see Adam's Jaguar parked in the driveway of his grandmother's house when she and Adam returned in Cody's Jeep. "Isn't that your car? How did it get here?"

He shrugged. "I made some arrangements. By the way, your car should be in a shop by now. I had it towed. We should have an estimate on repairs by tomorrow or the next day."

Her jaw dropped. "How did you manage that so quickly? With the condition the roads are in, and the horrible weather we've had lately, there must have been long waiting lists for wrecker service and repair shops!"

"I have a few connections," he said, turning off the Jeep's engine. "Be careful getting out, in case there are any more slippery spots. Grab the diaper bag—I'll take Melissa in."

"But I—"

But Adam had already gotten out of the vehicle.

Jenny buried her face in her hands in exasperation.

When they entered the house, they found Cody's feet sticking out from beneath the kitchen sink, while ominous clanging sounds filled the kitchen. Cody, it seemed, was fixing a small leak in one of the pipes, to Adam's apparent consternation.

Adam immediately knelt to offer his cousin plumbing advice, which set off a good-natured squabble when Cody pointed out that Adam probably hadn't held a wrench in his entire adult life.

Ignoring her grandsons' banter, Granny Fran welcomed Jenny with a warm smile and a barrage of anxious questions. "Did everyone check out all right? How's Melissa? What did Dr. Cooper say about you, Jenny?"

"You knew about Dr. Cooper?" Jenny asked.

"Of course. Adam mentioned last night that he'd called her. She's a lovely woman, isn't she?"

"Yes, she's very nice," Jenny replied absently, giving Adam a reproving frown. He'd remembered to tell his grandmother about the appointment he'd made Jenny, but he hadn't thought to tell *her?*

"And everything checked out all right?" Granny Fran repeated.

"Melissa and I are both fine," Jenny assured the older woman. "There's nothing to worry about."

"Oh, that's good news. I was sure everything was fine, of course. After all, Adam was taking care of you. But it's nice to have official confirmation."

Jenny managed a smile. "Thank you for being concerned. Now, if you'll excuse me, Melissa's getting hungry again. I'll take her to the guest room."

Adam glanced over his shoulder. "Need any help?"

"I think I can manage this on my own," she answered dryly, cradling the fussing baby in her arms.

He nodded and turned back to Cody. "You're turning that the wrong way," he said.

"I can handle it, Adam. Back off," Cody replied cheerfully.

Jenny took advantage of the opportunity to make her escape.

She really needed to be alone for a while, she thought wearily. Adam was an exhausting man to spend a day with.

"She looks tired," she heard Granny Fran say behind her. And then she added in a stern voice, "Adam, have you been steamrolling her again?"

"Of course not," Adam protested. "I just—"

Jenny didn't linger to hear the rest of his logical explanation.

Half an hour later, Jenny sat on the bed in the guest room, rocking her upper body and softly singing a lullaby. Melissa lay drowsily in her arms, replete from nursing, her tiny dark eyes focused on her mother's face.

Jenny had never been more utterly content.

A quiet tap on the bedroom door interrupted the idyllic interlude. She lifted her head. "Come in."

She wasn't surprised when Adam opened the door and looked in. "Have you finished nursing her?"

"Yes. Come on in."

Adam studied the baby as he approached the bed. "She looks content," he said with a smile. "She seems to have recovered nicely from her first outing."

"I think she enjoyed it," Jenny agreed. "She loves attention, doesn't she?"

Adam's smile deepened. "We've spoiled her already." He didn't seem to notice how naturally he said "we."

Jenny noticed.

Without asking permission, Adam sat beside her on the edge of the bed, his thigh only inches from Jenny's. He stroked Melissa's curls and spoke a few nonsense words to the baby, and Jenny watched him surreptitiously, wondering how he could talk gibberish and look so dignified at the same time.

He looked up suddenly and their eyes met. Jenny resisted an impulse to quickly look away.

"We need to talk," Adam said.

She knew what he wanted to talk about. He'd been remarkably patient about giving her time to consider his job offer, but it was obviously time for her to make a decision.

They couldn't continue in this limbo much longer.

"You want an answer," she said.

"We really should get this settled," he agreed.

Jenny took a deep breath. She'd spent so many hours worrying about this, trying to decide whether she'd be making a terrible mistake accepting his offer. On the one hand, it seemed ideal. A place to live, a safe environment for Melissa, a job that provided benefits and allowed her to be with her child.

Jenny didn't worry about the responsibilities of the job; she was certainly capable of cooking and cleaning and marketing. She *did* worry about moving in with Adam Stone, even if only as his employee.

Even if she ignored the tug of unwanted attraction she'd felt for him from the beginning—and that was hard enough to manage—there were still so many other potential problems. His annoying tendencies to take over her life, for example.

She didn't need anyone making decisions for her, especially when it came to her child. And she didn't like to think that he was offering this position because he felt responsible for her—or worse, because he pitied her.

"If I accept," she said, steadily holding his gaze, "there are certain conditions I want to make clear."

He narrowed his eyes. "What conditions?"

"First—are you absolutely sure you need a housekeeper? I refuse to accept charity—from you, or from anyone."

"We've talked about this before," he reminded her. "I need a housekeeper. Granny Fran can verify that Mrs. Handy was with me for several years before she retired."

"That won't be necessary. I just wanted to hear it again."

"Fine. You've heard it. Now what?"

"I don't want you taking over my life," she said bravely. "I don't want you making any more doctor appointments for me, or for the baby. When my car needs repairs, I'll call a mechanic. I'm an adult, Adam, not a child, and I don't need a caretaker. If I accept your offer, the only instructions I will accept are those that you give as my employer. My personal life is strictly that. Clear?"

He was frowning, but he nodded curtly. "Clear. What else?"

"It won't be a permanent arrangement. It's only until I get back on my feet and you find another housekeeper. As you asked, I'll give notice when I'm ready to move on, but I don't want you trying to stop me when I decide the time is right."

"What else?" he asked.

She noted that he hadn't exactly agreed. She supposed she could assume that he accepted her terms.

"While I'm under your employ, I want you to treat me exactly the same way you treated Mrs. Handy," she continued. "I don't expect to take meals with you or socialize with your friends and family. No special favors. I'll be your housekeeper, nothing more."

"As it happens, Mrs. Handy and I often shared meals—when I was home to eat them," Adam said silkily. "We enjoyed conversing over dinner. Does that surprise you?"

"No, of course not," she replied. Though, of course, it did.

She wouldn't have thought Adam was the type of man who would enjoy a quiet dinner with the household help.

"What else?" Adam prodded.

She bit her lip and tried to remember any other concerns. "That's all—I guess. Unless something else occurs to me later, of course."

"Why do I get the feeling that I'm the one being interviewed for this position?" Adam grumbled, as though to himself. And then he shook his head and lifted an eyebrow. "Well? Are you accepting or not?"

Jenny took a deep breath. "I'm accepting."

He looked pleased. "Fine. We'll leave first thing in the morning. Granny Fran wants us to spend one more night with her before we move on."

"When are you expected back at work?" she asked curiously.

"I'd planned to spend the rest of this week at the cabin," he admitted.

"I'm sorry I ruined your vacation for you," Jenny said, with genuine regret.

He made a face. "I wouldn't have lasted the week, anyway. I was already getting bored when you showed up. As far as I'm concerned, you and Melissa were the high point of my leave."

Touched, Jenny smiled at him. "That's a nice thing to say."

"I can be nice on occasion," he reminded her.

"I know. When you remember to be."

He chuckled, patted Melissa's head again and stood. "It's all settled, then. You won't regret this, Jenny."

Jenny remained silent. She truly hoped he was right.

"Granny Fran said to tell you to feel free to take a nap, if you want. She'll have dinner ready at around six."

"Shouldn't I offer to help her?"

He shook his head. "She loves this. Besides, Cody and I can give her a hand if she needs help. Get some rest. I'm sure you're tired."

As a matter of fact, she was, though she was reluctant to admit that he was right—again. She settled for a nod.

Standing by the bed, Adam hesitated, then startled her by gently touching her cheek, reminding her of the way he'd touched Melissa. "I'm glad you accepted my offer," he said. "I think this is going to work out very well. For both of us."

He left her then, closing the bedroom door behind him.

Jenny looked dazedly down at her now-sleeping baby. Several long minutes passed before she realized that she was holding one hand against her own cheek.

Funny. Her skin still felt warm where Adam had touched her.

They left Granny Fran's right after breakfast the following morning. Since Adam's Jaguar wouldn't hold all the luggage and baby things, Cody piled the excess in his Jeep, intending to follow them to Adam's house in Little Rock. Both Cody and Granny Fran had seemed pleased, but not particularly surprised, that Jenny had accepted Adam's job offer.

"I'm glad we'll be seeing each other again," Granny Fran told her as they prepared to leave.

Jenny smiled. "So am I." She had grown amazingly fond of Adam's grandmother during the past two days.

"Now, remember, don't let Adam push you around. If he gets out of hand, you just give me a call. I'll take him down a peg or two for you."

Cody chuckled in response to his grandmother's advice to Jenny. "She's probably the only one who *can* take Adam down a peg or two," he added. "Unfortunately it's always been only temporary."

"I'm surrounded by critics," Adam grumbled. "You ready to go, Jenny?"

She nodded and cradled the bundled-up baby closer to her heart.

It was surprisingly hard to leave this cozy little house where she'd been welcomed so sweetly. She wasn't afraid of what awaited her, she assured herself bravely.

She was only a bit nervous.

Granny Fran brushed a soft kiss against Melissa's cheek. "Goodbye, my angel," she said in a crooning manner. "I'll see you again soon."

And then she rose to kiss Jenny's cheek, almost as tenderly as she had the baby's. "Take good care of yourself, dear. Please don't hesitate to call me if there's anything I can do for you."

Jenny felt her eyes sting. She couldn't remember the last time she'd been embraced with more honest affection. "Thank you, Granny Fran," she said shyly, using the nickname for the first time. "For everything."

Adam kissed his grandmother, spent five minutes or so admonishing her about her health and her safety and finally allowed her to shoo him away. He and Jenny walked out while Cody was still bidding his grandmother a devoted farewell.

"You've been very quiet," Adam observed half an hour later, just a little over halfway to his house. "Are you tired?"

Jenny had been looking over the back of the seat to make sure Melissa was sleeping peacefully in her snug, rear-facing safety seat. In response to Adam's question, she turned back around. "No, I'm not tired. I've had plenty of rest the past few days."

"Is something bothering you? Would you like to talk about it?"

She shook her head. "Nothing's bothering me," she assured him. "I just haven't had anything to say."

Adam searched her face briefly, then looked back at the road ahead. He knew she hadn't been entirely truthful with him. It was obvious that something *was* bothering Jenny. He suspected she was nervous about arriving at his house. Moving in with him, actually.

He certainly couldn't blame her for that.

Despite the perfectly respectable circumstances, it was hard for him to remember that Jenny would be staying with him strictly as domestic help. It still stung a bit to remember how brutally clear she'd made it that she didn't want anything more from him.

Yet something told him it wasn't going to be easy for him to view her the same way he had the stern, portly Mrs. Handy.

Not that she wouldn't be perfectly safe with him, of course. Adam had no intention of allowing his feelings to grow into more than the mild affection he'd developed for her during the past few days.

Okay, so he was crazy about her kid. That was only normal. Nearly everyone liked babies.

And, sure, he found Jenny attractive. He wasn't blind. Any fool could see that she was gorgeous.

And yeah, all right. He admired her courage, her self-sufficiency, even her stubborn independence. She took chances, admitted her mistakes, picked herself up and kept right on going. Other than a few perfectly understandable hormone-driven lapses, she hadn't whined or panicked or begged for assistance.

She had every intention of making her own way in the world, raising her baby. All very admirable, if a bit misguided.

She considered herself his housekeeper. Nothing more.

He considered her a friend. Nothing more.

Time would tell which description—if either—best described the tentative bond between them.

Adam parked in front of an impressive, redbrick and white-trim Georgian house in an exclusive west Little

Rock neighborhood. "Welcome to your new home," he said.

"Temporary new home," Jenny murmured, whether to remind him or herself, she couldn't have said. She studied the dignified, formally symmetrical structure with hidden awe. Though it was almost modest in comparison to some of the mansions they'd passed, it was still a bigger house than Jenny had ever lived in before.

This was where she and Melissa would be living for the next few months? This was the house she would be responsible for keeping?

Oh, heavens.

"It's—very nice," she said inanely.

Adam didn't seem particularly bothered by her lack of enthusiasm. "Let's get you and the baby inside and then I'll start bringing in your things," he said, reaching for his door handle.

Jenny had a sudden, insane urge to run. As fast and as far as she could go. She felt almost as though her life would change forever, in some dramatic, potentially dangerous way, the moment she stepped through that stately, wood-and-leaded-glass front door.

She took a deep breath and told herself to stop being ridiculous. It was only a job, she reminded herself, and Adam only an employer.

She could handle this.

She hoped.

Cody didn't linger after he helped Adam carry in all the bags. He explained that he had to get back to Percy, to tend to his own business there. His partner, he added, was probably more than ready for Cody's help by now.

Cody kissed Melissa's little cheek, and then did the same with Jenny

"We'll be seeing each other again," he promised.
"Soon."

She smiled. "Good. I'd like that."

Adam cleared his throat and motioned toward the door.
"Come on, Cody. I'll see you out."

They left Jenny standing alone in Adam's house.

The place had obviously been professionally decorated. Colors, patterns, fabrics, materials—all blended
into a soothing harmony of terra-cotta and cream—elegant, without being overly feminine. Equally lovely and
restful paintings hung on the walls. Jenny was sure each
was worth a great deal, though she wasn't familiar with
the artists. What few baubles and knickknacks there were
had obviously been chosen for aesthetic, rather than sen-
timental value.

The overall effect was expensive, but a bit cold.

It was a gorgeous house. Jenny just wasn't at all sure
she would call it a home.

She held her baby and stood very still in the middle of
a huge, sunny, high-ceilinged gathering room that should
have been warm and comfort inspiring, but somehow
wasn't. She'd never seen a house that looked less welcoming for a newborn.

Adam had silently rejoined her and was watching her
closely. "What's wrong?"

She quickly shook her head. "Nothing."

He frowned. "Jenny. I know you well enough by now
that I can tell when you're trying to hide something from
me."

She didn't much like the sound of that.

If he knew her this well after only a few days, would he
be able to read her mind after another couple of weeks?
That didn't seem fair, since she could so rarely even guess
what Adam was thinking.

Telling herself that her nerves were making her fanciful, she cleared her throat. "Actually I was wondering if you're sure you know what you're doing bringing a baby into this lovely house," she said candidly.

He shrugged. "Melissa's no trouble. And, as I've explained, I'm not here much. Don't you think the two of you will be comfortable here?"

Comfortable? She doubted it.

Safe? Maybe.

She supposed she would settle for that.

As Adam had already explained, the master suite was on the ground floor, at the back of the house. The other four bedrooms were upstairs. As Jenny and the baby followed Adam through the upstairs hallway, she had the impression that it had been quite a while since anyone had climbed the stairs at all, except, perhaps to dust and vacuum.

"Did Mrs. Handy stay up here?" she asked curiously.

"Actually, Mrs. Handy lived in her own house across town. She was here from nine to five on weekdays, off on weekends."

Jenny's eyes widened. "You led me to believe she was a live-in housekeeper," she accused him.

He shrugged. "Practically. What's the difference?"

"Aren't you worried about what people will say about me living here?"

"No," he answered bluntly. "I never worry about what people will say."

He opened a raised-panel door. "This is the largest of the upstairs bedrooms. Perhaps you'd like this one."

Jenny glanced past him, noting the four-poster bed, the delicate little vanity, the paintings and crystal accoutrements. A little sitting area with a real fireplace. Even a rocker. "It's lovely," she said. "But—"

"Fine. It's yours. I'll go get your things."

"But Adam—"

"Make yourself at home. You can either pick one of the other bedrooms for Melissa, or we can set up a crib in here with you until she's older. Look around and think about it while I'm downstairs. Take your time."

He was gone before she could respond. He had a bad habit of doing that—making pronouncements and disappearing.

Jenny would have to work on correcting that if they were going to be living together—er, working together— well, whatever it was they would be doing.

Jenny was fully prepared to make dinner that evening, getting an immediate start on earning her salary, but Adam refused to allow her to do so.

"One more night of rest won't hurt you," he said. "We're finally back in civilization, so let's take advantage of it. I'll call for takeout. Do you like Chinese food?"

"I love it," she replied. "But—"

He was already heading for a telephone. "I'll just order an assortment of dishes. That way there will certainly be something you like."

"But, Adam—"

He was gone.

Jenny sighed, the soft sound seeming to echo through the big den, and looked down at Melissa, who was watching her as though to see what her mother planned to do next. "The man is impossible," Jenny grumbled. "Utterly impossible."

Melissa crossed her eyes as though in complete agreement. And then she yawned.

Jenny couldn't help smiling. At least Melissa was accepting their new surroundings easily enough, she thought ruefully. She really should take a cue from her daughter.

Chapter Ten

They ate in the breakfast room just off the kitchen, deciding that Chinese takeout was a bit too casual for the formal dining room with its glittering chandelier and glossy table for twelve.

The kitchen was actually Jenny's favorite room in the house. The cabinets were natural oak, the countertops cream-colored Corian, the appliances big and functional. The window over the ceramic sink held thriving herbs in small matching pots, and there was a rack over the island cook top for copper-bottomed pans.

"Mrs. Handy decorated in here," Adam admitted. "She wouldn't let my decorator through the kitchen doorway."

"Good for her," Jenny murmured.

"Don't you like the rest of the house?"

She nodded, not wanting to hurt his feelings—if, of

course, that were possible. "It's very nice. But this room is my favorite," she added.

Adam glanced around and smiled a little. "Yeah," he admitted. "Mine, too."

"Did your mother have a kitchen like this when you were growing up?" Jenny asked, spearing a grilled shrimp with her fork.

Adam laughed. "If you knew my mother, you'd realize what a silly question that was. As far as I know, my mother never stepped foot in a kitchen after she married my father. Dad came from a wealthy family, so their first household—a veritable mansion, of course—included a cook, a full-time housekeeper and a gardener."

He was still smiling faintly when he added, "Mother adapted to a life of leisure very naturally, though Granny Fran has always claimed all that money ruined the hard work she'd done to raise Mother to do for herself."

"So you were raised in luxury," Jenny said, permitting herself to tease him a bit, just to see how he reacted.

"Yes, I was," Adam answered unselfconsciously. "But, to be honest, I was never happier than when I stayed at Granny Fran's little house in Malvern. I liked sleeping over at my aunt and uncle's house, too. With their three kids, it was usually a bit chaotic there, but always fun. It was quiet at my house, especially after my father died when I was eight."

Jenny was touched by the hint of wistfulness in his deep voice. She wondered if he realized how much he'd just revealed to her, all with one word.

Quiet.

It must have been quite lonely for a little boy growing up with a difficult, embittered mother in an elegant, "quiet" mansion.

She suspected that Adam had never really gotten over that loneliness. He was still living in all-too-quiet luxury.

"I'm leaving early for the hospital tomorrow morning," Adam told her after dinner. "You'll probably have the house to yourself most of the day. I'll leave the number of my answering service. If you need me at any time, all you have to do is have me paged. I don't want you doing any heavy cleaning, definitely no vacuuming or heavy lifting—it will be a few weeks before you're up to that yet."

"You aren't paying me to be a houseguest, Adam," Jenny retorted. And then she wondered if his former housekeeper had addressed him so casually. "Maybe I should call you Dr. Stone."

"You do and I won't answer. You'll call me Adam."

His no-nonsense tone informed her that, to him, that issue was settled.

"As for your duties," he continued. "Light housekeeping is all you should be doing for the next few weeks, and that's all the place needs right now, anyway. I'll do the vacuuming for a while—I've been doing it for the past couple of months, anyway. That leaves dusting and straightening to you, as well as laundry and cooking. Between those responsibilities and taking care of the baby, I'm sure you'll be more than busy enough."

"I still don't feel right about taking full pay from you unless I'm earning it," Jenny said fretfully.

"Trust me, you'll earn it," he assured her, breaking into one of those rare, full grins that made her insides feel all funny and quivery. "Some would say putting up with me was a full-time job in itself."

Her mind temporarily emptied, Jenny couldn't think of anything clever to say in return. She settled for "mmm."

Sitting in her infant seat at one end of the table, Melissa began to squirm and fuss softly, her tiny fist going to her mouth.

"Looks like she's getting hungry again," Jenny said with a shake of her head. "She certainly has a healthy appetite."

"You go feed her. I'll clear this stuff away," Adam said.

She didn't argue, since she knew it wouldn't do any good. Instead she nodded and glanced at her watch. "I think I'll turn in early after I feed her. I'm sure she'll be awake several times during the night."

"I'm sure you're right. You'll call me if you need anything?"

She nodded and stood. "Good night, Adam."

He rose when she did. "Good night, Jenny. Sleep well."

He glanced at the baby, then grimaced humorously. "As well as can be expected, anyway."

Jenny chuckled and gathered Melissa into her arms. She felt Adam watching her as she left the room.

She was enclosed in her own beautiful room, nursing her baby and rocking in front of the empty fireplace, when she thought wistfully that she rather missed the tiny cabin in the woods, a cozy fire for warmth and Adam sleeping on the floor close beside her.

"...and what if something had happened to me while you were gone, hmm? You know my health isn't good. And you leaving me here alone with my heater out in the middle of a winter storm, and..."

Adam closed his eyes, pinched the skin above his nose between his right thumb and forefinger and tried not to let his mother's droning telephone lecture get to him.

He'd waited until late afternoon to call her, since he knew he would only be hearing a continuation of the complaining monologue he'd already heard several times. It took all the patience he had not to snap at her and hang up the phone.

He sat in his office, behind his uncharacteristically clear desk. Since he hadn't been expected in for a few days yet, and had no appointments scheduled for the rest of the week, there wasn't that much for him to do.

For the past hour, he'd been fighting an urge to leave early and go home to check on Jenny and Melissa. He didn't know exactly why he hadn't; he'd had a vague idea that maybe Jenny needed time alone to settle in and get comfortable in his house.

He hadn't stopped thinking about her all day. He'd told himself repeatedly that he was simply concerned about her—as anyone would be. Nothing more to it, of course.

"I still just can't understand why you didn't at least leave me a telephone number where you could be reached," Arlene finished in a near whine.

"You know why, Mother," Adam said bluntly. "You would have called it several times a day, and I needed a break. Granny Fran would have let me know if you'd really needed me."

"Granny Fran," Arlene repeated in a huff. "I told Mother several times that I needed your help with my heater, and she refused to even call you for me. I all but begged her for your number, and she wouldn't give it to me."

"I asked her not to," Adam reminded her. "Sorry, Mother, but that's the way it was. You were perfectly capable of taking care of the heater problem yourself, and you did so. So give it a rest, all right?"

Arlene sighed gustily. "Sometimes you can be very difficult, Adam."

So can you, Mother. So can you. But Adam kept the words to himself.

"At least come have dinner with me this evening," Arlene said, the invitation issued as more of an order than a request. "Grace is preparing trout almondine. I know it's one of your favorites."

Adam winced. "Thanks, Mother, but I'd better not tonight. I've hired a new housekeeper and I'm sure she's preparing dinner. Give me a bit more notice next time, okay?"

"A new housekeeper?" Arlene pounced on that announcement. "Who is it? Why didn't you tell me you were replacing Mrs. Handy? I'm sure I could have helped you locate someone suitable. How did you find this woman? I hope you didn't go to one of those domestic employment agencies, Adam. You never know about the people you find off the streets that way."

If he'd thought it would do any good, Adam would have beaten his head against his desk in sheer frustration at his mother's constant faultfinding. He knew it wouldn't help, however. He'd tried it.

"I'm perfectly capable of hiring my own housekeepers, Mother."

"Who is she? How much are you paying her?"

"Her name is Jennifer Newcomb and it's none of your business how much I'm paying her," Adam replied.

Arlene was too accustomed to Adam's occasional curtness with her to take offense this time. "Jennifer Newcomb? Is that Mrs. or Miss?"

"Ms." Adam corrected her, having no intention of telling his mother the personal details of Jenny's life.

"She's a single mother and she has experience with housekeeping. I'm sure she'll work out quite nicely."

"A single mother? Adam, this doesn't sound promising. Where does she live? How did you find her?"

Adam wished he could evade the subject of where Jenny would be living, but he knew his mother would find out eventually. "She's going to be staying in one of the upstairs bedrooms," he said lightly, ignoring her latter question. "I've explained to her that I'm rarely home, so she and her daughter will have plenty of privacy. She's going to clean house, cook meals, do the laundry and marketing, run errands when necessary. You said yourself that I needed to replace Mrs. Handy, Mother, and I've decided you were right. I do need help with the house."

Torn between gratification that he'd admitted she was right about something, and concern at everything else he'd said, Arlene stammered for a moment. "But, Adam—a live-in? With a child? Oh, dear, I'm sure you've made a mistake," she finally concluded.

"Well, that remains to be seen, doesn't it?" Adam said with forced cheerfulness. "If it doesn't work out, I'll take care of it, Mother. Don't worry about it."

"But—"

"Look, I really have to go. I have a lot of calls to make before I can leave the office this evening."

"But, Adam—"

"Goodbye, Mother. I'll talk to you tomorrow." Adam cradled the receiver before she could protest any further.

It was just before six when Adam returned home. Jenny was waiting at the door for him, her hands on her hips, temper flashing in her eyes.

He suspected he knew what had set her off this time. "I take it the delivery truck arrived?"

"The delivery truck arrived," she agreed grimly. "Adam, how could you order all those things? There's no way I can afford all this stuff now!"

"Jenny, be reasonable," he said wearily, without much optimism that she would easily comply. "The baby can't keep sleeping in a dresser drawer—or in your bed. She needed a crib."

"Did she also have an immediate need for a changing table? And a high chair? And a stroller? And an automatic swing? And an entire wardrobe of baby outfits? Not to mention the toys and boxes of diapers and the monitor system and—"

Adam broke in with an impatient shake of his head. "I just called the store this morning and told them to send around everything we'd need for a newborn," he explained. "What's the big deal?"

"What's the big deal?" Jenny repeated, looking stunned. "There must be hundreds of dollars worth of stuff sitting in the den! I can't begin to pay for it. It'll probably take everything I have to repair my car. And I still haven't been billed for the doctor appointments Melissa and I had yesterday."

"Er—those are already taken care of," Adam said. "And so is your car. As for paying for this stuff—forget it. I ordered it, I'll pay for it."

Jenny's mouth opened, then closed again. "If you really think I'm going to let you pay my bills and buy my daughter's supplies, like I'm some sort of—of kept woman, you can just think again. I want it taken back. All of it. And I fully intend to reimburse you for the doctor appointments. Is that clear?"

Adam knew better than to grin, though her use of the term "kept woman" deeply amused him. He couldn't help thinking that it sounded just like something Granny Fran would say.

Jenny was eyeing him suspiciously, her eyes going even darker. "Don't you *dare* be amused at me," she snarled. "I am very serious."

"I know you're serious, Jenny," he said soothingly, thinking longingly of a cup of coffee and the morning paper he hadn't yet had a chance to read. He seemed to spend most of his time lately soothing agitated women, he silently bemoaned.

"If it's important to you to reimburse me for the appointments, then do so. No rush, just make it whenever you feel comfortable about it. As for the things I bought Melissa, they're gifts to her, not to you. I delivered her, and that makes her very special to me. You didn't seem to mind taking shower presents from your friends in Dallas—why would you refuse to accept these things from me?"

"That's—that's different," Jenny said, her voice lowering.

"Why is it different?"

"Because—they were my friends. And no one person spent so lavishly."

"I like to think I'm your friend, too," Adam said a bit coolly. "After all we've been through together, I wouldn't have thought that was too much of an assumption on my part. As for the cost of my gifts, I have the money and this is what I wanted to do with it. It's not charity, Jenny, no matter what you've decided in that stubborn, suspicious mind of yours. I just wanted to buy a few nice things for Melissa."

Jenny threw up her hands. "You aren't being fair. I know you're fond of Melissa, but—"

"I'm crazy about her." Adam corrected her with a smile. "And, for your information, I sent Rachel the same things when Paige was born. Oddly enough, she claimed it was too much, too, and she worried that I was being charitable because she and Ray were a young married couple with a rather limited income at the time. I can't understand why either of you would deny me the chance to do something nice for your kids."

Jenny made a sound of impatience. "Stop doing that."

"Doing what?"

"Making me feel guilty for yelling at you. It doesn't matter how good your intentions were, Adam, the problem is that you've acted on my behalf again without consulting me first. I've told you I don't want you to do that."

"Well, actually, I acted on Melissa's behalf," he muttered. It wasn't as though he'd sent Jenny diamonds or lingerie or anything, he thought wearily. What could possibly be inappropriate about gifts of diapers and baby furniture?

"I don't want you doing that, either," Jenny said evenly. "Melissa is my responsibility, Adam, not yours. I'll take care of her."

"Fine," he said irritably. "Send the stuff back if you want. I can't make you keep it."

She bit her lower lip. "Well—"

He could see her vacillating. He took immediately advantage. "I'd like Melissa to have the things. I really would. But if it makes you uncomfortable—"

"All right," she said with a sigh. "I can see you really want her to have them. I don't want you to think I'm not grateful, Adam. I am. It touches me that you've grown fond of Melissa. But, please. Don't do anything like this again. Not without talking to me first.''

''Okay. Fine. Whatever you say.''

She surprised him then by laughing. It was only a little chuckle, but a laugh, nonetheless. ''Somehow that just doesn't sound right, coming from you.''

Adam smiled. ''Where's Melissa?''

''She's in the den, asleep in her infant seat, surrounded by all her new possessions.''

Adam nodded and headed for the den. He expected Jenny to follow, but she stayed behind. ''I'll finish dinner,'' she said. ''I'll let you know when it's ready.''

Adam smiled in satisfaction when he entered the den and saw Melissa sitting contentedly in her seat. She seemed to be just waking from her nap; she roused fully when he knelt beside her. Her dark eyes fixed on his face, and Adam fancied he saw a gleam of recognition in them.

''Hi, kid. How was your day?'' He was already unbuckling the safety straps on her seat as he spoke.

Melissa didn't answer, of course, but she seemed pleased to be picked up and held.

''How do you like your stuff?'' he asked, cradling her in the crook of his left arm while he scanned the neat piles of goodies. ''I'll set your crib up after dinner. There should be a musical mobile in one of these boxes. I bet you'll like that, hmm?''

Melissa kicked her feet as though in anticipation.

Smiling, Adam carried the baby to an overstuffed rocker-recliner and settled in with her.

It was amazing, he thought, how holding a baby could be so relaxing after a long day at the office. He set the rocker into lazy motion and began to tell Melissa about his day.

Jenny found them like that when she entered a short while later to announce that dinner was ready. Her steps faltered at the sight of Adam holding her baby, and looking utterly content.

Maybe he really had grown fond of Melissa, she found herself thinking. Maybe he really had bought the baby supplies just because it had made him happy to do so. To be honest, she really couldn't think of any other reason for him to have bought them.

Adam was a generous, if high-handed, man. His intentions were good. It was just his methods that were questionable.

Jenny had fully intended to serve Adam his dinner in the dining room and then slip into the kitchen to eat her own meal. She had told herself repeatedly during the day that it was time to get their relationship on a pleasant, but strictly professional basis. Employer, employee. Nothing more.

His bond with her child had already blurred the lines between personal and professional.

He scowled when she proposed her dining arrangements. "Nonsense," he said. "I'll eat in the kitchen with you. I'd look pretty stupid sitting at that huge dining room table alone."

Jenny was too tired to bother arguing.

She wouldn't win anyway.

Adam was very complimentary about Jenny's cooking. She wasn't particularly flattered that he seemed rather surprised that she could.

After dinner, Adam carried the new baby items upstairs. At Jenny's request, he set the crib up in one corner of her room. The extra things he set in the bedroom next door, for her to utilize as she needed them.

Jenny lay the baby in the crib on her back. Adam wound up the musical, farm-animal mobile he'd attached to one rail. He and Jenny stood shoulder to shoulder, leaning over the other rail as they watched Melissa stare in fascination at the colorful, slowly revolving toy.

Adam chuckled. "I think she likes it."

"I think you're right," Jenny agreed. She glanced up at Adam, then blinked, suddenly realizing just how closely he stood to her. So close their shoulders brushed when they moved. She went very still.

Adam's smile faded. Their eyes locked.

Jenny's mouth went dry.

Adam lifted a hand and brushed a strand of hair away from her cheek. The touch of his fingers against her skin made her tremble.

She didn't want to think about why.

"Want to watch TV with me tonight?" Adam asked. "There's probably a movie on cable."

"I—er—" She was tempted. But scared. She didn't want to step too far over that invisible line she'd drawn between personal and professional. "I think I'll stay up here this evening. I have some letters to write. I told some of my friends I'd let them know when the baby came."

The warmth seemed to fade in his eyes. "Fine," he said, shifting a couple of inches away. "I'll see you tomorrow then."

She swallowed and nodded. "Good night, Adam."

"Good night. Sleep well." He didn't look back over his shoulder when he left the room. He closed the door behind him, perhaps with a bit more force than necessary.

Jenny let out a long, deep breath.

"Your mother," she told Melissa wryly, "is an idiot. But I hope I'm not foolish enough to fall for Adam Stone. No matter how nice he can be when he tries."

Melissa made a sound that might have been a snort.

Chapter Eleven

Carrying Melissa in a padded sling against her chest, Jenny moved through Adam's house late Thursday afternoon with a dust cloth in one hand and a can of dusting spray in the other. The sling, of course, had been among the mountain of baby supplies Adam had provided. Jenny had quickly discovered that it was one of her favorite gifts. She liked having Melissa so close to her, and Melissa seemed content to ride along during her mother's light housekeeping duties.

There really wasn't much to do to the house. Apparently Adam had had it thoroughly cleaned just before he'd left for his disrupted vacation. But Jenny conscientiously wiped down every surface she could reach, telling herself there was no reason to wait any longer to begin her duties.

Besides, it gave her a great excuse to explore the rest of the house. The elegant dining room. The medical-book-lined study that Adam obviously used as a home office. In the prim parlor stood a gorgeous grand piano that looked as though it had never been played. The huge, window-lined gathering room could have been casual and comfortable with just a few minor changes. The four upstairs bedrooms, each beautifully decorated, each hauntingly empty. The upstairs lounge that could easily have been a teenager's game room or study area.

She hesitated before going into Adam's suite, but then told herself that she was only doing her job by dusting in there, as well. She opened the door and tiptoed in.

She wondered if Adam had had a personal hand in decorating this part of the house. For the first time, she caught a glimpse of his personality in his furnishings.

She would bet he spent most of his time here when he was alone in the house.

The bed was enormous, supremely inviting. The massive triple dresser was haphazardly cluttered with keys, spare change and a pair of reading glasses she'd never seen him wear, even at the cabin. She smiled, wondering if he was too vain to wear them, or simply couldn't remember to do so.

The sitting room was an L-shaped extension to the bedroom. A well-worn recliner faced a small fireplace. A book lay open, facedown, in its seat. A mystery novel, of course. A newspaper lay on the floor beside the chair. The walls were lined with bookcases, the shelves crowded with books, almost all works of fiction, in contrast to the medical tomes in the study. An entertainment cabinet held a television, a VCR, a stereo system with a CD carousel and an impressive number of CDs of an eclectic mix.

Jenny had noticed that there were no photographs displayed anywhere in Adam's house. She found them now, marching neatly down the fireplace mantel. The frames, of course, needed dusting—or at least she told herself they did as she studied each photograph.

There was one of a small boy who looked endearingly like Adam—probably five or six years old—with two adults. His parents, she would guess. The man looked very nice. Adam's dark hair and eyes, but an easy, lazy smile that made her suspect he hadn't been as intense and serious as Adam was.

The woman, surely Adam's mother Arlene, looked pretty much the way Jenny had pictured her. Not a hair out of place, face meticulously made-up, clothing expensive and tasteful. She had one hand on her husband's shoulder and one on her son's, and she looked very proud of them. Jenny felt a touch of sympathy. The woman looked as though she'd loved her husband very much. It must have been very difficult for her to lose him so soon after this portrait had been made.

Did Adam feel the same sympathy for his mother? Was that why he seemed so patient with what had been described to Jenny as quite difficult behavior now?

She put the portrait down and picked up another. A pretty, brown-haired woman and two small children posed self-consciously for the camera. The woman bore a faint family resemblance to Adam. Her dark eyes held a touch of sadness.

Rachel, Jenny thought. Adam's favorite cousin, who'd been widowed very young. And these must be her children, Paige and Aaron. Cute kids. She set the photo back down, hoping that the sadness had left Rachel's eyes now that she'd found love again.

The other photo was a snapshot that had been enlarged to a five-by-seven. It appeared to have been taken very recently. Granny Fran sat proudly in the center, surrounded by her grown grandchildren. Adam stood behind her, wearing his faint, enigmatic smile. Jenny looked quickly away from him, annoyed that her heart rate had increased in response to even that brief glimpse of him.

The woman she'd already guessed to be Rachel stood at Adam's left. Cody knelt beside his grandmother's chair, his bright blue eyes gleaming with mischief, his gold-tipped hair attractively disheveled. He really was gorgeous, Jenny thought dispassionately. She'd grown to like him during the short time she'd spent with him. So how come her pulse didn't do anything strange when she looked at *him,* hmm?

The other young woman in the photo had to be the other cousin, Celia. She had Rachel's dark hair and Cody's blue eyes and bright smile, and the combination was incredibly striking. Breathtaking, actually.

It was a lovely family. No wonder Granny Fran looked so proud.

Jenny replaced the frame on the mantel and stood looking at the grouping thoughtfully. So much of Adam was revealed right here, she mused. His family was so important to him. She suspected that his work and his family were really the only two things he cared deeply about.

Did he often sit in his chair in his room, looking at those photos and thinking of how alone he was here in this big, empty house? Or was he perfectly content to be alone, as long as he knew his family was well cared for?

Melissa squirmed in the sling, bringing Jenny out of her thoughts. She patted the baby's back. "We're finished in here for now," she said, turning away from the mantel.

The chime of the front doorbell stopped her before she'd made it all the way to the kitchen, where she'd intended to make herself a cup of tea and put up her feet for a few minutes. She hastily stashed the dusting supplies out of sight and altered her steps to take her to the front of the house.

"If this is another deliveryman with a stack of gifts— for either of us—I'm going to have Adam Stone's hide," she told Melissa, who only watched her somberly from the depths of the blue gingham sling.

The caller wasn't a deliveryman.

A middle-aged woman with immaculately styled gray-frosted hair, meticulously applied makeup and tastefully expensive clothing stood beneath the front portico, an Etienne Aigner purse clutched in her perfectly manicured hands.

Jenny knew immediately who she was.

Adam's mother wasn't ill-bred enough to gape at Jenny, but she came close. It obviously took her a moment to recover from her surprise. "You're the housekeeper?"

"Yes. I'm Jenny Newcomb. May I help you?"

The woman was staring at the wriggling bundle strapped to Jenny's chest. "Is that an infant you're carrying?"

Jenny fought down a surge of irritation. "This is my daughter, Melissa. And you are—?" she asked, though she already knew.

The woman drew herself up to her full height. "I am Mrs. Jason Stone," she announced. "Dr. Stone's mother."

"It's very nice to meet you, Mrs. Stone. Ad—er—Dr. Stone isn't home right now, but I'm expecting him soon. Would you like to come in and wait for him?"

"I believe I will." Mrs. Stone swept past her with a flourish.

"Perhaps you'd like to have a seat in the parlor," Jenny suggested, at a loss as to what to do with the woman.

"May I bring you a cup of tea? Or would you prefer coffee?"

Mrs. Stone slipped out of her coat and turned to Jenny. "I'll have tea, thank you. And I'll take it in the breakfast room."

Jenny swallowed and nodded, reaching for the coat. "I'll hang this up for you," she murmured, opening the coat closet beneath the stairs.

Mrs. Stone watched her closely. "I see you know your way around the house. How long have you worked for my son?"

"This is my first week," Jenny said, wondering if Adam had told his mother any details about how they'd met—one week ago today, to be exact.

She closed the closet and moved toward the kitchen to start the tea, one hand supporting Melissa's back. Mrs. Stone followed right at her heels.

Oh, Adam, please hurry home! Jenny sent out the silent SOS without much hope of it being received.

Adam entered his house that evening with more enthusiasm than usual. "Jenny? Hey, Jen? Guess what?" he called out, anxious to tell her that her car repairs were underway, and that her insurance company was taking care of everything.

"If you are bellowing for your housekeeper, she's upstairs, Adam. Nursing her child, I believe."

Adam froze in response to his mother's voice. He turned slowly, finding her standing in the doorway of the den he'd just entered. She was watching him with an expression that warned him he was in for one of her grand performances.

"Mother. What are you doing here?"

"I just wanted to see you. It has been two weeks since you've visited me," she reminded him.

Adam knew exactly why she'd chosen today to drop in unannounced. She'd wanted to check out his new housekeeper.

Jenny, I'm sorry. I should have warned you.

"I take it you've met Jenny?" he asked unnecessarily, after perfunctorily kissing his mother's smooth, scented cheek.

"Yes. We've met. I persuaded her to have a cup of tea with me."

Adam managed not to wince. "And?"

Arlene sighed. "And now I know why you hired her. You've taken in another stray, haven't you, Adam?"

Avoiding her eyes, Adam motioned her toward a chair. "I don't know what you're talking about," he muttered as he settled onto the couch after she was seated.

"Now, Adam, you know better than to try to fool me. It was the same when you hired Mrs. Handy. We both knew her medical problems made her totally unsuited for the job, but you knew she needed the money for her medicines until she was old enough for social security, so you hired her."

"Mrs. Handy was a very good housekeeper," Adam said defensively. "She was a great cook."

"You had to hire someone to come in twice a week to help her do the heavy cleaning," Arlene reminded him.

He shrugged. "That has nothing to do with Jenny."

"Doesn't it? She has a baby, no husband, and probably no money. She was very evasive about her family, so I assume she has no one to turn to with her problems. It's quite obvious that you've hired her because you feel sorry for her. Honestly, Adam, someday that soft heart of yours is going to get you into trouble. Someday you're going to try to help someone who will only take advantage of your generous nature."

Adam had to bite his tongue to keep from pointing out that his mother had been known to take full advantage of that "generous nature," herself.

"I hope you were polite to her" was all he allowed himself to say.

Arlene lifted a regal eyebrow. "Of course I was polite to her, Adam. I resent your implication that I would be deliberately rude—to anyone."

"You didn't give her the third degree, did you? Jenny has a right to her privacy, Mother."

"I only asked a few questions, simply trying to get to know her a bit. When I saw that she didn't like answering questions about her background, I stopped asking them."

Adam swallowed a moan. "Mother—"

"Now, don't start one of your lectures. I assure you I said nothing to upset her. She seems like a pleasant young woman," Arlene conceded. "And her child is very sweet, though I'm surprised that you were willing to bring an infant into your beautiful home. Still, I suppose the baby's too small to do much damage now, and Jenny assured me she intends to remain here only for a few months."

Adam didn't want to talk—or even think—about Jenny leaving. "She has a job here for as long as she needs one."

"Of course. Still, it might be better if you help her find another place to stay. She is a single young woman, and people might talk. *I* know, of course, that she is hardly your type, and that your interest in her is purely philanthropic—you're so like your dear father, bless him. But few people know you as well as I do, darling. They might think—"

"I don't care what 'they' might think, whoever 'they' might be," Adam said crossly. "And stop implying that I'm giving Jenny charity. She will earn every penny I pay her, I assure you."

He was tempted to ask exactly what she'd meant by saying Jenny was hardly his type—Adam didn't even know what his "type" was—but he decided to leave that alone. He foresaw all sorts of potential pitfalls in *that* discussion!

"Stop being so prickly, Adam. I haven't criticized you for hiring her. I was simply surprised to discover that she's so young and—well, everything else."

"Everything else" being Melissa, Adam assumed. He practically bit a hole in his tongue to keep quiet. He'd learned years ago that the best way to end an uncomfortable discussion with his mother was simply to shut up. She didn't like it when he wouldn't respond to her. She would soon take the hint.

She did. Arlene had a few other complaints to share with him—someone in her garden club who'd offended her, the problems she'd been having with her new cook, the discomfort she'd been having with her bursitis. Adam made his usual pretense of listening patiently, nodding his head occasionally, while wondering how soon he could get to Jenny to find out how badly his mother had upset her.

"Well, I can see you're going to be in one of your quiet moods," Arlene grumbled after another few minutes. "I suppose there's no reason for me to stay any longer."

"Sorry, Mother. It's been a long day and I still have some paperwork to finish tonight."

"Jenny assured me that she's made you a good dinner. I'm sure you need it after a hard day at work."

Adam rose quickly. "I'll see you out."

"I do hope the child doesn't keep you awake at night with her crying," his mother said fretfully as they made their way to the front door—much too slowly for Adam's satisfaction. "A busy surgeon needs his rest."

"The child has a name, Mother. It's Melissa. And this house is well soundproofed. The—er—Melissa doesn't bother me at all."

"Good. Now make sure Jenny sends your suits to Park Lane Cleaners. They're the only ones I trust with my clothing. And tell her not to use pine-scented cleaners or air fresheners. They always make you sneeze. And don't forget..."

Adam had his hand at the small of his mother's back—a gesture of affection, he assured himself. He wasn't really trying to push her out of the house.

He barely gave her time to get her coat on the way out.

Jenny was sitting in the rocker with her baby when Adam burst into her room.

She lifted an eyebrow. "You do own the house, Adam, but I still wish you'd knock when you come into my room."

"Sorry," he said impatiently, brushing off what he considered a minor complaint at the moment. "What did my mother say to you?" he demanded. "Did she upset you?"

He couldn't read Jenny's expression. "No, she didn't upset me," she said. "She was very gracious."

Adam grimaced. He could just imagine how gracious his mother had been. Something along the line of the Queen Mother granting a brief, civil conversation to a parlormaid. "Jenny, about Mother—"

Jenny was looking down at the baby as she continued. "She's very proud of you. She thinks you're the best surgeon in the country—the world, probably. She told me how you disdain 'nip-and-tuck' surgery, and prefer to specialize in more serious reconstructive surgery, such as after disfiguring accidents. She said you're considered an expert on making delicate corrections on small children with genetic disfigurements.''

"Yes, well, mothers tend to brag."

"Mmm. She's particularly proud of the contributions you've made to your community—a Stone family tradition, she told me. Anonymous charitable donations, donating your medical expertise for particularly needy patients. Taking in strays. You—um—never mentioned that Mrs. Handy was practically an invalid.''

Adam was furious—with his mother for running her mouth and with Jenny for listening. "Damn it, Jenny, don't start this again. I did *not* hire you out of charity.''

"Didn't you?" Jenny stood and tenderly laid the sleeping baby in her crib. And then she turned to Adam, still not quite meeting his eyes. "I'll turn the kitchen monitor on while I serve dinner, in case she wakes up. I'm sure you're hungry. Dinner will be ready in—"

He caught her shoulders in his hands. She fell silent and looked up at him with that still-unreadable expression. It was all he could do not to shake her.

"Stop that," he snapped. "Stop shutting me out."

Temper that matched his own flared in her eyes. "What do you want from me?" she demanded. "Total compliance? Undying gratitude? Well, sorry, but I—"

He smothered her words beneath his mouth. It wasn't something he'd planned—or had even considered—but almost before he realized it he was kissing her. And reveling in it.

Jenny went very still. For a moment, she didn't respond at all.

And then her mouth softened beneath his.

Adam groaned and pulled her closer.

Jenny responded to the kiss only briefly. She pulled away with a gasp.

"Please," she whispered, turning her face away. "Don't do this. I can't— It isn't—"

Adam kept his hands on her shoulders, this time to steady her. He wondered if she could feel the fine tremors in his fingers. He found that he really didn't care if she did.

"I'm sorry," he said, his voice gravelly. "I didn't mean to upset you."

Her face was pale. "Why did you hire me, Adam?" she asked, the words almost too soft for him to hear.

He started to tell her again how badly he'd needed a housekeeper. How he'd planned to hire someone all along. He fell silent when the glib words refused to come to him. Finally he drew a deep, not quite steady breath and admitted frankly, "I don't know, Jenny. It just seemed like a good idea at the time."

She groaned.

He dropped his hands, stuck them deep into his pockets to keep them out of further trouble. "Look," he said bluntly. "Let's just forget the past ten minutes ever happened, okay? You work for me—and you'll damn well earn your pay. Starting with dinner. I've put in a long day and I'm starving."

His brusque, bossy tone seemed to steady her. She lifted her chin, ran a hand through her curls and moved another step away from him. "Fine," she said, a bit curtly. "Go wash up. Dinner will be ready in twenty minutes."

As he nodded and headed for the door, Adam reflected that Jenny could sound every bit as brusque and bossy as he could when she wanted. He rather liked that.

But then, there was very little about Jenny Newcomb he *didn't* like. Including the delectable taste of her.

Damn it, Stone. What the hell are you getting yourself into here?

Jenny put Adam's kiss very firmly out of her mind. She didn't think about it as she put the finishing touches to dinner. She didn't think about it when she poured herself a glass of cold water and gulped it down without stopping to breathe. She didn't think about it when Adam reappeared after washing up for dinner.

Since she was *not* thinking about the kiss, she couldn't imagine why her face flamed at the sight of him.

"Sit down," she said, motioning toward his chair at the table. "I'll serve."

He frowned suspiciously. "You are eating with me, aren't you?"

She'd thought about telling him she'd eat in her room. She'd even thought of a good excuse—that she wanted to be close to the baby. But Adam would surely have pointed out that the monitor sat right beside them to pick up the faintest peep from Melissa's crib, and he would have been convinced that she was avoiding him only because he'd kissed her. He would never believe she hadn't given the embrace another thought.

"Yes," she said in resignation. "I'll eat with you."

He nodded in satisfaction. "What can I do to help?"

"Just sit down," she ordered. "I can handle this."

She was referring, of course, to dinner. Nothing more.

During the next weeks, Adam and Jenny settled into a routine of sorts. Particularly after his surgery schedule was reestablished, Adam left very early in the mornings—sometimes before eight o'clock. He was usually home around 6:00 p.m. for dinner, and he always called when he would be late.

There were four occasions when he didn't come home until late. He always told her in advance so she wouldn't prepare dinner for him. Though Jenny assured him that it wasn't necessary, he always gave her a brief explanation of where he'd be for the evening. A dinner party at his mother's house. A medical seminar. A fund-raiser for the local children's hospital. A professional organization meeting.

He never mentioned whether he was accompanied by dates to any of those functions, and Jenny didn't ask. She realized to her chagrin that she really didn't want to know.

She had succeeded so well at putting their kiss out of her mind that sometimes as much as half a day would pass without her remembering it. When the memory did creep back into her unwilling thoughts, she always firmly pushed it away, refusing to dwell on it.

At least, not much.

As Jenny's strength returned, she put more energy into her housekeeping. The exercise was good for her, anyway, she figured, and she wanted no doubt in anyone's mind that she earned her pay. She scrubbed floors, cleaned light fixtures, dusted baseboards, oiled and buffed every inch of exposed wood, polished brass and silver.

Adam noticed everything she did. He always complimented her on her work, and then fretted that she was trying to do too much. She brushed his concerns aside, telling him that she was perfectly capable of doing her job.

Her car was repaired and returned to her, and she began to run the errands he'd listed as part of her responsibility—marketing, dry cleaning, and such. At first it was a bit awkward getting Melissa bundled up and loaded into the car seat and stroller, packing a diaper bag for every possibility. Jenny quickly became more adept at it, so that it soon seemed second nature to her to take her daughter everywhere with her.

Adam worried about that, too. "Little Rock traffic can be hazardous," he warned repeatedly. "Don't go out at rush hour, or during lunchtime. Don't wander into the bad neighborhoods—some of them aren't safe even in daylight."

He insisted on paying for her gas and car expenses; after all, he argued, she was doing most of this for him.

Again, Jenny managed to soothe him with breezy reassurances, and then proceeded exactly as she wanted to.

On Valentine's Day, Adam came home bearing flowers for Jenny. Red roses. He'd purchased a fluffy white teddy bear with a cheery red bow for Melissa.

Jenny hadn't even realized the date. Flustered by his gift, she accepted with stammered thanks. He shrugged, smiled and told her that he'd sent flowers to his mother, grandmother, cousins and secretary. He couldn't neglect the two ladies in his own household, he'd added casually, dangling the teddy bear playfully above Melissa's fascinated eyes.

Jenny left him playing with the baby while she put her roses in water. She buried her face in the fragrant blooms, inhaling deeply. She loved roses. How had he known?

Biting her lip, she reminded herself sternly that she shouldn't read anything more into the gift than what he'd said. He'd bought a lot of flowers for the occasion. Must be something he enjoyed doing.

She wondered how many other women had received Valentine's Day tokens from the eligible doctor.

And then she had to fight off the wholly inappropriate wave of jealousy that accompanied the question.

Oh, Jenny, you're headed for trouble again. You idiot.

* * *

The telephone rang on a Friday afternoon in late February. While Melissa sat in the baby seat on the floor of the kitchen, experimenting with the cooing sounds she'd only recently begun to try, Jenny had been chopping vegetables for one of Adam's favorite dishes. She sighed and wiped her hands on a dish towel.

"I hope he's not calling to tell me he won't be home for dinner," she murmured aloud as she reached for the phone. "Ten more minutes and this will be ready to go into the oven. Stone residence."

"Jenny? Hello, dear, it's Granny Fran."

Jenny smiled in delight. "Why, hello. How are you?"

"I'm fine, thank you. And you?"

"Fine. I'm sorry, Mrs. Carson, Adam isn't home yet, but I'm expecting him within the hour. Shall I have him call you when he gets in?"

"Actually I called to talk to you," the older woman explained. "And what's this Mrs. Carson? I'd so much rather have you call me Granny Fran."

"If you like," Jenny agreed, a bit shyly. "You wanted to talk to me?"

"Yes. I wondered how you were settling in to your new job. And, of course, I want to know how my little angel is doing."

Touched that Granny Fran had been thinking about her, Jenny leaned against the counter and smiled down at Melissa. "Your little angel is growing so fast you wouldn't believe it. She's thriving. She's starting to make a few little babbling sounds, and I'm almost sure she's trying to smile."

"How adorable. I must have Adam bring you both down to visit me soon."

"We would like that," Jenny said honestly. "And I'm sure Adam doesn't need an excuse to come visit you."

"And what about you? Are you feeling well?"

"Yes. I've found a gynecologist here in Little Rock, as well as a pediatrician Adam highly recommended. Melissa and I are both scheduled for our six-week checkups next Friday."

"Adam's treating you well?"

"Yes, of course. He's a very considerate employer," Jenny said carefully.

"Oh." For some reason, Adam's grandmother didn't seem particularly satisfied with that answer. "He calls me from his office once a week, you know. He tells me he's very satisfied with your work. He says you're a wonderful cook."

Jenny was glad Granny Fran couldn't see her blush. "That's very kind of him."

"Adam rarely says anything he doesn't mean, as I'm sure you know by now," his loving grandmother said indulgently. "He's grown very fond of little Melissa. He talks about her often every time we chat."

That didn't surprise Jenny. "Yes, he does seem fond of her," she admitted. "He plays with her every evening before I put her down for bed. He's very good with children. I hear he's particularly adept with his youngest patients."

"Oh, yes, Adam loves children. He really should have some of his own soon, as I've told him repeatedly. He'll be thirty-nine in June. It's well past time for him to start his family."

Jenny cleared her throat. "Yes, well, um—" She couldn't think of anything else to say.

Either by accident or understanding, Granny Fran changed the subject. "I suppose you've met my daughter, Arlene, by now. Adam's mother."

"Yes. She's dropped by a time or two." Always with a long list of instructions for Jenny. Adam's favorite foods. His dislikes. The best dry cleaner and butcher. Warnings about Adam's allergies to certain foods and cleaning products. When Jenny had asked him about them later, Adam had irritably denied having any allergies at all.

"I hope she isn't being a problem for you," Granny Fran said.

"Not at all," Jenny assured her. "Mrs. Stone has been quite gracious to me."

"Mmm. I love my daughter dearly, Jenny, but I'm well aware that she can be a pain in the rear. I have to say it's at least partly Adam's fault. If he just wouldn't cater to her the way he does—"

"She's his mother." Jenny broke in gently. "He loves her."

Granny Fran was quiet for a moment, and then she chuckled. "Yes. He does. How sweet of you to understand."

Jenny hung up a few minutes later with a faint smile that soon faded. It had occurred to her that Adam's lovely grandmother was trying her hand at a bit of matchmaking. She'd all but invited Jenny into the family. Jenny deeply hoped Granny Fran hadn't been sending such unsubtle hints toward Adam.

Surely Granny Fran could see what a mismatched couple Adam and Jenny would be, even if Adam *should* be interested. Which, of course, he wasn't. Not really.

Even if he had kissed her like a man who was very interested, indeed.

Chapter Twelve

Adam and Jenny were spending a quiet Sunday afternoon at home in his den. Lunch had been eaten, the dishes cleared away. Adam had turned on the television to watch a basketball game. He gave only half his attention to the game, the other half was reserved for Melissa, who lay contentedly in his lap, gumming her fist.

Jenny sat in a chair nearby, reading the Sunday newspaper. She was particularly interested in an article about a local business college that specialized in computer training. The school had evening classes available and even provided in-house child care for its students.

Perhaps she should look into it, she thought. She couldn't go on indefinitely working as Adam's housekeeper, and her lack of computer training was a major drawback in the contemporary job market.

"Jenny? Jenny, look!"

Adam's urgent whisper drew her head up sharply. "What is it?"

Adam was leaning over the baby, grinning broadly. "Look at Melissa. She's smiling. A real smile."

Jenny dropped the paper and hurried to see for herself. Sure enough, Melissa was gazing up at Adam, her tiny mouth curved into a toothless smile. Her tiny feet flailed happily in response to his voice.

"She *is* smiling," Jenny said, sitting close beside Adam and leaning toward the baby.

"Yeah. At me," Adam pointed out smugly.

Jenny frowned. He was right. Melissa had given him her first smile. After all those long nights of nursing and walking her, she thought with a touch of resentment. No wonder so many mothers griped because their babies said "Da-Da" before "Ma-Ma."

"Smile for Mommy, darling." She cooed, blocking the baby's view of Adam's face.

Obligingly Melissa grinned again, this time obviously for her mother's benefit. Jenny's heart warmed.

Adam chuckled. "Wise move, kid," he informed the baby. "Better stay on Mom's good side."

"She *would* have smiled at me first, if I'd been holding her," Jenny informed him loftily, a bit giddy from happiness. "She was probably thinking of me when she smiled the first time."

"Yeah, right," Adam retorted. "She was looking at *me*. Melissa knows who brought her into this world."

"Who carried her for nine months—er—a little over eight months?"

"Who changed her first incredibly smelly diaper?"

Adam and Jenny were looking at each other as they conducted their mock argument, still sitting so close that their faces were only inches apart. Adam's gaze lowered to Jenny's mouth, and held. "She has your dimples," he said.

Jenny immediately felt self-conscious. She stopped smiling. "Does she?"

"Yeah. And your dark curls. I think her eyes will be a darker brown, though."

"Possibly."

Adam looked back at the baby. His voice was a bit too casual when he said, "I suppose she looks a little like her father."

Jenny studied Adam's profile. The firm cut of his jaw. The slight softness of his lower lip. The length and thickness of his dark lashes. That intriguing little bump on his otherwise perfect nose. "I can't remember what he looked like," she said, with complete honesty at that moment.

Adam slanted her a smile. "I'm glad to hear that," he said huskily.

Jenny swallowed, suddenly aware of how very closely they sat. Shoulder to shoulder. Thigh to thigh.

She could feel his warmth. His strength.

His dangerous appeal.

Adam lifted one hand to Jenny's cheek. "If Melissa turns out half as lovely as her mother, she can count herself fortunate," he murmured.

Jenny flushed. "Don't flirt with me," she said gruffly. "It's not your style."

Adam's smile was just a bit mocking. And a whole lot seductive. "How do you know it isn't my style?"

"It just isn't. Not with me, anyway."

"Because you work for me?" The question was at least half-serious.

She refused to smile. "Because I'm all wrong for you."

His thumb traced a lazy path across her lower lip. Jenny couldn't help remembering that kiss she'd been trying so hard to forget. She looked into his eyes and knew that he remembered it, too. That he wanted to kiss her again.

She shivered.

"Why are you all wrong for me, Jenny?"

Melissa sneezed and Jenny latched on to the distraction. "I have a baby."

"Yes, I know," Adam said gravely, cradling Melissa securely with his free hand. "Maybe you've noticed that I don't mind your baby."

"I come from a very blue-collar background," she said. "I've scrubbed filth out of rental trailers."

"I never had to do that," he agreed. "But I once spent a summer cooking hamburgers for a fast-food chain. Mother hated the very idea, but Granny Fran thought it would be a character-building experience."

"And was it?" Jenny asked, momentarily diverted.

Adam grinned. "I met lots of girls."

She sighed and shook her head.

"Tell me why else you think you're wrong for me," he said, prodding her relentlessly.

"Everything," she said simply. "You're a doctor—a well-known surgeon, for heaven's sake. I'm a housekeeper—and not very well qualified for that. You have a big, loving family. I haven't spoken to my parents in a year. You're rich, I have only a few thousand dollars to my name. And I—well, I've made some really stupid mistakes." She finished with a touch of bitterness.

"So have I, Jenny. But letting any of your frivolous arguments change my feelings about you would be the dumbest mistake of my life."

He slowly closed the very short distance between them, his mouth hovering only an inch above hers. "I've been attracted to you from the first moment I saw you," he said. "Even when you were cold and wet and miserable and heavy with child. You were no less beautiful to me then than you are now, slim and dry and stubborn. Only now I have the advantage of knowing you, and admiring you and respecting you. And the attraction has only gotten stronger.''

Jenny's throat felt tight, her eyes hot. She hadn't expected this, hadn't known he felt this way. But was it real, or was he only being affected by circumstances?

Even worse, did he still feel sorry for her? Was this attraction—or pity?

She couldn't bear for it to be pity. ''Adam...'' she whispered, wondering how to begin.

She was spared by the sound of the doorbell.

She drew a deep, shaky breath and told Adam she'd get the door.

It could only be his mother, she thought fatalistically as she headed for the front entryway. That was just the way her luck went.

And if Adam needed any more convincing argument of how wrong he and Jenny were for each other, she was quite sure his mother would be only too willing to provide it. In spades.

Instead of Adam's mother, Jenny found a man, a woman and two young children waiting at the door. She recognized the woman and children immediately. She'd dusted their photograph often enough.

''You're Adam's cousin Rachel,'' she said without stopping to think. And then almost winced at her lack of tact.

Rachel smiled curiously. ''Yes, I'm Rachel Fletcher.'' She said the last name—which Jenny knew to be new to her—with pride. ''And you are?''

"Jenny Newcomb. Dr. Stone's housekeeper," she added, trying to sound a bit more conventional. "Please, come in. Ad—Dr. Stone is in the den. I'll tell him you're—"

She quickly discovered there would be no opportunity for her to formally announce the callers. The two children had already dashed past her.

"Uncle Adam! Uncle Adam!" the little boy was calling. "We've come to visit you."

"Paige, Aaron, wait!" Rachel began, moving to grab them.

Her husband held her back. "They're already gone," he said ruefully. "Maybe we'd better have a talk with them about visiting etiquette on the way home."

Rachel nodded her dark head in agreement. Her brown eyes were focused with interest on Jenny. "Cody and Granny Fran have told me about you," she said. "They tell me you have an adorable little girl."

"She's with Adam," Jenny admitted, abandoning the more formal address. It seemed a bit silly, under the circumstances.

"I'm Seth Fletcher," Rachel's sandy-haired, green-eyed husband said, holding his hand out to Jenny. "Nice to meet you."

Rachel groaned as Jenny and Seth shook hands. "I'm sorry, I should have introduced you. I don't know where my own manners have gone."

Jenny smiled. "Shall we join the others?" she suggested, motioning toward the den.

They found Adam surrounded by children. Melissa was still in his lap, kicking and smiling, while Paige and Aaron sat on the couch at either side of Adam, making silly faces at the baby.

"Mama, look at the baby," nine-year-old Paige said in delight. "Isn't she beautiful?"

"Look, Mama, she's got my finger," six-year-old Aaron added, giggling. "She's holding it tight."

Rachel quickly introduced her children to Jenny, then rushed over to admire the baby. "She really is precious." She cooed, already reaching to take her from Adam. She paused to look at Jenny. "Do you mind? I adore babies."

Jenny assured Rachel she was welcome to hold Melissa.

His hands freed, Adam hugged his niece and nephew, then stood to shake hands with Seth. "How's it going?" he asked.

Seth nodded, a deep glow of happiness clearly visible in his bright green eyes. "Couldn't be better," he said, his tone utterly sincere as he glanced from his wife to her children.

Rachel looked up from the baby for a moment. "Hello, Adam," she said with a smile of apology for ignoring him.

He kissed her cheek. Jenny heard that by-now-familiar softness in his voice when he spoke to his cousin. "Hi, Rach. You look great."

"I feel great," she assured him. "I've never been happier."

"Good for you. Did you meet Jenny?"

Rachel nodded and smiled at Jenny. "Yes, we introduced ourselves. Granny Fran and Cody both told me how beautiful your new housekeeper is, but neither of them did her justice."

Jenny was annoyed with herself for flushing again. She seemed to do that a lot lately, she thought.

"We won't stay long," Seth assured Adam. "We had lunch with my parents today and the kids insisted on dropping by to say hello to you on our way back." He glanced at Jenny. "My parents live only a few blocks from here," he explained for her benefit.

"I'm glad you came by," Adam replied. "Why don't you stay for dinner? Jen, we have some steaks or something we can throw on the grill, don't we?"

Jenny noticed that Rachel looked up from the baby again at that. She knew that Rachel must have noticed Adam's rather possessive use of the word "we." He'd made Jenny sound like much more than a housekeeper.

"Of course," she replied with a forced smile, tempted to call him by his title to remind him of her true place in his household. She didn't—not because it would embarrass him, but because she figured the hint would go right over his arrogant, dark head.

"Thank you, but we can't stay," Rachel said. "Paige has a report to finish before school tomorrow, so we have to be on our way."

Paige groaned loudly. "I want to stay and have dinner with Uncle Adam," she protested. "And the baby."

"Your mom did try to get you to work on your report yesterday," Seth reminded his stepdaughter good-naturedly. "You assured her you'd have plenty of time to work on it this evening. Next time maybe you'll remember to get the necessary stuff out of the way early so you'll have time to relax and have fun afterward."

Paige hefted a heavy sigh. "Okay, Dad," she grumbled.

Jenny noted the gleam of pride that lit his eyes when the little girl called him Dad. She also noticed that he was having a very hard time keeping his stern, parental expression.

She suspected that Paige and Aaron both had their new stepfather wound around their little fingers, and that he was struggling valiantly not to spoil them because of it. Probably with their mother's help.

The family stayed for almost an hour. Jenny served soft drinks and cookies—Rachel insisted on helping her—and then allowed herself to be persuaded to join them as they sat in the den and chatted.

"Have you signed the final papers on your company yet, Rachel?" Adam asked, keeping one eye on Paige and Aaron, who were kneeling beside Melissa's infant seat, laughing at the faces she made for their entertainment.

"Yes, on Friday," she replied. She turned to Jenny. "My first husband left me a waste-hauling business when he died several years ago," she explained. "I've recently sold it to have more time to spend with Seth and the children."

"Now that you're not working, Mama, can we have another baby?" Paige asked innocently. "A little girl, like Melissa?"

"I'd rather have a brother," Aaron argued, then looked self-consciously at Jenny, as though concerned he'd offended her. "But Melissa's real nice," he assured her.

Jenny smiled at him.

Rachel had turned a bit pink. "We'll—um—discuss babies later," she said, avoiding her cousin's amused eyes.

They left soon afterward. Paige and Aaron kissed Adam, then planted smacking kisses on Melissa's chubby cheek.

Rachel bade a fond farewell to her cousin, cooed one last time at the baby, then clasped Jenny's hand. "I'll be seeing you again," she said, the words sounding more like a promise than a wish.

Seth shook hands again with Adam, complimented Jenny on her beautiful baby, then ushered his new family out amid a flurry of chatter and laughter.

Adam's house seemed very quiet when the visitors were gone.

"Whew," he said, making a production of mopping his brow. "Those kids are full of energy, aren't they?"

Jenny nodded. "Melissa seemed to enjoy watching them."

"Yeah. Maybe we should think about putting her in a play group in a few months so she'll have other children to play with," Adam suggested seriously.

There was that "we" again—along with an assumption that Jenny and Melissa would still be around in a few months, and Adam still taking an active role in making decisions for them.

Jenny sighed. "I'd better start dinner," she said.

"Jenny."

She glanced warily over her shoulder. "Yes?"

He stood watching her, his hands in his pockets, his dark eyes narrowed intently. "We haven't finished our discussion. Not by a long shot."

"I know," she admitted. "But would you mind if we table it for now? I—I really need to start dinner."

Without detaining her again, he watched her leave the room.

Adam brought up the next difficult subject over dinner. "Tell me about your quarrel with your parents, Jenny."

He didn't phrase it as a request. This time he was determined to find out the whole story.

It had become all too important for him to do so.

As he'd expected, Jenny's expression immediately shuttered. "Why?" she countered, already looking defensive.

"I have to know," he said simply.

"Why?" she asked again.

"You're the one who said your problem with your parents is one of the obstacles between us. How can I know what I'm up against unless I hear the entire story?"

"You aren't up against anything," she argued. "I was simply pointing out how close you are to your family, especially in contrast to my own. I saw that again this afternoon, while your cousins were visiting. I've never had that tight bond you seem to have formed with your family."

"Not even with your parents?"

"My parents are the only family I have," she answered with a cool shrug. "And, no, we've never been especially close."

"Tell me, Jenny."

She sighed. "You aren't going to drop it until I do, are you?"

"No." He didn't smile at her plaintive tone.

Though her dinner was only little more than half-eaten, she set her fork down, as though the subject had destroyed her appetite. Adam regretted ruining her meal, but he couldn't wait any longer for this.

"My parents were both in their early forties when I was born," she began. "They'd been married for years and had finally decided they wouldn't be having children. And then I showed up."

"They should have been delighted."

"I don't think they were. They'd both resigned themselves to being childless, and I think they rather resented having their schedules so terribly disrupted. Both of them are a bit obsessive about schedules, I'm afraid. Dad's a preacher—the old hellfire-and-brimstone type, you'd probably call him. He's always been involved with small, poor churches that could hardly afford to keep him on, which is why he supplemented the family income with rental property.

"Mother is a retired librarian. It's almost as though she tried to fit the stereotype. She worships order, quiet and tidiness. None of which are typical of toddlers, obviously. And I was a handful—stubborn, noisy, curious, restless. Neither of my parents quite knew what to do with me."

"So what *did* they do with you?" Adam asked, watching her intently.

She shrugged. "They tried their best to tame me. And they succeeded, eventually. At least outwardly. I tried very hard to conform to their standards, to be the restrained, proper lady they'd raised me to be. I was so eager to please them that I didn't outwardly rebel until my early twenties, when I met a man my father didn't approve of. I don't know, maybe that's why I was attracted to Tommy in the first place."

"Tommy?" Adam repeated with a frown.

She nodded. "He had a ponytail and an earring. My father nearly had a heart attack on the spot when I introduced them. Tommy wasn't really a bad sort. We just didn't have much in common after the initial attraction wore off. Dad couldn't resist pointing out that he'd predicted a bad ending to the relationship, and I got mad and decided to finally break away. That was when I moved to Dallas."

"And met Carl," Adam said glumly.

"Well, not right away. I found and lost a few jobs—my career training had been sketchy, to say the least, since

Dad doesn't believe in women having careers. He only tolerated Mother's work because they so badly needed the money.

"Anyway," she continued doggedly, "I met Carl almost two years ago when I started working for the company where he was a supervisor. I had just begun to patch things up with my parents, who'd finally accepted that I wasn't going to move back home and let them watch out for me.

"Then, just over a year ago, my father showed up unexpectedly at my apartment one evening and met Carl. He hated him on the spot. The feeling was mutual. I accused Dad of not giving Carl a chance, of disapproving because he was divorced and rather liberal thinking. I told him that I was an adult and he had no business trying to run my life. We ended up yelling at each other—again. Dad left my apartment in a rage, and I haven't spoken with him since."

"And your mother?" Adam asked, trying to keep his reactions to her tale out of his voice.

"I called her a week later. She told me I should have listened to my father, and that she would be willing to talk to me when I was ready to apologize to him. I hung up on her."

"And you haven't called back."

She shook her head, her own face expressionless. "A few months later, Carl had dumped me and I found out I was expecting a baby without benefit of marriage. Do you really think I would call them under those conditions? Can you imagine what they would have said?"

Adam could see why Jenny had been so resistant to his well-meant advice. She would have resisted anyone she saw as taking over her life the way her father had tried to do. She couldn't have known how different he was from the man she'd described—at least, not initially. She certainly should know better now.

"You should call them, Jenny. Give them another chance. They might surprise you." He tried to make it sound like a suggestion, rather than a directive, though it wasn't easy for him.

He was much more accustomed to giving orders and having them followed with little question.

She shook her head, so hard her curls bounced around her face. "No."

"Why not? They haven't talked to their only daughter in over a year. They probably bitterly regret the rift between you. I'd bet they've been praying for a call from you."

"To tell them I've had an illegitimate child? I hardly think so."

Adam scowled. He didn't like the term she'd used to describe the baby he'd come to love, technically correct though it might be. "I'm sure they would soon grow to love Melissa," he argued. "She's their only grandchild. They'd be crazy not to want to know her."

"I would be crazy to call them and open myself up to their abuse again," Jenny retorted obstinately. "I won't do it, Adam, and I don't want you badgering me about it."

"But—"

"I mean it, Adam. I've told you the whole ugly story, but now the subject is closed. Permanently. Okay?"

"Jenny—"

"Okay?" she repeated, a tenacious spark in her eyes.

He sighed. "Whatever you say."

He would drop the subject for now, he assured himself. But that didn't mean it was permanently closed. Jenny would never be able to plan for her future until she'd made peace with her past. And if he had to insist that she face that past—well, it wouldn't be the first time.

She would understand, and forgive him, once she realized that he was only acting in her own best interest. Hers, and her daughter's, he added self-righteously.

As though in response to his thoughts, Melissa began to squirm and fret in her seat, gumming her fist to indicate that it was time for her own dinner.

Jenny excused herself. "I'll take care of the dishes later," she added, reaching for her baby.

"You take care of Melissa," Adam told her. "I'll get the dishes tonight."

"That's my job, Adam."

"Don't argue with me about this, Jenny," he said wearily. "I really don't want another argument with you tonight."

She lapsed into silence and carried Melissa away.

Adam could feel the resentment lingering behind her, and he suspected she was still irked with him for insisting that she tell him more than she'd wanted him to know about her family problems.

He dismissed that possibility with a wave of his hand. She'd soon realize that it had been necessary for him to know the whole story, he assured himself. After all, he couldn't even begin to work on a solution until he'd understood the problem.

And now he thought he understood.

He reached for the dirty dishes, his analytical mind already creating and studying different approaches to healing Jenny's heartache over her estranged family.

Jenny was in the den, rocking the now-fed baby to sleep when Adam rejoined her, leaving a spotless kitchen behind him.

She looked up when he entered. "You mentioned that her eyes are a darker brown than mine," she said.

He remembered. "Yes."

"She has my mother's eyes," Jenny told him, and there was the faintest trace of pain in her low voice.

Adam's heart twisted for her.

He was only more resolved now to do anything he had to do to solve Jenny's problems.

Chapter Thirteen

Something changed during the next two weeks. Jenny couldn't have defined exactly what it was, but it had something to do with the way Adam looked at her. The difference in his voice when he talked to her.

He wanted her. He was no longer making an effort to disguise it.

And yet he did nothing to frighten her, nothing to make her think he wanted any more than she was willing to give. He wasn't rushing her, wasn't pushing her, wasn't even putting his feelings into words. He hadn't kissed her again, though he touched her more often now than he had. Very light, casual, nonthreatening touches—a graze of his hand against hers, an encouraging pat on the shoulder, a brush of his knuckles against her cheek.

The touches were affectionate, tender, seductive—and yet she was fully aware that he would have stopped immediately if she'd asked.

She didn't ask.

She found herself pausing in her housework to stare into space and think of him. He disturbed her sleep by invading her dreams, charming and wooing her. She woke trembling and hugging her pillow, an odd, hungry emptiness inside her.

She was falling for him. Hard. Or maybe she'd fallen for him on that icy, wet night when he'd taken her out of the cold and into his warmth.

She strongly suspected that what she was feeling for him was love. Real love this time, not the shallow infatuation she'd felt before.

And it petrified her.

She was cleaning out the refrigerator in his kitchen, Melissa kicking contentedly in her automatic baby swing nearby, when the telephone rang early on a Friday afternoon. Suspecting it might be Adam, Jenny took a deep breath and answered on the kitchen extension. "Dr. Stone's residence."

"Hello, Jenny, it's Mrs. Stone."

The only person in the world who could make Jenny more nervous than Adam. His mother.

"Hello, Mrs. Stone. How nice to hear from you," she lied.

"I called to ask if Adam has mentioned how much he loves honey-baked ham. I wasn't sure if you know that's one of his favorite meals."

"No, I didn't," Jenny said patiently. "Thank you for telling me."

"He particularly likes it with sweet potatoes. Now, Jenny, dear, you mustn't buy those cheap hams. The flavor just isn't the same and they're much too fatty." She named the source she deemed most suitable.

"They're a bit more expensive, but Adam can certainly afford it, and he does deserve the best," she added.

"Of course," Jenny dutifully replied.

"I understand from his secretary that he's eating dinner at home much more often than he did before you came to work for him. Marcie said he's leaving the office earlier than he used to, and that he isn't working as many weekends as before."

Jenny hadn't realized that. She wondered if Adam were spending more time at home to be with her. The thought warmed her, despite her concerns.

"Dr. Stone is still a very busy man," she said. "He leaves very early each morning and he comes home so tired. I know he carries a heavy load at the hospital."

"Yes. My son is an important man. It's because of him that many formerly horribly disfigured people are able to lead normal, happy lives."

"It must be nice to make that kind of difference in the world," Jenny said wistfully.

"Mmm. Tell me, dear, what are your career plans? I only ask because you once told me your job for Adam was to be temporary."

Jenny wondered if she should take that as a hint. And then she chided herself for being paranoid. "I've been looking into night classes at a career college here in Little Rock," she said. "They offer several computer courses."

"Computers? You want to work with computers?"

"I don't know what I want to do, exactly," Jenny admitted. "But most jobs these days seem to require computer training, and I have little experience with them."

"I see. Well, I think you should make every effort to get your training, then. I know Adam will help you in any way he can. Adam has always liked to see deserving young people better themselves."

Jenny's chin lifted at the implication that she needed Adam's help. Biting back the instinctive disclaimer, she reminded herself that Arlene was Adam's mother and naturally thought that he was indispensable.

"Adam is very fond of you and your child," Arlene said a moment later. "I know he wants the best for you both."

Jenny didn't think she was being paranoid this time. Arlene seemed to be trying to find out if there was anything more to Adam and Jenny's relationship than she'd been told. Specifically, it sounded as though she were trying to discover how Jenny felt about Adam.

"Dr. Stone is a good man," Jenny said rather primly. "I couldn't have asked for a more thoughtful employer. I'm sure his next housekeeper will feel equally fortunate to work for him."

Arlene seemed satisfied with that—at least for now. She reminded Jenny again about the honey-baked ham and then murmured an excuse about how very busy she was before disconnecting the call.

Jenny felt drained when she hung up the kitchen phone. Automatically she checked on Melissa and then went back to her refrigerator cleaning.

She couldn't help wondering why Arlene's call had left her so depressed. Surely Jenny hadn't started to believe her daydreams about Adam. Surely she hadn't truly forgotten all the reasons why a happily-ever-after ending was so unlikely for them. Surely she hadn't allowed foolish love to blind her to grim reality.

If she had, it had taken only that one call to remind her of the truth. Arlene Stone had made the folly of those daydreams quite clear.

She swiped irritably at her streaming eyes. The fumes from this cleaner must be stronger than she'd realized, she told herself, refusing to admit her tears could be caused by anything else.

"What's this about you signing up for night classes at a career college?" Adam demanded that very evening. It was the first thing he said when he came home to find Jenny in the kitchen, putting the finishing touches to dinner.

Startled, she turned quickly, clutching a wooden spoon to her chest. "Adam!" she scolded. "I wish you wouldn't do that. You almost gave me a heart attack."

He brushed the remonstration off impatiently. "Have you signed up for night classes?" he repeated.

"I called and asked about the courses, but I haven't actually signed up yet," she replied. "How did you know?"

"I talked to my mother this afternoon." And he had been in a hurry to get home ever since. Arlene had made it sound as though Jenny was getting ready to move out at any moment.

His mother had seemed to approve of the possibility. She'd made it clear, in her own subtle-as-a-bulldozer manner, that she was afraid Adam was getting a bit too attached to his housekeeper and her child. Not that she was a snob, she'd added, but he had to see how unsuitable it was. Jenny was years younger, and from an entirely different background. Not to mention that she had a child to worry about.

Adam had ignored everything his mother had said after she'd hinted that Jenny was preparing to move on.

"Your mother called here earlier," Jenny explained. "She wanted to tell me where to buy your favorite brand of ham."

Adam didn't want to talk about food. "Why didn't you tell me you were looking into night classes? What kind of classes are they? When did you start planning this?"

"You're the one who suggested that I could attend classes while I worked for you," she reminded him, rather defensively. "You mentioned it the first time you offered me the job."

"Well, yeah, sure," he said, stumbling a bit. "But I didn't think you'd consider it so soon. Melissa's barely two months old. You've only just recovered from having her."

"Adam, I've been fully recovered for weeks, and you know it. I passed my six-week physical with flying colors. If I can run a vacuum and do heavy cleaning, I can certainly handle a few classes."

"And Melissa? What are you planning to do with her while you're gone?"

"The school I called has child care available on the premises. They employ licensed child-care workers, and the students are free to check on the children whenever they like."

Adam was shaking his head long before she finished speaking. "Just because someone has a license doesn't mean she's a dependable caretaker, especially for a baby as small and fragile as Melissa. If you're going to do this, you'll leave her with me. But I still don't know why you can't wait a few more months before you jump into something like this."

"The sooner I start my training, the sooner I'll be prepared to find another job," Jenny explained. "And I certainly wouldn't expect you to baby-sit Melissa while I attend classes. If I don't like the child-care facilities available at the school, I'll hire someone else."

"You aren't leaving Melissa with a total stranger," Adam said flatly. "And I don't know why you're in such a damn hurry to find another job, anyway. What's wrong with this one?"

"This one is temporary," she snapped in return, her fists on her slender hips, the wooden spoon still clutched in her right hand. "It always has been. I told you from the beginning that I would work for you only until I was able to support myself and my child. On my own."

It was only then that Adam realized why he utterly detested the idea of Jenny taking those classes. He'd been seething about it ever since his mother had mentioned it, but he hadn't really stopped to analyze his reaction. Now he knew.

The more training Jenny received, the more qualified she would be for another job. She would be leaving then.

She wouldn't need him anymore.

He asked himself if he was being fair to her. He couldn't blame her for wanting something more than cooking and cleaning. Not that she'd seemed unhappy in the job so far, but maybe she was getting tired of the routine. He couldn't imagine that a clerical job, even one that used computers, would be any more interesting—but maybe Jenny thought it would be.

Whatever she wanted, he shouldn't stand in her way.

"When do the classes start?" he asked.

She seemed to relax a little. "Not until next month."

He nodded. "Let me know what you decide to do, when the classes meet. I'll arrange to be free those nights to take care of the baby."

She threw up her hands. The wooden spoon went flying, clattering against a wall and dropping to the tile floor. She ignored it. "You are *not* going to baby-sit!" she repeated.

"Yes," he answered implacably. "I am."

With that, he turned on one heel, walked to the swing and lifted Melissa into his arms. She smiled broadly at him, greeting him with the soft babbling she'd begun in the past week or so. He kissed her soft cheek. No stranger was taking care of this baby, he thought determinedly.

"Adam—"

"Melissa and I are going to watch TV until dinner's ready," he said, turning toward the door.

He heard Jenny sputtering behind him. He didn't pause to find out what she was trying to say.

Dinner was eaten with cool civility. Neither of them mentioned the night classes. Adam told Jenny a little about his day; she mentioned a problem she was having with the clothes dryer. He promised to have someone out to look at it the next day.

They cleaned the kitchen together. Afterward, Jenny took the baby upstairs, nursed her and put her down to bed in the bedroom next to her own. Adam had moved the crib in there a few weeks earlier, when Jenny had decided Melissa would sleep better in a room of her own.

Jenny paused before going back downstairs. It wasn't even nine yet, and she didn't want to spend the rest of the evening in her room, reading or watching television alone. But she didn't want to get into another quarrel with Adam, either.

In the end, she decided she'd rather risk another quarrel than to spend the evening without him.

He was sitting on the couch in the den. The television was on, but the volume turned down so low Jenny couldn't hear it. A book lay on the end table, but he didn't seem to be interested in reading it. He looked lost in thought. So very far away.

He looked up when Jenny came fully into the room. His expression cleared, and he smiled. "I wasn't sure you'd come back down this evening," he said.

A bit self-consciously, she shrugged and slipped her hands into the pockets of the comfortable, purple fleece slacks she wore with a matching fleece top. "It's a little early to turn in," she explained.

He patted the couch. "Come sit beside me."

She hesitated, then walked slowly to his side. She sat as far away from him as space permitted.

He reached out and hauled her closer. "We can't talk when you're sitting so far away," he explained when she gasped at his unexpected action.

"What—what did you want to talk about?" she asked, noting that he kept his arm around her shoulders.

"I want to apologize," he said gravely. "I was out of line earlier, and I'm sorry."

She certainly hadn't expected an apology. "You were rather brusque," she admitted. "I couldn't understand why my taking night classes seemed to annoy you so much."

"I know."

"Is it because I didn't talk to you about it before I looked into it?" she asked hesitantly, the only reason she'd come up with on her own. "I know you like to help with things like this, but I really am capable of making decisions on my own, Adam."

He nodded, then said, "That wasn't it."

"Was it because you're worried about Melissa? That isn't necessary, either. I wouldn't leave her with anyone I didn't trust. Surely you know that."

"I'm not worried about Melissa. I'll be keeping her myself," he said.

She sighed. "Adam—"

"Let's not get into that argument again," he said quickly. "That wasn't what was bothering me, anyway."

"Then what *was* bothering you?" she asked, bewildered.

"I don't like to think about you leaving," he said simply. "And I hadn't realized you were getting so impatient to do so."

She stared at him. "You think I'm impatient to leave here?"

He nodded, his gaze focused broodingly on her face. "Aren't you?"

She shook her head. "No," she whispered. "I like it here. Very much." And wasn't *that* an understatement! "But—"

Something sparked in his eyes. "But?"

"I know we can't go on like this indefinitely. I have to start preparing myself to leave—to find another job," she added quickly, in case he thought she meant an emotional preparation.

"As far as I'm concerned, you have a job, and a home, here for as long as you like," Adam told her, his voice deeper than usual.

Her throat felt tight. "That's very kind of you. But—"

"I'm not being kind, Jenny. I'm being as selfish as always. I don't want you to leave. Haven't I gotten that through to you yet? And it has nothing to do with your skill as a cook or a housekeeper, though you've done an excellent job with both."

She twisted her fingers in her lap, achingly aware of the weight of his arm on her shoulders. She didn't quite know what to say, what, exactly, he was implying.

He seemed to sense her confusion. "I want you, Jenny. I've told you before. Maybe you didn't believe me. But it's true. I want you more than I've ever wanted another woman. I care about you. I don't want you to leave me."

Jenny swallowed hard and looked down at her fingers. Her vision was blurred by unshed tears.

"Am I making you uncomfortable?" Adam demanded. "If you don't want to hear this—if you don't feel the same way I do—tell me now. You'll still have your job and your home, but I won't bother you again personally. Or at least, I'll try not to," he added wryly. "I can't promise the subject won't ever come up again. I'm only human."

"You—you aren't making me uncomfortable," she murmured. "But—"

"But?" There was a quick note of hope in his voice.

"I'm scared."

He went very still. "Of me?" he asked after a moment. "Surely you know I would never hurt you. Not deliberately."

How could she explain what really frightened her? That she'd heard words like these before, from men who looked and sounded as sincere as Adam. That she'd been hurt before, badly hurt.

But not as desperately hurt as she would be if Adam pulled away from her the way those other men had.

She had given her affection before, but she knew now she'd never truly lost her heart. Her feelings had been hurt, her ego crushed—but her heart had remained intact.

Adam could shatter it.

"I don't think you realize how badly you *could* hurt me," she said, looking away from him.

Very tenderly, he turned her face back to his. "Jenny—"

One tear escaped to trickle down her cheek. "I've made so many mistakes," she whispered.

"Not this time," he promised, drawing her closer. "This time, I'll take care of everything."

So typically Adam. So confident that nothing could go wrong if he were in charge. Even in matters of the heart, Adam considered himself infallible.

And Jenny found that as frightening as anything else she had to worry about.

She started to tell him so.

His mouth got in the way.

Jenny gave in to the inevitable and wrapped her arms around his neck.

Adam murmured something that might have been approval. And then he devoted his full attention to kissing her.

Jenny hadn't suddenly decided this wasn't a mistake. She still firmly believed it was.

She hadn't come to the conclusion that a happily-ever-after ending was possible after all. She still didn't believe it was.

She didn't even try to convince herself that Adam had fallen as deeply, irrevocably for her as she had for him. She didn't accept that for a minute.

What she *had* decided was that she might as well stop fighting him—stop fighting herself.

She was in love with him, exasperating and arrogant and bossy as he could be at times. And, even though this was probably the biggest mistake she'd ever made, it was much too late for her to change course now. Had, perhaps, been too late since she'd recklessly agreed to move in with him.

"It's not a mistake, Jenny," he muttered, and she didn't know if he was reading her mind or repeating what he'd said earlier.

It didn't seem to matter just then.

"Shut up and kiss me again, Adam," she murmured, sliding her fingers into his hair.

He grinned briefly. "You just love giving me orders, don't you?"

"It's such a rare treat for me," she murmured.

His grin turned piratical. And then he kissed her again.

And Jenny decided that this was an even more gratifying treat.

The big bed in Adam's room looked even more enormous that night when he led her to it. Jenny gulped silently and fought down a surge of panic.

Was she really ready for this?

Adam raised her icy, trembling hand to his lips and kissed it. "Trust me," he murmured.

It sounded so simple when he said it. So natural.

So easy.

She trusted him, because she had no choice. She only hoped that this time—just this once—she'd given her trust wisely.

Still holding her hand, he set the wireless nursery monitor on the nightstand and turned it on. He listened intently for a moment, then turned to her with a smile. "She's sleeping like a baby," he murmured.

She smiled faintly at the lame joke and wondered how she could possibly *not* trust him. What other man would be so conscientious about her baby at a time like this? What other man could have seen her at her worst, as Adam had, and still want her?

There simply was no other man like Adam.

She drew a deep breath and found that she was no longer afraid. She opened her arms to him.

She hadn't expected Adam to be a gentle lover. She'd never considered him a particularly gentle man.

And yet he was.

She certainly hadn't expected patience. Not from him.

Yet she discovered that he had a wealth of patience hidden beneath that brusque, driven facade.

She hadn't expected him to tremble. Adam didn't strike her as a man who was ever unsure of himself. Who was ever in less than full control.

And yet she felt the tremor in his fingers when he brushed her face, his strong, bare body poised above hers.

"I don't want to hurt you," he murmured, his voice tight with the control he exerted over himself. "You're still recuperating."

Touched by his concern for her, even when she could see the need that was driving him, she reached up to him. "You won't hurt me," she assured him in a breathless whisper. "I'm fully recovered. And I want you. Now."

He made a strangled sound deep in his throat and pressed slowly forward.

Jenny gathered him close.

This, she thought with her last flash of coherence, was where he belonged.

She never wanted to let him go.

Jenny had never been happier than she was during the weeks that followed her first night in Adam's bed. It was March, and the first signs of spring made their appearance—buttercups, forsythia, japonica, pear blossoms, a few early azaleas. The air turned warmer, and it was no longer necessary to bundle up in coats and heavy sweaters to venture outside.

Adam continued to work a heavy, demanding schedule, but when he wasn't working, he was with her. Melissa was growing and thriving, a happy, healthy baby who couldn't have asked for more attention than she received from Adam, Jenny and the members of Adam's family who had taken to dropping in more often than they had when he'd lived alone.

Jenny enjoyed all of them. For the first time since she'd broken with her own parents, she tentatively began to feel like part of a family again. Arlene wasn't pleased when she finally realized that Adam and Jenny had become much more than employer and employee, but she accepted it gracefully enough, if not with as much enthusiasm as Jenny would have liked.

It could have been worse, she told Adam one evening after Arlene joined them for a painfully polite, though satisfyingly cordial, dinner. Arlene could have made an ugly scene, dramatically threatened to disinherit Adam or something like that.

Adam had only laughed and assured her that he'd known all along that his mother wouldn't risk showing open disapproval of anything he did. She wouldn't risk driving a wedge between her and her son—she depended entirely too much on him. Jenny realized that he was right the day Arlene appeared with an expensive outfit for Melissa that she claimed she'd seen in a children's boutique and simply hadn't been able to resist.

It was quite obvious that Arlene had bought the gift primarily to please Adam. And it worked. He thanked her warmly for her gesture, and Arlene bustled away with great satisfaction that she was still in favor with her son. Jenny was rather amused by the whole thing. She'd finally come to understand that Arlene lived with a secret, painful fear of losing her adored son the way she had his father.

That was certainly a fear Jenny could identify with.

Everything was so perfect that it scared her silly.

Adam still irritated the hell out of her at times. She supposed that was inevitable. His was just that sort of personality. She loved him, but there were times she wanted to smack him.

He told her ruefully that he understood. She wasn't the only one who felt that way about him, he confessed. He'd try to do better.

He didn't change. Jenny admitted to herself that she loved him anyway.

She'd never quite had the courage to say so to Adam. Maybe because he'd never said the words to her.

He wanted her. He told her that often enough. He thought she was beautiful. He admired her mind, her spirit, her competence in the house and the kitchen, her painstaking care of her daughter, her easy acceptance into his beloved family.

But he never told her he loved her.

They argued seriously about only two subjects—her enrollment in the career college, and her stubborn refusal to contact her parents.

Adam saw no reason for her to "knock herself out" taking night classes in computer usage.

"You're working all day taking care of the house and Melissa," he argued. "Then you take these classes two nights a week and come home so tired you can hardly move. Why are you doing this to yourself?"

"I want to know how to use computers," Jenny said repeatedly. "If I don't, I'll never get a decent job."

"You don't need a job," he replied, obviously trying to be patient and logical. "I'll take care of you, and Melissa. God knows I have plenty of money for all of us."

Jenny had squared her chin, narrowed her eyes and informed him that she wasn't a kept woman and she didn't intend to be treated as one. "I earn my way," she told him coolly. "I don't need anyone to 'take care' of me."

Though he'd scoffed at her use of the dated terminology, Adam had soon realized that it wouldn't do him any good to argue. Jenny had no intention of changing her mind. She couldn't persuade him, however, to allow her to put Melissa into child care. Adam made certain that he was home every Tuesday and Thursday evening in time to watch the baby while Jenny attended her classes.

No stranger, he said flatly, was taking care of their baby.

Jenny had found herself unable to remind him that Melissa wasn't really their baby. She hadn't been able to say anything at all. She'd been too busy fighting off a wave of longing that Melissa really had been theirs.

As for her parents, Jenny refused to even discuss them with him. Adam told her again and again that she was being stubborn, foolish, overly proud and willfully obtuse. She told him to mind his own business.

"You'll regret it," he warned her. "Your family is too important to ignore, Jenny. You'll realize that someday and it will be too late for you to make amends."

His words had hurt her, but she'd obstinately held her position. Just the thought of calling her parents and telling them that she'd had a child out of wedlock, and was now living without benefit of marriage with yet another man, was enough to make her shudder. She'd been enough of a disappointment to her parents. She didn't need another painful reminder of how she'd failed to live up to their unrealistic expectations of her.

"I can't call them," she told Adam quietly, following one of their noisier and more heated "discussions" about the subject. "I know you mean well. I know you don't really understand. But I can't call them."

He sighed, ran a frustrated hand through his hair and then took her into his arms. "We'll let it go for now," he promised. "Give it a little time. Maybe you'll change your mind."

She kept her doubts to herself, and gratefully accepted Adam's assurances that he wouldn't nag her about it any further.

She was beginning to hope, she realized. It was a shaky optimism, at best, but she found herself starting to believe there was a chance that a lifetime commitment to Adam was not as unlikely as it had once seemed.

Other than those few disagreements, they got along so well. They were compatible in so many ways. They were good friends, and passionate lovers.

She prayed that one day they would be even more.

For the first time in years, it seemed as though Jenny might finally come out ahead. That she'd taken a risk and hadn't made a mistake. That everything she desired most in life was close at hand.

And then, on one particularly beautiful spring afternoon, Adam ruined everything.

Chapter Fourteen

It was a Saturday afternoon in April. The sky was cloudless, a blue so brilliant it made Jenny blink. Spring flowers were in bloom, their colors bright and cheerful, and the new leaves on the trees added a background of mint green. Jenny hadn't seen a more beautiful day in years—or had she simply not stopped to notice?

It was warm, and a soft breeze caressed the skin bared by the loose, scoop-necked white cotton blouse she wore with a colorful broomstick skirt. A wide leather belt cinched her slender waist. She'd let her hair grow a bit; soft, dark curls bounced around her neck. She felt light, feminine. Happy.

So happy it was almost frightening.

She'd been shopping. Melissa was growing so quickly that she'd outgrown all her clothes. Adam had convinced Jenny to leave the baby with him for the afternoon while she shopped for a new infant wardrobe. They'd had a few words about who would pay for that wardrobe. They'd finally compromised. Adam had given her his credit card and had said they'd split the cost when the bill came in.

Though Jenny expected another argument then, she'd finally given in. She was tempted to stick the card in her purse and leave it there, but Adam seemed so eager to buy things for Melissa. Knowing how much he'd grown to love the child, Jenny didn't have the heart to completely deny him that pleasure.

Her arms loaded with packages, a smile on her glossed lips, Jenny entered the house through the back kitchen door from the garage. She dumped the packages on the kitchen table. She couldn't wait to show the adorable garments to Adam, she thought with a smile. He got such a kick out of seeing Melissa dressed in ruffles and ribbons. Of course, she'd picked up a few rugged little play-suits, too.

She plucked a cute, lop-eared stuffed dog out of the pile and carried it with her as she went in search of Adam and Melissa. She expected to find them in the den. She did.

With her parents.

Jenny froze in the doorway, unable at first to believe her eyes. Her father and mother sat side by side on the couch, Adam in the recliner closest to them. Melissa sat in her grandmother's lap, babbling and looking pleased with all the attention she was currently receiving.

Adam was the first to notice that Jenny had joined them. He rose immediately, moving toward her with an outstretched hand. His eyes held a mixed message— apology, anxiety and an unmistakable demand for her to behave herself.

Looking into those dark eyes that had become so dearly familiar to her in the past months, Jenny felt her heart break.

She'd trusted him. And he—like the men before him—had callously betrayed that trust.

She took a deep breath, made a mental vow that she would get through this without falling apart and squared her shoulders. Ignoring Adam's extended hand, she stepped past him without a word to him.

"Mother. Dad. This is a surprise," she said, and she was pleased that her voice sounded cool and composed.

Esther Newcomb, a thin, wispy-gray-haired, inexpensively dressed woman in her sixties, looked up quickly. Behind her plastic-framed bifocals, her once-dark eyes—now faded to a soft chocolate—were damp with unshed tears. "Jenny," she said, her own voice tremulous.

Herb Newcomb, reverend and rental property owner, stood to greet his daughter. Slim except for a round paunch of a tummy, only a couple of inches taller than Jenny, almost entirely bald other than a half circle of steel gray curls, he wore a shiny brown suit, a white shirt and a tie that Jenny remembered giving him for Father's Day at least a decade earlier. His lined face was set in an unreadable expression, but he spoke affably enough. "Hello, Jennifer. You're looking well."

She swallowed, making no move to touch him. "So are you."

The moment was painfully awkward. Herb cleared his throat. "We know you weren't expecting us. Dr. Stone called and explained your situation to us. He thought it was time we put the past behind us and made amends in our family. Your mother and I agreed."

Jenny flicked an angry glance at Adam. "Dr. Stone thought that, did he?"

Adam didn't wince at her tone, but she saw the flicker of his eyelashes before she turned away from him.

"I see you've met my daughter," she commented.

"She's so beautiful," Esther said, clutching her granddaughter's tiny hand. "I can't get over how much she looks like you did at this age."

"She has your mother's eyes," Herb said, looking toward the child.

"Yes, I know." Jenny sighed. "Sit down, Dad."

He waited until she was seated in a nearby chair before he settled on the edge of the couch. "Why didn't you tell us about the baby?" he asked, getting straight to the point.

"I didn't think you would want to know," Jenny replied bluntly.

Her mother made a choked sound of protest.

Herb only nodded. "I can understand why you would have thought that. But you were wrong. We're your parents, Jennifer. We love you. We would never have turned you away if you'd come to us for help."

"I didn't need your help," Jenny replied immediately. She didn't like the image his words evoked—her getting herself in trouble and crawling to them to take care of it. Maybe she hadn't gotten by completely on her own these past months, but she'd done her best to earn her way.

She'd thought she'd finally found a place for herself. She'd been wrong again. But damned if she would admit it now, in front of her parents.

"I know there have been hard feelings between us in the past," Herb conceded, obviously trying to meet her more than halfway. "I know I've been at fault in many ways. It was hard for me to accept that you're a grown woman, with the right to make your own choices. I can't honestly say I approve of all the choices you've made—"

He glanced at Adam, and Jenny wondered how much her father suspected about her present living arrangements.

But then Herb sighed almost imperceptibly and continued, "But I will concede that your decisions should be your own. As your mother has pointed out, I've been stubborn and inflexible and I almost lost my daughter and the chance to know my granddaughter because of it. I'm sorry, Jennifer. I'd like for you to give me—give us—another chance. I can love you for who you are—if you're willing to do the same for me."

Jenny's throat tightened. There had been so many times she'd dreamed of hearing her father say those words. It was a bittersweet pleasure to hear them from him now. Her emotions were so battered by Adam's betrayal that she could hardly deal with anything else at the moment.

"Please, Jenny," Esther said quietly. "Forgive us. We love you."

Jenny closed her eyes for a moment, then took a deep breath and looked at her parents again. The years were taking a toll on them. Her father had once seemed so big and intimidating, so all-powerful. Now he looked old and a bit frail. And—for the first time in her memory—unsure of himself.

She knew that Adam was watching her very closely, waiting to see how she would respond to her parents' entreaties. She could almost feel his gaze on her.

She couldn't look at him.

"I'll forgive you," she told her parents, "if you'll forgive me. I know I've been difficult for you to understand. And I know I've disappointed you in many ways. But I've never stopped loving you. Either of you."

Esther caught her breath in a sob.

Herb exhaled deeply, as though he'd been holding his breath.

Adam murmured something that might have been approval.

As though aware that she wasn't the center of attention at the moment, Melissa crowed and pumped her arms.

Her ploy succeeded. Everyone immediately turned to admire her. Both Herb and Esther made it clear that they were claiming their granddaughter. Jenny wondered if she'd ever really doubted that they would.

She would have called them eventually, she realized now. When she was ready.

Adam had had no right to make that decision for her, no matter how well it had turned out.

"Jenny." Herb glanced from her to Adam, as though aware of the tension between them. "I hope you know that you still have a home with us. We would love for you and Melissa to go back to Texas with us."

Adam moved restlessly in his chair, and started to speak. Jenny sensed that he bit the words back with an effort.

Still looking at her father, she shook her head. "Thank you, but no. I need to be on my own now, Dad. I'll come to visit, of course. I want Melissa to know her grandparents. But I have to make my own way.

"As a matter of fact," she added deliberately, "I've been taking some classes and I'm looking for a new job. I'll be moving into a place of my own soon."

"What the—"

Jenny spoke over Adam's exclamation. "I'm not even sure I'll be staying in Arkansas," she added. "But I'll always let you know how to reach me from now on. We won't lose touch again," she promised her parents.

That seemed to satisfy them.

"We have to catch a plane back home soon," Herb said after another half hour of catching up.

"You aren't staying over for a few days?" Jenny asked, a bit disappointed. Now that she had been reconciled with her parents, she didn't want to tell them goodbye again so soon.

"I can't stay," Herb answered. "I have to preach in the morning. Are you sure you can't return with us? At least for a few weeks?"

"I can't," Jenny answered gently. "But soon."

"We'll hold you to that."

They left twenty minutes later. Melissa was getting sleepy, rubbing her eyes and clutching her new stuffed dog beneath her nodding head.

"I'll put her down for a nap," Adam told Jenny, taking the baby with a familiar ease that she knew her parents noticed. "You see your folks off. Melissa and I will be fine until you get back."

She nodded, still not meeting his eyes. Her parents thanked Adam for calling them, kissed the baby, then reluctantly said goodbye to her.

The Newcombs had planned to take a cab back to the airport, the way they'd arrived. Jenny wouldn't hear of it. She insisted on driving them.

They talked about Adam during the twenty-minute ride. They wanted to know how Jenny had met him. Apparently he'd told them little more than that he employed Jenny as his housekeeper and that he'd heard about her family estrangement and had wanted to help them make amends, for Jenny's and Melissa's sake.

Jenny briefly explained about the car accident that had brought her to Adam's attention—only three months earlier. It seemed so much longer.

How could her life have changed so drastically in only three months?

"He's obviously very fond of you and Melissa," Esther said tentatively. "I had the impression that he has become more to you than an employer."

Jenny shook her head. "He's been a good friend to us," she said, deliberately keeping all emotion out of her voice. "But that's all there could ever be between us. I'll be moving out soon, living on my own. As busy as Adam is, I doubt that I'll see him much after that."

It took all the strength she had just to say it. Heaven only knew how she'd survive actually leaving him. But somehow, she would find the strength.

She had no choice.

Her parents' flight was called only minutes after Jenny delivered them to the gate. She embraced both of them, her eyes filling with tears. "I love you," she said. "Thank you for coming."

"We love you, too," Herb said, his own eyes suspiciously bright. "You'll call us if you need us?"

"I'll call."

"God be with you, darling," Esther said, clinging to Jenny as long as she could before her husband gently pulled her away. "Give Melissa a kiss for me tonight."

"I will." Jenny dabbed at her eyes and waved her parents out of sight.

She cried as she made the lonely drive back to Adam's house. She wasn't crying over the goodbyes that had just been said—but the one that still lay ahead.

That one would be even harder, because it would be permanent.

Adam hardly gave her a chance to get back in the door before he confronted her. "Why the hell did you tell them that you were moving out?" he demanded.

She'd prepared herself for this before she'd gotten out of her car. She'd carefully dried her tears, squared her shoulders and made a firm vow that she would not yell, would not cry, would not let him see that she was dying inside.

"I told them the truth," she said coolly. "Must I remind you yet again that this job was only temporary from the beginning?"

He stared at her as though she'd lost her mind. "Who's talking about a job? I'm talking about *us!*"

"There is no 'us,' Adam. Whatever we might have had—it's over."

His eyes narrowed. At any other time, she might have been intimidated by the ominous look that hardened his dark face. As it was, she was too miserable and determined to feel anything more.

"What do you mean it's over?" he asked, his voice quiet. Silky. Dangerous.

"Just what I said. Over. I'll be moving out tonight."

"The hell you will."

She tossed her head. "You can't stop me."

Adam threw up his hands, visibly frustrated. "Damn it, Jenny, why are you doing this?"

He didn't even know. That hurt her as badly as anything he'd done yet.

Sadly she shook her head. "I just think it's for the best, Adam," she said softly. "Please, don't fight me on this. Just let me go."

"I'll be damned if I will." He drew a quick, sharp breath. "Was it something your parents said during the drive to the airport? Does it bother them that we've been living together without being married? I mean, I understand why they'd feel that way—and they're probably right. We should be married. Actually I've been meaning to suggest that soon, anyway. It would be much better for you and the baby if we—"

That did it. She forgot her lofty intentions to stay calm and cool and rational.

She hadn't been this furious since—since—

She'd *never* been this furious.

She hit him. Doubled her fist and punched his arm as hard as she could. And then she planted one small hand against his broad, hard chest and shoved.

"How *dare* you?" she yelled, and there was nothing calm, cool, or rational about her voice. "You are the most arrogant, the most obtuse, the most infuriating, the most thickheaded male I've ever run across in my life. And let me tell you, I've encountered some real pigs, but you, Dr. Adam Stone, take the cake!"

Still stumbling from her not-insignificant shove, Adam quickly righted himself and planted his fists on his hips. Now he really *was* looking at her as though she were insane!

"Jenny—"

"Be quiet! I refuse to listen to any more of your pompous lectures about how you know what's best for me. You think you're so damn perfect, so damn *right* about everything, but this time you were wrong, Adam. You couldn't have been more wrong," she added bitterly.

"Because I called your parents without telling you? Is that what this tantrum is all about?"

She hadn't thought she could get any angrier. His incredulous expression proved her wrong.

"You had no right to call them!" she shouted, her cheeks wet with wrathful tears. "How could you do that? How could you interfere in my family without even bothering to discuss it with me? How could you hurt me like that, when I trusted you?"

"Jenny—"

"As for your oh-so-gracious offer of marriage—"

She told him exactly what he could do with it.

"This is ridiculous," Adam said, his own voice cold, aggrieved. "Your rift with your parents was hurting you. I couldn't stand to see you hurting, so I did something about it. Are you going to try to tell me that you're sorry you've made up with them?"

"I'm not going to tell you anything," she muttered, not caring that she sounded childish. "It's none of your business."

"Of all the—" He shoved a hand through his hair. "Look, maybe we'd both better cool off before we say anything we'll both regret."

She only glared at him, still so upset she was trembling.

"I'm going out for a while," he said abruptly. "If I stay, we'll only yell at each other some more. While I'm gone, you can calm down and think about this. Everything I did was for you, Jenny. And I meant what I said about getting married. I certainly wasn't trying to patronize or offend you."

She remained stubbornly silent.

Adam hesitated, then moved as though to touch her.

"Jenny—"

She flinched.

He dropped his hands. "I'll be back later," he said, his face hard.

She watched him go through tear-filled eyes.

She knew she wouldn't be there when he returned.

"Goodbye, Adam," she whispered when the door slammed behind him.

* * *

Adam figured three hours was plenty long enough for Jenny to calm down.

Women, he thought, *try to please them and look what happens. A guy just can't win for losing.*

He shook his head as he parked his car in front of the house. He'd put it into the garage later, after he and Jenny had settled this.

He climbed the front steps with his jaw set in determination. He'd thought a lot about what Jenny had said, and he conceded that she had the right to be angry that he'd taken her family matters into his own hands. He'd half expected her to be annoyed by what she'd always called his arrogance.

But surely by now she could see that he'd had her best interests at heart. And hadn't it all worked out for the best? He'd seen the tentative joy in her eyes when her father had apologized so sincerely to her. He didn't think Jenny and her parents would ever fully understand each other—they were so very different, not unlike him and his own mother—but it was obvious they loved each other. It was ridiculous for them to let foolish pride stand between them.

Surely Jenny would admit that now.

As for his marriage proposal—he grimaced. Okay, so he'd handled that badly. A woman wanted candles and flowers and all that folderol when a man proposed. He should have known better than to just blurt it out during a quarrel that way.

His only excuse was that he'd never proposed to anyone before.

There'd never been another woman he'd wanted as his wife.

"Jenny?" he called out as he stepped into his foyer. There was no answer.

"Jenny?" He headed for the kitchen, assuming she was in there, making dinner.

But the kitchen was empty, the stove cold. As far as he could tell, nothing had been prepared for dinner.

He began to frown.

She had to be upstairs with Melissa. Suddenly impatient, he sprinted for the staircase, taking the stairs two at a time. "Jenny?"

Melissa's room was unoccupied. The crib sat silent and empty, the colorful mobile dangling above it. Melissa's favorite stuffed toys, which usually lined the windowsill near the crib where she could see them, were gone.

Adam went very still, staring blindly at that empty crib. And then he turned, very slowly, and walked to Jenny's door. His hand wasn't quite steady when he lifted it to knock.

"Jenny?"

There was no answer.

Sick with dread, he turned the knob.

She was gone.

Chapter Fifteen

Adam nearly went insane during the long night that followed Jenny's departure.

His emotions swung wildly. He was angry with Jenny for walking out on him, after all he'd done for her. He was bitterly disappointed that what they'd found had meant so little to her. He was offended that she hadn't realized that he'd only wanted what was best for her and her child. And he was terrified that something would happen to one of them without him there to take care of them.

He spent the evening calling every motel in central Arkansas. Jenny hadn't registered in any of them—at least not under her own name. He couldn't think of anywhere else she might have gone.

He didn't go to bed that night. He paced the big, empty quiet rooms of his house, his footsteps sounding loud in the utter silence. He couldn't seem to settle long in any particular room— Jenny's presence was too strong in all of them.

The kitchen, where they'd shared so many casual, comfortable meals, Melissa lying in her infant seat at one end of the table.

The den, where they'd spent long, peaceful hours reading, watching television, playing with the baby.

Melissa's room. The one Adam had begun to think of as the nursery. The crib he'd put together, the mobile he'd attached to the rail, the toys he'd bought her, now lying abandoned in the silent room.

His bedroom, where he and Jenny had spent long, passionate nights in each other's arms. Where he'd discovered a depth of pleasure he'd never experienced before her. A wealth of tenderness he hadn't known he possessed.

The place had never seemed so big. So cold. So joyless.

It was only a house. While Jenny and Melissa had lived there, it had been a home.

Early the next morning, he called her parents. Jenny wasn't with them. Nor had they heard from her.

He spent all day Sunday trying to find her. By late afternoon, he finally made a decision to contact a private investigator, and damn the cost. He was already reaching for the telephone when it rang.

He snatched it up. "Jenny?"

"It's Granny Fran, Adam."

He tried not to sound disappointed. "How are you?"

"I'm fine. I probably shouldn't be calling you—you deserve every minute of worry you've probably had—but I couldn't stand it any longer."

At first he didn't understand . . . and then it hit him. "Jenny's with you?" he asked quickly, hopefully.

"Yes. She didn't know where else to go. And she knew I would be here for her if she needed me."

Adam pinched the bridge of his nose between his thumb and finger. His shoulders sagged. The relief was almost overwhelming. A sleepless night and hours of worry had taken a heavy toll on him that evening.

"Is she all right?" he asked wearily.

"She's physically unharmed, if that's what you're asking. And Melissa's fine, too."

"Thank God. Look, I'll be there in an hour and—"

"You'll do no such thing. I didn't call you so that you would come here, Adam. I only wanted to ease your mind. I knew you would be making yourself sick with worry about them. Now you can relax and go back to your busy, important life."

Oh, hell. Granny Fran was incensed. She always got that chilly tone to her voice when he'd displeased her, ever since he'd been a kid.

"You could at least hear my side of the story before you start chewing me out," he said, aware that he sounded a bit like that sullen boy who'd fallen out of her apple tree.

"That isn't necessary. I already know exactly what you would say. In your mind, you were utterly justified in calling Jenny's parents without her knowledge or her consent, and arranging a meeting she wasn't at all prepared for. You knew how she felt about it, but you went ahead with your own plans just because you thought it best—and you are always right, aren't you, Adam?"

"Gran, it was hurting her to be at odds with her family. None of them could take the first step toward a reconciliation. All I did was help them meet halfway. It turned out fine. Jenny's father apologized, and she agreed to stay in touch with them from now on. I could see in her eyes that she was glad the reunion had finally taken place."

"It should have been *her* decision, Adam. You should have discussed it with her first. By taking away her choice, you implied that she wasn't capable of handling her own affairs. That hurt her very deeply."

"I'm sorry. I didn't mean to hurt her. I only wanted to help," Adam repeated.

"No, Adam. You wanted your own way. As always. Whether anyone else agreed with you or not. And this time, your thoughtless arrogance caused a great deal of pain. That poor child..." Her voice trailed off.

Adam swallowed. "Let me talk to her. Please."

"She doesn't want to talk to you. She didn't even want me to call you. She finally gave me permission to do so only because she knew it would ease my mind. Jenny is a very special woman, Adam. She's bright and capable and independent. She deserves better than to be treated like a helpless, dependent child who must be guided for her own good."

Adam started to protest that he hadn't treated Jenny that way. That he had never treated her that way. The words caught somewhere in his throat.

Was that the impression his actions had given her?

"I want her back, Gran."

She paused to digest his words before asking, "Why?"

"I miss her."

His grandmother sighed through the wires. "I'm sorry, darling. That just isn't good enough."

And for the first time in his life, his adoring grandmother hung up on him.

Adam called his grandmother's house several times during the next week. Each time, Granny Fran lovingly told him that he was being a nuisance and then refused to make Jenny speak to him. She warned him not to show up on her doorstep. She wouldn't let him in, she said regretfully. Not while Jenny was with her, asking for sanctuary.

"Sanctuary," Adam muttered disgruntledly, stalking through the halls of the hospital where he most often operated. Patients, visitors and hospital staff scattered from in front of him, perhaps warned by his expression that he was in no mood to be detained.

"Sanctuary," he repeated. "You'd think I was a marauding Hun or something."

"Er—sorry, Dr. Stone. Did you say something to me?" a nervous young nurse asked, clutching a clipboard to her skinny chest.

He glared at her. "No," he barked.

She gulped and scurried away.

Adam exhaled in self-disgust. There really was no excuse for taking his bad mood out on his associates.

He was finished here for the day. He might as well go home.

The only problem was, he didn't feel as though he had a home to go to.

It was sometime during that near-sleepless night that Adam finally realized just how badly he'd messed up. He wasn't infallible, it appeared. And when he failed, he did so spectacularly.

He'd had no right to try to arrange Jenny's life. No matter how well-intentioned his motives had been. He'd called himself helping her, but he'd hurt her. Badly.

He'd ruined everything.

His chest ached. His arms felt hauntingly empty. He remembered how they'd felt filled with a cooing, sweet-smelling, satin-skinned baby. The baby he'd come to think of as his own. And then he recalled the dazzling, delicious sensation of holding Jenny in his arms. And he was almost ripped apart by a wave of sheer longing.

For the first time in his life, Adam was in need of help. He'd gotten himself into a terrible mess, and he couldn't get out of it by hiring someone to take care of it, or by making a few quick, imperious decisions.

There was only one person who could help him. Jenny. And he'd driven her away.

And this time, he didn't know if there was anything he could do to make everything right again.

A week after she'd slipped away from Adam's house, Jenny sat in the living room of his grandmother's cozy little cottage, playing with Melissa. Granny Fran sat nearby, laughing at the faces Melissa was making in response to her mother's teasing. It was a pleasant, cozy scene.

Jenny wished she could truly enjoy it.

She knew she wouldn't be able to stay here much longer. She'd imposed on dear Mrs. Carson long enough. But she'd been so emotionally battered, so heartsick and lost when she'd left Adam's house that she hadn't been able to think of anyplace else to go. She'd gotten into her car, and found herself headed for the only place she knew where she would be welcomed with simple, unconditional affection. And she had been.

"She's such an intelligent baby," Granny Fran said enthusiastically. "Look at her trying to imitate you. I swear, she'll be talking in complete sentences before she's a year old."

Jenny smiled. "Maybe not quite that early. But she does seem bright, doesn't she?"

"Extremely. And beautiful, too."

"And you say that with total objectivity," Jenny said gravely.

The older woman laughed softly. "Of course not. I can't be objective about anyone I love. I think everyone in my family is bright and beautiful."

Jenny's own smile faded. Every once in a while it occurred to her that she and Melissa weren't really a part of Granny Fran's family. That it would soon be time to move on.

It would hurt her almost as much to leave Granny Fran as it had to leave Adam. Not quite, of course. But almost.

A sudden pounding on the front door made her sit up with a gasp. It was silly—but she was almost sure she knew whose fist was rattling that door.

Granny Fran seemed to have the same suspicion. Wide-eyed, she looked at Jenny. "I was afraid his patience would wear out soon," she said, almost apologetically.

Jenny moistened her lips. "You think it's Adam?"

The door quivered again beneath another impatient assault.

"Oh, yes," Adam's grandmother said ruefully. "I'm absolutely sure it is."

Jenny groaned. Why was Adam here? Why couldn't he just accept that it was over? Was it so hard for him to admit that he couldn't always have things his way?

She didn't even try to delude herself that she'd hurt more than his sizable ego when she'd left him.

"I'll send him away," Granny Fran said, rising to her feet.

Jenny stopped her with an outstretched hand. "No. That won't be necessary. I'll see him."

She couldn't have forgiven herself for coming between Adam and his beloved grandmother. This was his family, not Jenny's. She had no right to keep them apart any longer.

She could handle this, she assured herself, wishing she could have expressed the thought just a bit more confidently.

Adam barely took time to greet his grandmother before he stepped past her, his eyes locked with Jenny's. She stared back at him, shocked by his appearance.

He looked terrible.

His hair was rumpled and in need of a trim. His white cotton shirt was wrinkled, and he wore old, tattered jeans that faithfully molded his lean hips and long, powerful legs. His eyes were deep set, heavy lidded, as though he hadn't slept in days. The lines around his mouth seemed to be carved more deeply than they had been before.

Had he been anyone else, she would have said this was a man in deep pain. A man in need.

But Adam Stone didn't need anyone, she reminded herself sternly. Adam Stone thought he could take care of everything himself, with a wave of his regal hand.

"Jenny," he said, and his voice sounded hoarse. "Are you all right?"

"I'm fine," she answered, refusing to be swayed by his appearance. The hunger in his dark eyes.

He wouldn't play her so easily this time.

He looked at Melissa. For a moment, Jenny's resolve quivered. The way he looked at the baby almost broke Jenny's heart—or would have, if he hadn't broken it already.

"Hi, sweetheart," he murmured, touching Melissa's cheek.

She grinned in delight at the sound of his familiar voice. She flexed her fingers in his direction, and he reached for her, gathering her close.

I won't cry, Jenny thought determinedly. I *won't!* But she had to look away from Adam and her daughter to keep the tears under control.

"I'm sure you want to talk to Jenny," Granny Fran said to Adam, reaching for the baby. "I'm going to take Melissa next door to visit Lila for a little while. All right, Jenny?"

Jenny wanted to beg her to stay, wanted to plead with her not to leave her alone with Adam. But, instead, she nodded. "Yes. Fine. Take your time."

Tucking the baby into one arm, Granny Fran paused to give her grandson a stern look. "Behave yourself."

"Yes, ma'am," he said automatically.

Jenny wondered if he was aware of how naturally the respectful words came to him.

The silence seemed almost palpable when Jenny and Adam were alone. He cleared his throat, and the sound almost echoed in the silent room.

Adam spoke first. "Would you like to sit down?"

She perched on the edge of the couch. He sat at the other end, half turned to face her, his hands gripped on his knees.

Jenny noted that his knuckles were white.

"I've missed you," he said, quietly.

She couldn't answer. She'd missed him, too, of course. So badly she'd thought she couldn't bear it at times. But she wouldn't tell him so.

"I've done a lot of thinking since you left," he went on. "I've thought about what I did, what you said. And I've realized how wrong I was. I'm sorry, Jenny. I shouldn't have called your parents without talking to you about it first."

She nodded. "All right. I accept your apology."

That obviously was not the answer he'd expected. "You accept my apology?"

"That's what I said."

He frowned, searching her face. She hoped he couldn't read her emotions there. "Does this mean you've forgiven me?" he asked.

"I understand why you did it," she said honestly. "I know you thought you were doing the right thing. As for forgiving you—no, I haven't. I'm sorry—but I can't."

She half expected him to start yelling again. Something along the lines of "Damn it, Jenny!"

Instead he sighed heavily, lowered his head and stared at his white-knuckled hands. "I was afraid of that."

Watching him out of the corner of her eye, she bit her lower lip. Something just wasn't right here, she thought warily.

Why wasn't Adam shouting? Why wasn't he telling her again how foolish she was not to acknowledge that his plan had worked exactly as he'd expected it to? Why wasn't he reminding her that he knew what was best for her?

Why did he look so sad?

"Adam?"

He looked up at her, his expression bleak. "I've destroyed everything, haven't I? Your feelings for me, your trust in me. I blew it."

She swallowed hard, past the lump in her throat. "Please," she whispered. "Don't do this."

He turned away. "I'm sorry."

Jenny twisted her fingers in her lap. What game was he playing now? What did he expect her to do, to say?

She couldn't stand seeing him like this. Tired. Depressed. Defeated. It just wasn't...Adam.

Tentatively she reached out to him. Her fingertips brushed his shoulder.

He trembled.

"Adam?" Jenny asked, his name little more than a breath of sound.

"I know you're capable of taking care of yourself, and your child. I know you don't...you don't need me to help you. But if there's anything you need—anything at all—I want you to feel free to ask."

She couldn't believe he was saying this. She hadn't expected him to give up so easily. Had she only hoped he would fight harder for her? Had she secretly believed he would win?

"All the things you left at my house belong to you," he continued. "Melissa's crib, her toys, the other things...they're yours. I'll see that you get them."

Unable to speak, she nodded.

Adam drew a deep, unsteady breath. "I have a few connections in Little Rock if you need a job or an apartment. I could help you get an interview. The rest, of course, would be up to you. I know you wouldn't want me to do any more."

He really was saying goodbye, she realized, stunned. He was letting her go.

Had she meant so little to him, after all?

Adam stood abruptly. "I didn't come here to make you uncomfortable," he said gruffly. "I only wanted to make sure you and Melissa are okay. And to let you know that if you ever need me, I'll be here for you. Always."

He turned and moved toward the door.

Jenny caught her breath. He really was leaving.

And she couldn't let him go.

She jumped to her feet, hurried after him. "Adam—"

He paused, one hand on the doorknob, his back turned to her. He seemed to be holding himself unusually stiffly. "Yes?"

"I— I—" *What?* What was left to say?

She drew a deep breath for courage. "I wanted to thank you for all you've done for me during the past three months. Taking me in, delivering the baby, giving me a job, a home. I owe you a great deal."

"You owe me nothing." He corrected her curtly, sounding more like himself now. "Everything I did, I did because I wanted to. Because I cared about you."

She wished she could see his face. She ached to touch him, to kiss him. Just one more time. "I cared about you, too," she whispered.

She heard him swallow. "I know," he muttered. "And I threw it all away."

He bent his head. His voice was gravelly. "I've rarely asked for anything in my life, Jenny. And I've damn well never begged. But, if I thought it would help, I would beg you to forgive me for the way I hurt you."

Her eyes widened. He sounded so humble. So sincere. So hopeless.

"I...I've tried to forgive you," she said. "I've tried to understand..."

He looked at her, a muscle working in his jaw. "You think I'm like your father, don't you? That I want to control you. To tell you what to do, who to be. But I want you to know that I never meant to be that way. That I would never do anything like that again, if you gave me a second chance. Or at least," he added with painful candor, "I would try. It's very hard to change thirty years of training overnight."

She twisted the hem of the blue knit pullover she wore with comfortable, matching knit leggings. She wasn't even aware that she was stretching the fabric out of shape. Fashion was the furthest thing from her mind at the moment.

"You *did* act a lot like my father," she agreed, struck by the comparison. "He always called himself acting in my best interest, taking care of me because he didn't consider me capable of looking out for myself."

"I know. And I did the same." He hesitated, then added, "But you forgave your father. You told him you love him despite his flaws."

She thought she saw the faintest glimmer of hope in his eyes. It gave her the courage to nod. "Yes. I forgave him. But my father met me halfway, Adam. He—he promised to love me, too. Just the way I am."

Adam's face softened. His eyes were bright, liquid. His voice husky when he said, "No one could ever love you more than I do, Jenny. And there's nothing about you that I would ever want to change."

The words almost rocked her on her heels. "You—you love me?" she repeated in an incredulous whisper.

"More than I've ever loved anyone," he answered simply. "It's the only reason I wanted so badly for you to be happy. My methods were wrong, but my feelings were genuine. I wanted to help you. It's all I've ever wanted to do for those I love."

Jenny was terribly afraid her knees were about to buckle. She put out a trembling hand and steadied herself against the wall. She studied his expression, trying to find any reason not to believe him.

He looked utterly sincere.

Her eyes flooded. "Oh, Adam."

"Maybe we could start over?" he suggested, diffidently. "If you could give me another chance, let me prove to you that I'm trying to change. That I won't ever hurt you again. Maybe, eventually, you can forgive me. Learn to love me."

"I love you so much it hurts," she said simply. "I have loved you for a very long time. Do you really think you could have hurt me so badly if I didn't love you?"

He made a choked sound, and moved automatically toward her. He caught himself short, stopping a few inches away from her. His eyes burned with emotion, searching her face with a desperate intensity.

"Can you give me another chance?" he asked, so softly she could hardly hear him. "I'm begging, Jenny."

The tears escaped her eyes to cascade down her cheeks. "Oh, please. Don't beg," she said, throwing herself against him. "I don't think I can handle that right now."

His arms closed around her, so tightly she could hardly breathe. She wouldn't have complained even if she'd been able to speak coherently.

"Jenny. Oh, God, Jenny, I love you. Please don't send me away."

His voice was so hoarse, so raw that her eyes overflowed again. But she managed a shaky smile as she looked up at him. "I can't send you away. Darn it, Adam, you need a keeper. Someone to take care of you—keep you from shooting yourself in your own foot with that overloaded ego of yours. I guess it's up to me."

His eyes very bright, he gave a low, unsteady laugh. "I'm not sure there was a compliment anywhere in there, but if it means you're giving me another chance, I don't care."

"I love you, Adam. I don't want to leave you again."

He kissed her. Hard. Heatedly.

Lovingly.

And then he kissed her again. And again. And again. Between kisses he muttered broken promises that he would never hurt her again, that he would never again make decisions for her without talking to her first, that he would never again be arrogant, or overbearing, or pompous or insensitive.

Jenny didn't believe him, of course. As he'd said, it wasn't easy to change thirty years of training overnight. But she believed that he loved her enough to try.

That was all she could have asked.

His hands swept her body, holding her close. "I've missed you," he murmured, allowing her a moment to breathe as he released her mouth and pressed hot, hungry kisses across her cheek and temple. "I've missed you so much I ached. I don't want to spend another night alone in that house, or in my bed. Come home with me, Jenny. Please."

There was that word again. Please. It sounded so sweet coming from him. "Yes," she said.

He swept her into a hug that left her feet dangling above the floor and threatened imminent damage to her rib cage. She locked her arms around his neck and hugged him back as hard as she could.

For once, she thought happily, she'd made exactly the right choice.

He finally set her down, though he wrapped an arm around her shoulders to keep her close. Almost as though he were afraid to let her go again.

"We'll get married as soon as I can make the arrangements," he said, his voice light again, his eyes clear and unshadowed. "It'll be a small wedding—your family and mine, maybe a few close friends. I'll call my attorney this afternoon to start proceedings for me to adopt Melissa. I

want her to have my name. I want to be her father. I love
that kid, Jenny. Surely you know that. I could never love
our own children any more than I do her. I'll never give
you or her reason to doubt that. After the wedding,
we'll—"

He paused, looking at her quizzically as she ruefully
shook her head. "What is it?" he asked. "What have I
said?"

"Adam, you're doing it again," she pointed out patiently. "You're planning our wedding, our future—and
you haven't even asked me if I want to marry you."

His eyes widened. A tinge of color stained his lean
cheeks.

Jenny had to bite the inside of her lip to keep from
smiling at his obvious chagrin.

Adam cleared his throat. "I *was* doing it again, wasn't
I?"

She nodded, not quite trusting her voice.

Anxiously he placed both hands on her shoulders. "I'm
sorry," he said penitently. "I didn't mean to break my
promises to you, especially not so soon. I got carried
away..."

"I know."

He gave her a sheepish smile. "*Will* you marry me,
Jenny? I love you so very much. I will always love you."

She reached up to touch his cheek. "I'll marry you,"
she murmured. "I love you, too."

"And Melissa? You don't mind if I adopt her?"

"I'm thrilled that you want to adopt her. She already
loves you, Adam. I couldn't have asked for a more perfect father for her."

He smiled and made a production of wiping his brow.
"That's settled, then. Let's go tell Melissa and Granny
Fran."

She was amused by his eagerness to share their news. "How do you think your mother's going to take this?" she asked a bit nervously.

He chuckled ruefully. "My mother has spent the past week yelling at me and calling me an idiot for letting you get away," he confessed. "She's very fond of you, Jenny, despite the funny way she has of showing it. I don't think anyone could know you and not love you," he added sincerely.

She blinked back a wave of fresh tears. She wouldn't cry again, she vowed, no matter how touched she was by Adam's words. She was too happy for tears now.

"Let's go find Granny Fran," she said, taking his hand.

He grinned and pulled her close. "Yeah. And then I'm taking my family home. To stay, this time."

Home. Family. Such beautiful words, Jenny thought with a blissful sigh.

She'd been looking for both for such a long time.

Epilogue

Frances Carson opened her mail eagerly, delighted to find an envelope of photographs in a cardboard mailer. She looked through them slowly, stopping often to *ooh* and *aah*. Melissa was growing so quickly, she thought, studying the smiling baby in the photos. Seven months old now, the child looked happy and healthy and pampered.

One photograph in particular made Frances smile and blink back tears. In it, Melissa rode on Adam's shoulders, clutching his hair and squealing with delight. Adam steadied the baby with his hands on her legs, his gold wedding band gleaming in the photograph. He wore a broad, happy grin. He looked very much like the young boy in Frances's most treasured memories.

Frances was so happy for her eldest grandchild. He was such a good boy, she thought proudly. He deserved to be happy, and she knew he was, now that he had a wife, a dear little girl. A real home.

She carried the photographs to her mantel, laying them there so she would remember to show them to her best friend, Lila Twining, later that afternoon.

Her attention turned to a framed photograph of a handsome young man with laughing blue eyes and a heartbreaking smile. Cody, she thought, touching the glass over his dear face.

Poor Cody. It must be so lonely to be the only single adult left in the family, she mused. She wondered if there was anything she could do to help him. Perhaps he'd like to meet the granddaughter of one of her friends, she thought.

She gazed at his photograph, contentedly making her plans.

* * * * *

Don't miss CODY'S FIANCÉE, *the next book in The Family Way series, coming in early 1996, from Silhouette Special Edition!*

COMING NEXT MONTH

#985 D IS FOR DANI'S BABY—Lisa Jackson
That Special Woman!/Love Letters

Eleven years ago, Dani Stewart had no choice but to give up her baby for adoption. Now she was determined to find her son—and the last thing she expected was a reunion with Brandon Scarlotti, the father of her child.

#986 MORGAN'S WIFE—Lindsay McKenna
Morgan's Mercenaries: Love and Danger

Everything was at stake when Jim Woodward accepted a dangerous mission to rescue his closest friends. Pepper Sinclair was along for the ride to ensure he got the job done—and to melt the ice around his enclosed heart....

#987 FINALLY A BRIDE—Sherryl Woods
Always a Bridesmaid!

Katie Jones never expected a proposal of marriage from the man who was once her best friend. She'd always loved Luke Cassidy, but once they said their "I do's," Katie learned a few secrets about her new husband....

#988 A MAN AND A MILLION—Jackie Merritt

A newly rich woman like Theo Hunter attracted her share of roguish attention—and town bad boy Colt Murdoch made no secret of his interest. Talk around town predicted Colt stealing Theo's land, but the only thing she was sure of losing was her heart!

#989 THIS CHILD IS MINE—Trisha Alexander

Eve DelVecchio and Mitch Sinclair hadn't seen each other in years, but the attraction between them still smoldered. Mitch was elated to find his lost love, but would Eve's secret jeopardize their second chance?

#990 AND FATHER MAKES THREE—Laurie Campbell
Premiere

Despite the wild attraction between them, Sarah Corcoran knew Nate Ryan was not her type. After all, she was single-handedly raising a teenager—but maybe footloose and fancy-free Ryan could be convinced to settle down....

Take 4 bestselling love stories FREE

Plus get a FREE surprise gift!

Special Limited-time Offer

Mail to Silhouette Reader Service™

3010 Walden Avenue
P.O. Box 1867
Buffalo, N.Y. 14269-1867

YES! Please send me 4 free Silhouette Special Edition® novels and my free surprise gift. Then send me 6 brand-new novels every month, which I will receive months before they appear in bookstores. Bill me at the low price of $2.89 each plus 25¢ delivery and applicable sales tax, if any.* That's the complete price and a savings of over 10% off the cover prices—quite a bargain! I understand that accepting the books and gift places me under no obligation ever to buy any books. I can always return a shipment and cancel at any time. Even if I never buy another book from Silhouette, the 4 free books and the surprise gift are mine to keep forever.

235 BPA ANRQ

Name	(PLEASE PRINT)
Address	Apt. No.
City	State	Zip

This offer is limited to one order per household and not valid to present Silhouette Special Edition® subscribers. *Terms and prices are subject to change without notice. Sales tax applicable in N.Y.

USPED-295   ©1990 Harlequin Enterprises Limited

Become a
Privileged Woman,
You'll be entitled to all
these *Free Benefits.*
And *Free Gifts,* too.

To thank you for buying our books, we've designed an exclusive FREE program called *PAGES & PRIVILEGES™.* You can enroll with just one Proof of Purchase, and get the kind of luxuries that, until now, you could only read about.

*B*IG HOTEL DISCOUNTS

A privileged woman stays in the finest hotels. And so can you—at up to 60% off! Imagine standing in a hotel check-in line and watching as the guest in front of you pays $150 for the same room that's only costing you $60. Your *Pages & Privileges* discounts are good at Sheraton, Marriott, Best Western, Hyatt and thousands of other fine hotels all over the U.S., Canada and Europe.

*F*REE DISCOUNT TRAVEL SERVICE

A privileged woman is always jetting to romantic places.

When <u>you</u> fly, just make one phone call for the lowest published airfare at time of booking— <u>or double the difference back!</u>

PLUS—you'll get a $25 voucher to use the first time you book a flight AND <u>5% cash back on every ticket you buy thereafter through the travel service!</u>